# THE FIRE WITHIN SITA

## RSVIKA TRIPATHI

To every woman who felt a fire burning within her each
time they said her character was stained.

To every woman who felt a fire burning within her each
time she was touched without consent.

To every woman who felt a fire burning within her each
time she was objectified.

To every woman who felt a fire burning within her each
time she was treated as an outcast.

To every woman who felt a fire burning within her each
time the world became a forest of hardships and a den of
demons.

To every woman who felt a fire burning within her, is
feeling a fire burning within her, will ever feel a fire
burning within her.

# Contents

# Contents

# Preface

I began this journey with a story about a woman born out of fire, a character that called me into this world of novel writing. My first book, "Draupadi's 13 Relations," was about a strong and unbreakable queen who, despite facing overwhelming odds, never weakened. Draupadi rose from the ashes of evil like a pure lotus, untouched and unscathed by the darkness around her.

Following that, I wrote about another resilient woman in "The 3 Illusions of Amrapali." This book traced the entire journey of a woman in love, a woman transformed by her experiences, a woman judged at every step by society, and yet, she stayed strong and ultimately transformed into a spiritual being.

Now, it feels only right to complete this trilogy by writing about another iconic woman whose life was a continuous journey of hardships and resilience. A princess, a queen, wise and compassionate—Sita embodies both humility and fierceness. Through her story, I aim to showcase that even a woman as gentle and compassionate as Sita can be remarkably resilient and fierce when faced with adversity.

"The Fire Within Sita" is the final book in my trilogy of resilient women from history and mythology. This book encapsulates a character who goes through everything, a tale of a complete and strong woman in all her totality. They say femininity is not anti-feminist, and this story reflects that truth. Sita's journey is one of endurance, strength, and unwavering spirit, showing that true femininity encompasses both compassion and resilience.

As my trilogy began with a woman rising from fire, it fittingly concludes with a woman stepping into it. This final chapter is a reflection of the enduring spirit of women who, despite all challenges, continue to shine brightly and fiercely.

# ACKNOWLEDGEMENTS

I would like to thank my father for instilling in me a love for literature, a love for writing from a very young age. I am forever grateful to my mother, who has been the biggest cheerleader for me, has always motivated me. To my late Baba, and late Nani, it was their love for books that imprinted on my heart. I am grateful to my Naana who has always motivated me by his words and the life he lived. Thank you, Dadi, for those spiritual insights that have always been helpful. I would extend my thanks to Reiki, Mithu, Misthi, Aira who helped me with the playful moments when this journey got a little tough. I would thank my friends, who trusted me and encouraged me.

# Prologue

A lady whose journey was fraught with difficulties and hardships, yet whose name often gets lost amidst the norms of an ideal woman. Ideal woman for whom? As per whom? Her character begins and ends with the title of 'an ideal woman.' As much as this sounds respectful and pleasant, it also traps her character.

Sita was so much more than that. She was not just a wife, not just a queen, not just a mother. She was a woman—a strong, resilient woman whose struggles, fears, and feelings have been overshadowed by the narratives of wars, ideal norms, and other characters.

This book aims to give voice to the feelings and thoughts of Sita. How did she feel? How did she perceive life? How did she remain resilient throughout her journey? This is not just a retelling of a narrative we've all heard. It's an exploration of Sita's inner world, her thoughts and emotions, of a woman who transcends the societal tags of an ideal woman, who carries an individuality of her own, and who stands resilient despite her life being filled with hardships.

We have known a narrative, we have known a tale, but this is not just a narrative or a tale. This is solely about Sita's thoughts and feelings, of a woman who is above the societal tags of an ideal woman, who carries an individuality of herself, who stands resilient despite her life being filled with hardships.

# I

Today carried a certain enchantment, a certain excitement, a beauty that transcends description, a beauty that makes all the words fall too short to describe. I couldn't quite tell what it was, but today just felt like the fresh rain droplets on a lotus flower on the dawn of a bright spring. The wind felt like it whispered secrets, gently tousling the strands of my hair as it passed. Above, the sky displayed a masterpiece of warmth and comfort, like hues painted by the very hands of divinity. The earth beneath my feet seemed to share in the jubilation, as if it, too, yearned to reach upward and touch the heavens, birds chirping merrily as if singing a song of celebration.

And oh, the sound of my anklets! Today, they resonated with a melody distinct from the usual. It was as if they, too, were caught up in the euphoria of the moment, they felt way more excited to dance than my feet felt to walk.

"Didi today you chanted the Gauri aarti so beautifully, it felt like Mata Parvati was herself present there to bestow her blessings" Mandavi's words brought me back from adoring today's evening.

"Mind your step Mandavi" I said hurriedly as I saw she was about to miss a step as we were stepping down from the Gauri temple. She stumbled a little but thankfully didn't fall. "Are you okay?" I still asked to reassure if she was alright.

"Of course, didi but today you sang really..." she was about to say something, maybe compliment me again, which she always did despite me telling her not to, Urmila interrupted "what do you mean by *today*, Sita didi always sing from her heart." Urmila had this thing to always interrupt Mandavi and irritate her. So, I was sure more than she wanted to compliment me by saying that, she wanted to get a reaction from Mandavi. They fought a lot, but yet they were inseparable.

"Wish you could do the same for at least a day, for at least one aarti, for at least a word, but your voice makes me think of...who is that cruel king we have been hearing about, oh yes Raavan." Mandavi said bringing a smile on my face, that here they go again.

"Sita didi, say something" Urmila pouted and complained about Mandavi. "Well, you started it Urmila." I said, I never took sides, because I knew that this moment they are fighting and the next they will be giggling together, besides I never wanted Mandavi and Shrutkirti to feel even for a second that they were our cousins, daughter of our father's brother. But since the day they were born, we have been together so I never wanted her to feel otherwise.

This reminded me, "where is Shrutkirti?"

"I don't know didi as soon were done with the prayers, she left" Mandavi replied making me realize my question was not just in my head, I had said it out aloud. I looked at Urmila if she knew anything but she still carried her angry expressions from her squabble with Mandavi.

"But where did she...oh there she is" I saw Shrutkirti coming with her usual smiling chirpy face.

She seemed too excited, which she normally is, but today there was something extra, she was exuberantly gleeful. As she approached us, I was about to ask where was she all this while but then neither did her bright wide eyes wait to notice my question nor did her mouth to speak the words.

"I saw one *Kaaki* a little upset during the prayers and I went to see if she was okay and then I walked her to some distance."

"...and that upset Kaaki makes you this excited and happy?" Urmila said, her expressions changing from angry to now confused, which was the emotion I too shared with her, surprised.

"No, it's not that. So, you know while I was on my way back, I saw two young men in Pushpvatika. They were with *Rajrishi* Vishwamitra" she said blushing and giggling.

"It's not right Shrutkirti to talk about other men in this manner." Mandavi said though I could sense a little intrigue in her eyes and tone.

"Not for meee." Shrutkirti replied in her defence, with her pitch sharpening at the last word to emphasise it. Shrutkirti has always been the expressive one.

"Since Sita didi's svayamvara is to take place in four days, so I was thinking to introduce her to potential husband, maybe those two men will participate and one of them can be Sita Didi's groom. Because trust me one of them is exactly what I feel like Sita didi's groom would be like. Calm composed, a certain *ojus* on his face, maturity." She said in an animated voice.

"Well, considering the qualities that you have described and the fact that they were with Rajrishi Vishwamitra, I am inclined to believe that they are the esteemed princes of Ayodhya" Urmila said smiling at me with a glint of mischief.

From our childhood, Ayodhya had been a recurring tale, where King Dashrath's generosity aided Mithila in times of need. Lately, news of his sons, particularly Prince Ram, student of great sages *Maharishi* Vashishta and *Maharishi* Vishwamitra, filled our ears. Amidst the havoc unleashed by demons across Aryavarta, Prince Ram emerged victorious, by defeating many demons. The desire to meet Prince Ram and inquire about the tales surrounding him, especially the socially debatable talk of his liberating Mata Ahalya from the curse, tugged at me. Yet, fate had other plans, and I never got an opportunity to satisfy this intrigue and hope, of meeting him. I never talked about this to anyone but Urmila. She always somehow knew when my mind was pondering something. And one day when I was just thinking about the prince of Ayodhya and his heroic tales, Urmila noticed it and forced me to share my thoughts. Urmila can be very assertive once she decides to know something or make one talk about something, she always turns out to be successful in her venture. But since that day, Urmila being Urmila, she took delight in teasing me. And today again she got her chance.

However, I knew I shouldn't be paying heed to this, I have never paid any attention to any man, or any talks about them except for of course legendary tales about Ram. A strange ray of hope however made my heart beat a little faster, maybe all those thoughts of intrigue towards him, all those hopes to meet him, were about to be fruitful. But then again, it was my Svayamvara in some days, and I shouldn't be thinking about any man, for my decision would then be biased. But just like this evening had a different feel, my thoughts too danced in an unusual fluttering manner.

As I was trying to define to myself what I actually felt at that very moment, I felt a grip on my wrist. It was Shrutkirti with her big round eyes looking at me with mischief and excitement. She then pulled me to make me walk with her.

"Where are you taking me?" I asked as she still had the hold on my hand.

"To ensure you catch a glimpse of them?" she mused, gently guiding me forward. I could have halted our progress, but something within me resisted the urge, and so I continued to move alongside her, with Urmila and Mandavi in tow. Although I sensed the need to interject, a modest form of resistance, I found myself hesitating. "What do you mean by 'to catch a glimpse'? You know I won't allow it," I asserted, attempting to sound stern. Yet, even as I spoke, my steps mirrored hers, allowing the wind to weave through my hair and tenderly caress my face.

"Oh, the words stumbled out in a tangled mess. I meant to lead you to greet Rajrishi Vishwamitra and seek his blessings," she clarified with a mischievous twinkle in her tone. Despite detecting the playful mischief in her words, I chose not to resist.

Without her realising, her grip on my hand tightened as we walked, causing my gold bangles to create a friction on my wrist. The air carried a subtle tension, a blend of anticipation and uncertainty, as we ventured closer to the possibility of encountering the princes of Ayodhya.

I then just gave up any resistance through my wors or expressions because one it would not be of any use since Shrutkirti seemed very firm in her decision, and second, I too wanted not to resist this natural pull towards.... *him.*

So, I walked with her catching up with her quick steps. I could already feel my cheeks blushing, a flush of heat running through my cheeks, but why was it, I couldn't understand, I have never felt this way before. My nature has always been steady, very rarely did my emotions and thoughts act in an untamed manner, once this happened when I came to know about my birth, and then it was only today that my feelings transcended thoughts.

*Sometimes you can't tame your thoughts to not make you feel a certain way, because in those moments even the thoughts are unaware of the feelings, it is just the feeling. your thoughts can't match up to the feeling that you are feeling.*

Shrutkirti hadn't even given us enough time to put on our footwear. The entire space around Gauri temple and Pushpvatika was covered with grass ad since it drizzle in the morning today the grass was moist. So, as we walked, the moist grass brushed my feet and gave a cooling soothing feeling. It was as if mother earth was herself encouraging me to go where we were headed by making this walk a soothing one.

Shrutkirti took a sudden haut making me bump into her and the same with happened with Urmila and Mandavi.

"What is it" Mandavi said a little frustrated.

"Hushhh...we are here now I don't want us to just go there especially Sita didi. Afterall she is the eldest princess of Mithila and I want her to look her best when she meets the eldest prince of Ayodhya." Shrutkirti said whispering.

I chose not to utter any words to this; I just folded my arms and gave her a stern expression while Urmila and Mandavi chuckled. The best things to remain quiet at times is you don't have to say anything but still the other person interprets your silence as per the situation in their own way. This is what happened with Shrutkirti.

She unfolded my arms and again said whispering, "of course, you always look your best didi, but we just came all the way almost running from Gauri temple so just a last moment touch-up."

Shrutkirti gently brushed away grass fragments that had stuck to my beige silk lehenga. The red velvet border, embroidered with golden threads. The kurti matched the lehenga's pattern, featuring detailed embroidery that paid homage to the art of our land. I have always been inclined to pastel shades, the made me feel more connected to the harmony of nature. Shrutkirti, always vibrant, donned a striking yellow sequin lehenga with a rose-pink kurti. Mandavi, always adaptable in her choices, with her wardrobe having a diverse collection of clothes in all shades and colours, opted for a cucumber green lehenga layered with organza.

Urmila, our rebellious one, defied conventions with her love for darker shades. Despite Mother's caution against red hues symbolizing marriage, Urmila confidently wore maroon, carmine, crimson, and today, a deep purple outfit. Her spirited choices occasionally drew scoldings from Mother, but Urmila never shied away from expressing her individuality.

Mandavi and Urmila took charge, assisting Shrutkirti to ensure everything met their standards of perfection. I finally let them be, finding joy in their enthusiasm. Mandavi, carefully, adjusted the locks of my long, thick, black hair, which cascaded in waves. Urmila, with her tight curls reflecting a carefree and rebellious spirit, inherited a different hair texture.

In contrast, Shrutkirti and Mandavi inherited their mother's shiny, straight, silk-like hair. As Mandavi tended to my hair, Urmila focused on positioning my jewellery. Although the adornments were already in place, Urmila, driven by her penchant for precision, made subtle adjustments. Personally, I preferred minimal jewellery, but the responsibilities of royalty dictated otherwise. Wearing these embellishments wasn't just a matter of personal choice; it symbolized the prosperity of our kingdom—a sentiment my father believed would resonate with the people of Mithila. Despite my father's reservations about such superficial displays, he acknowledged their significance in connecting with the people and showcasing the prosperity of our land through the attire of Mithila's royal family.

After they were contended with their little activity, I sighed and said, "well, that was not necessary, and you..."

"Oh, there they are, come" Urmila interrupted as she held my hand and made me walk forward.

Before I could think, before I could comprehend, before I could process myself into what was happening and what I should do or how I should act or what to expect, I stood as Urmila halted beside me. There was silence for a moment, no more sound of our anklets, no ore chuckles from my sisters. Then, slowly my eyes fixed upon him, to see him standing right in front of me, Raghunandan, prince of Ayodhya, Ram.

# II

Sunlight kissed Raghunandan's ebony hair, turning it into a halo of molten gold. The air around him shimmered, as if his very presence infused the atmosphere with warmth. As my eyes met his, my heart thudded a frantic rhythm against my ribs. The complexion of his face was a mysterious depth, a rich, dark hue that held secrets and untold stories. It was as if his skin carried the weight of infinite depths, unfathomable and endless. Gazing at those dark brown eyes, akin to the vastness of deep oceans, caught breath in my throat. His eyes were like a thousand sunlit dawns that held an ancient wisdom A strange sensation bloomed in my chest, like a wildfire threatening to consume me, and also like butterflies fluttered within me.

*In that sunlit moment, a thousand suns bloomed within me, and yet I felt strangely chilled, as if plunged into the depths of his gaze.*

He wore a saffron coloured cotton *Dhoti*, had a large bow which he held with his right hand and a quiver he carried diagonally on his back. His shoulders, broad enough to bear any burden, seemed etched by both wind and water, his body gave a new meaning to grace and power. Yet, it was his face that stole my breath, a face that reflected empathy, that glowed with what felt like humbleness. He looked strong but in a way that makes you feel protected.

*He felt like the sunrise which had power to banish the night, chasing away any fears I might have harboured.*

It felt like the earth had shifted beneath my feet, tilting my world towards this man bathed in sunlight. The sandalwood scent that clung to him, earthy and intoxicating, made me feel so comfortable, like I have known him for so long.

*It felt like he was the home and my soul has been the wanderer which yearned for this safe place.*

His subtle smile, felt like the sun breaking through storm. His lips, the colour of ripe berries, curved ever so slightly. Time seemed to lose all meaning, the world around me faded into a muted blur. In that moment, there was only him, a beacon of warmth and strength in the midst of the unknown. I was so encaptivated in his beauty that I didn't realize until now that his eyes have also been also directed at me and I felt my cheeks flush a feverish crimson. Tears, unexpected and warm, spilled from the corners of my eyes. I blinked, startled, then wiped them away, only to find more welling up. But it wasn't the sting of sadness that pricked my eyes, but a strange, sweet ache, a blossoming of something long dormant. My eyes, it seemed, had glimpsed a haven they didn't know they'd been searching for, and the floodgates of joy had opened.

"*Pranam.* We came here to meet sage Vishwamitra and seek his blessings." Shrutkirti's high pitched eager voice brought me back to reality, from the transcend like state I have been in since I saw Raghunandan.

I then again gave a little gentle pat on my cheeks to make sure no one noticed my tears and as I gently looked at Raghunandan again, his lips curved a little more in smile as he looked at me, as if to tell me *he saw those tears.*

"*Pranam devi.* Oh, he just left, you are a minute late." I heard a voice that sounded strong and manly and yet filled with so much energy like an active young boy. It was from the young man standing next to Raghunandan. He was similar in hight to Prince Ram, just inched shorter, had a fair skin and a well-built physique just like Prince Ram. He was just like a mirror reflection of prince ram with only some slight differences, and it was obvious to me that he must be Prince Ram's brother Prince Laxman.

"Well, that's sad, we really wanted to meet him" Urmila said smiling as if some unsaid task was accomplished.

"I am sorry but your words and expressions don't match." Laxman pointed out.

"I beg your pardon" Urmila said with an evident tone of being offended.

"Well, you said you were sad but then you said it while smiling" Laxman's words brought a smile to my face, finally someone who said what he felt, someone just like Urmila, to match up to her sense of sarcasm and upright nature.

"Well, well..." for the first time I saw Urmila stumped not knowing what to say further other than 'well'

"Well, our sister Sita didi, eldest princess of Mithila, daughter of King Janak and Queen Sunayana" Mandavi interjected keeping her hand on my arm and gently stepping a step back.

I then looked at Laxman, though I wanted very much to catch a glimpse of Raghunandan again, but I composed myself and looked at Laxman as he joined his hands bowed and said pranam. He then said, "My eldest brother, Ram bhaiya, prince of Ayodhya son of King Dashrath and Queen Kausalya."

I the looked at Prince Ram again, our eyes met and we gently bowed to each other, slightly nodding our head. We said nothing because,

*it felt like our eyes already communicated a thousand words, and so our lips hesitated to ruin the communication of our eyes.*

"And who must you be with the great prince of Ayodhya." Urmila said in and interrogating manner, clearly upset from the last conversation.

"I am Laxman, prince of Ayodhya, son of Queen Sumitra. If you would have heard me clearly devi...umm...devi, then I clearly said I am the brother of ram bhaiya." Laxman said in a crisp voice which led Urmila to say something but then she decided otherwise and simply rolled her eyes.

To not make this conversation awkward, I said, "well very glad to meet you" I said as I looked at Prince Laxman and then for a second at Ram. I could look at Prince ram all day but I also constantly reminded myself of the svayamvara, though it was becoming harder, still I needed to compose myself. I then looked at Laxman again and said, "she is my sister Urmila" as I looked towards Urmila who didn't look at Laxman this time. "My sister, shrutkirti and Mandavi" I introduced them as they exchanged bows, except Urmila.

"Urmila let's be nice to our guests now" I said to Urmila. Before she could say anything, we heard a familiar voice, "of course, especially when the guests are so special. The land that has been there for Mithila in the tough times." It was my father.

My father walked towards us with Rajrishi Vishwamitra. We bowed to Rajrishi Vishwamitra and sought his blessings. My father's attire has always been modest, at least for a king. He didn't wear too much jewellery. Since he was a

Rajrishi, he maintained his attained status of sage while being a king.

The two princes of Ayodhya bowed to my father. Raghunandan then said, "I feel immensely blessed to meet you, King Janak. It is our honour that we got to meet you, Rajrishi."

A little confused my father said, "one thing I can say for sure is I have no appearance of a king." He then laughed slightly and then continued, "how did you know who I was."

"The appearance of a wise man is difficult to hide respected king Janak. The wisdom in your eyes, the calm in your voice, the aura surrounding you, the scent of entire Mithila from you, I don't think there is anyone who can't tell that this greatness is of King Janak." My father smiled at this and hugged Prince Ram.

At this very moment I could definitely say that more than my father, I was happy. I immensely felt myself admiring Price ram even more. For a daughter whose father has been her greatest support, the greatest man she has ever looked up to, for that daughter whenever someone respects her father, she can't help but admire that person. That person becomes dear to her. Daughter takes pride in her father and when someone respects that pride, she feels the most respected and happy.

"We get to hear about your great accomplishments very frequently, Raghunandan and Sumitranandan. You are truly great men there's no doubt in that" Father complimented.

"We are just the reflection of our parent's upbringing, our teachers' teaching, and a result of the blessing from great people like you." Raghunandan replied.

He had such calm voice, his voice was like a balm to aching, restless heart. His words could remedy any broken soul. He had this certain steadiness in the way with which he talked. One would just crave to listen to more and more of what he had to say.

My father evidently very pleased with this interaction said to Rajrishi Vishwamitra, "I am very grateful to you that you brought the princes of Ayodhya with you"

"If you don't mind me asking how long will you be staying here in Mithila?" father asked Raghunandan.

"We are here with our *Guru* so whatever he says, we are bound to follow that."

"Then Rajrishi Vishwamitra kindly enlighten us with this." Father then directed the question at Maharishi Vishwamitra who till now was just standing there calm, composed. I was always inspired by this quality of great sages, they didn't say anything or talk anything until it was very important or someone asked anything, they would stand with so much integrity.

Rajrishi Vishwamitra then replied, "we will stay as long as fate wants us to", and then he slightly smiled.

To this father joyously said, "then kindly give us an opportunity of proper hospitality, it's my daughter Sita's svayamvara in four days, kindly attend it."

My heart skipped a beat at these words as Urmila poked my arm with her elbow, but my impulsive action was to look at Raghunandan. He had that kind of beauty that can never get old, each time you look at him, your heart will flutter the same. I thought just a look at him made me heart beat fast and maybe my heart couldn't race any faster than this was proved wrong when Raghunandan looked at me at the mention of svayamvara. I have always been intrigued when I heard the tales of prince ram, I always knew I had this wish to meet him, but only after I met him, I realised that this was something more, there was some thread pulling me towards him, it was not just an intrigue, but something more, but what.

"Your mothers have been looking for you" Father said and I realised that was our que to go back to palace. My sisters and I then nodded in bow to all our guests and with that we turned to return to our palace. Urmila, Mandavi and Shrutkirti clustered in front of me as they giggled and discussed something. However, as we walked a few steps, I still had this desire to look again, once more at Raghunandan. I never know when we would get to meet again, but something in my heart said, this couldn't be our last interaction, there had to be something more. I turned back to look but they were gone at some distance, I could only see the strong back and integrated walk of Raghunandan.

# III

I couldn't sleep all night after that interaction with Raghunandan. It was a feeling I had never felt before. My inner mind was in a complete turmoil, I knew I shouldn't be giving so much thought to a man especially when I had my svayamvara, I shouldn't be thinking of any other men. But my thoughts were not of 'other men' but only of *him*. I just couldn't help it; I felt a connection with him.

*In certain gazes, one finds not reflection, but completion, a piece of the soul long missing finally finding its rightful place.*

My thoughts were all over the place, I could not think clearly, this morning brought the same confusion. Usually, my father cleared all my confusions, all my doubts, but this was something I couldn't discus with him, neither I wanted my mother to know, because she would get tensed for even the little things, and now that she was already busy and tensed with preparations of svayamvara, I didn't want to bother her more.

Sleep, that fickle friend, shunned my embrace all night. I tossed and turned, a prisoner of my own restless thoughts. Hours bled into one another, each tick of the clock a taunt echoing in my silent room. Finally, just as exhaustion began to steal its way around the edges of my mind, a faint glow tinged the eastern sky. Dawn was approaching, unwelcome and unwanted, a grim reminder of the sleepless night I had endured. I thought like always the rising sun would give me certain clarity but no the clouds in mind resembled the cloudy sky outside, the only difference was the sky till had certain sunrays but in my mind, I had no light to clear the confusing clouds. Wait! Light, I know just the person to help me with this of course other than my father, someone who is just as wise and bright as the sun, Mata Gargi.

I have known Mata Gargi since I was 9, and from that day I have been a huge admirer of her. I always looked up to her, I wanted to be like her, strong, powerful, not afraid of adversity. She was a learned woman who wouldn't hesitate from saying what was right. I was awestruck that day when I saw her debating Rishi Yajnavalkya on metaphysical topics. For a nine-year-old girl, the topics were out of my understanding but the way she dared to question the learncd rishis, the way she communicated her ideas left me aw struck. She then became the first ever woman to be a guru, my guru. This is a thing that I loved about her most, when traditions and "rules" demanded a woman to act a certain way, she took a stand for herself she stood for what was right, she made a mark for all the women.

Though Mata Gargi is my guru, still I always had a closer bond with her, more emotional, she felt like a mother figure to me, she would always know if ever there was a turmoil in my mind, like a mother. But the chaos that was now in my head, I had never experienced this before.

I then freshened up and got dressed to go and meet her. I chose to go for a pastel lavender coloured lehenga with cotton base and net frilled layers. The kurti too had flared net sleeves, I adored this dress for its comfort and just how refreshing it looked and helped. I informed mother that I was going to meet Mata Gargi, and then cautiously tried to go and meet her so that none of my sisters accompany me, because I wanted this talk with Mata Gargi to be very personal so that I could very comfortably communicate whatever it was that was in my mind. But I wasn't so lucky.

"Where are you going?" Urmila said just as I was about to step out of the main door.

"To get some fresh air, for a little walk." I replied, I couldn't lie to her, so I just fudged the truth.

"I'll come with you then. And maybe we might get to meet Prince Ram again." She said and raised her eyebrow. She always did this thing when she wanted to tease me, she would raise one eyebrow.

Mention of Raghunandan's name was enough to make my heart beat race. Just the thought of him, oh wait, I had to go and meet Mata Gargi. So, I tried to think of something to not make her come along.

"Oh yes absolutely we might meet him and also of course Prince Laxman." I felt a little mischievous, now even I had a name to tease Urmila with, after her little altercation with Laxman. And as expected she grimaced and walked away waving her hand.

I then quickly made me way to Mata Gargi's ashram to finally share whatever it was that has been disturbing me, all the new feelings, the thoughts of Raghunandan that just won't leave my mind, his beautiful face, his calm soothing voice, but also the guilt that I was about to get married and thinking all this was wrong, but the again all this was not in my control.

I decided that I will get a clear direction once I discuss with her, but now that I was here, I felt shy to talk to her about this. To be fair I didn't know how to exactly give words to my uncleared, tangled thoughts. What will I say to her, what will I ask? Should I be straightforward or talk indirectly.

"No greetings today I believe" Mata Gargi's words made me realize that I had already reached the ashram and was just standing there pondering all by myself.

"Oh, Pranam Mata Gargi" I bowed to her and sought her blessings, but still those thoughts consumed my attention and I was only physically there, still trapped in my thoughts.

"Sita, Sita" Mata Gargi called out in a slightly higher pitch which made e realise she has been saying something but I didn't hear her the first time.

I looked at her and then simply walked towards the adorable little lamb who was exuberantly playing with straws. Few days ago, I saw her wounded all by herself, I looked around and nowhere could I see her mother so I brought her to Mata Gargi's ashram and we healed her. Now her wound was almost healed, and that little lamb who was timid when I first saw her, was today jumping in glee. Someone would say this was because of the aid we did, but I knew it was also because of the home she got in Mata Gargi's ashram. This place had such effect on people.

*More than the physical aid sometimes it's the soul that needs the healing.*

"How is she doing, my adorable little beauty?" I said inn regard to the lamb asking Mata Gargi. After a pause, a pause of maybe observing me, which I felt, she said,

"She is doing perfectly alright Sita, but what about you?"

"What about me?"

"You tell me. You know pure hearts like you can't hide what's going on inside you. You can't pretend or lie." She said as she sat and gestured me to sit alongside her.

"Well, I wasn't trying to hide anything, it's just that I don't know how to share, what to say." I replied being completely honest.

"Sita how can you forget the thing I have taught you about saying what you feel, owning up to your thoughts. And since when did you feel awkward in sharing things with me. I am all ears, tell me my child, what is it that is troubling you."

I craned my head in both directions to make sure no one else was there because in someone's presence I could not deliver my thoughts to her and secondly, I didn't want my thoughts to be delivered to entire Mithila after being manipulated. My father has always said, the more people get to know something you didn't say to them directly, the more wrong interpretations they will have, and as a princess I had certain responsibilities and I can't just let people weave rumours. I loved people of Mithila, I know they loved us as well but sometimes the rumours spread not out of hatred but also out of concern, but in whichever case, it would be harmful not just for me but for my entire family, especially when svayamvara was just around the corner.

I took a long breath and finally began, "so you know I have svayamvara in three days, and it's not right to think about any man, and all my life I had no thought of any man. But now" I hesitated for a moment, I could feel my cheeks going red again, I could feel the heat on my cheeks, I continued again,

"But from the very moment I met this wonderful man, I couldn't help but think about him. It's like his image, his personality, hi aura has imprinted on my heart. He is so humble, so respectful towards elders, and most of all, one would just feel so comfortable and at the same time so mesmerised in his presence. But all these thoughts are also driving me into guilt, I feel like this is wrong, I know that this is wrong, but I also feel some sort of connection to him which I am not able to neglect."

Before I could say anything else, she said, "so you met Kausalyanandan Ram."

I was taken aback, how did she know, I didn't even mention his name.

"Yes, but how did you know?"

She smiled, paused for a moment, looked at me carefully and said, "my child I have known you since you were a little girl, I know your nature, your likes, your inclinations, I know the type of man that will capture your attention. And I have met Ram, and I know that he is the man that would resonate the most with you, with your soul."

I stopped listening to anything else the moment she said 'I met ram' and I just wanted her to take a pause in what she was saying so I could ask,

"You met him? You met Raghunandan?"

My voice came out more like a squeal which was very unlikely of me. Even Mata Gargi was amused at the tone with which I said, I could see the amusement in her expression, though she tried to act subtle, but still her lips curved a little more than 'slightly' as she said,

"Yes, I did meet him."

I waited for her to say something more but she didn't, she waited for me to ask further, so I repeated the same question or rather confusion that was going on in my mind.

"Well, yes, it is Raghunandan that I can't stop thinking about, whose magnetic personality has just embedded in my heart. I just can't help it, but I also feel guilty about it."

"My dear Sita, banish any whispers of guilt that may flutter around your heart. To feel touched by Rama's presence is not a sin, but rather a result of the kind of man he is. I have seen brave warriors and humble sages, and I can tell you with certainty – Rama is all of these, he is a noble man with the strength of a warrior, empathy and wisdom of a saint, and has virtue of great kings. He wears his princely cloak with grace, not arrogance, and his lineage, instead of inflating his ego, fuels his humility. To meet him is to be etched in his memory, for his very essence leaves an indelible mark on the soul. Hence, it is not just you Sita, but everyone, every man, every woman, every child, every elderly, despite all ages and genders, whoever once meet prince ran can never erase that interaction from their memory because there is something divine in Ram, something magnetic. So, there should be absolutely no guilt for he has a personality that can create an impact on anyone's and everyone's heart."

As I heard Mata Gargi's words my smile widened with all the praise, I heard about me as if I felt the proud as she praised him. But maybe she read something in my eyes, maybe she saw a sign of hope or expectation, not quite sure what but she said, "But Sita, I want you to not have any prior expectations from anyone, about anything. I understand that Kausalyanandan's personality is such that one is bound to admire him, but also remember that you are a princess who has a svayamvara in coming days, so you shouldn't be biased, even if the personality like his makes your heart biased, tell your mind to not have expectations."

A little confused I asked, "so you mean I should force myself into not thinking about Raghunandan?"
She looked at me as if I was a little child who is naïve and is looking for answers. I waited for her to say something, but she just smiled. She then got up and said, "Sita, one can force their mind but how will you force your heart which is innocent, which is unaware of the worldly rationalities. I

am suggesting you to steady your mind. I am asking you to have *faith in fate.*

*Faith is one thing that acts as your anchor when your life seems a storm.*

So, my dear Sita, have faith." She paused and then continued again,

"But Sita, always remember to have faith in fate, not in people. As much as faith in fate will not only give you hope and steady your mind, but it will also manifest into something beautiful. But faith in people if shattered will shatter your capability to ever hope again, to ever have faith again." After she said those wise words, I pondered about it.

I knew that if I come to Gargi Mata carrying a burden of doubts, I will definitely walk out the ashram satisfied. Just a brief interaction with her, and she always knew the right words to calm my uneased mind.

Now finally, instead of running away, I accepted my adoration for Raghunandan,

*He's like the dawn, painting a new sky onto the canvas of every soul he touches. You can't help but wake to his light.*

And all my questions about my future groom, my hope for him to attend the svayamvara, the outcomes of the svayamvara, I left these on fate.

"Contended?" Mata Gargi asked looking at me. I realised I hadn't said anything in a while and was just looking into space.

"Ye..." before I could complete my sentence, Mandavi entered huffing and puffing, "Sita didi, *badi maa* has asked you to come, we have some guest sages, they want to meet you."

"Oh sorry, pranam Mata Gargi" she said as she acknowledged Mata Gargi standing right next to me.

Mata Gargi nodded in return, I knew now we couldn't have any more conversation about this now but it was fine because my heart was actually contended, I was at ease regarding this now. So, I looked at Mata Gargi and nodded in pranam. She embraced me in a hug and said, "at every step in your life Sita, no matter how hard your life gets, always remember,

*When shadows engulf and hope dims, faith becomes that ember glowing and rekindling the fire of spirit in the ashes of despair.* Hold onto your faith strongly for it will give you steady mind, and a steady mind can do wonders in the harshest of situations."

"Sure Mata. But won't you attend my svayamvara ceremony? Your words are hinting that this is the last time we are meeting."

She gave a slight laugh and said, "how can I miss my dear Sita's svayamvara ceremony. But I know you will be busy and crowded with so many people and thoughts. We might not get this peaceful, calm atmosphere to exchange words."

I don't know why but Mata Gargi's words overwhelmed me, tears welled up in my eyes, it hurt me like a sting with the thought that this same old life is about to change, I will no longer get to share things with Mata Gargi, listen to her words of wisdom, this ashram, my life will completely change, I realised,

all my present will just become a memory that I can only visit in my thoughts but never in the real world, it will just disappear from the real world, and that feeling was haunting.

Mata Gargi observed the glistening tears in my eyes, yet she chose silence, perhaps understanding the inherent nature of this overwhelming moment. A subtle acknowledgment passed between us, for I could see the moisture in her own eyes, though no tears betrayed her composure. In response, she offered a gentle smile, accompanied by a comforting pat on my shoulder.

Her understanding gaze and the shared emotion lingered in the air, unspoken yet profoundly felt. With a nod of respectful farewell, she bestowed her silent support, allowing me to depart with Mandavi. The unspoken exchange left an indelible imprint, a bridge of shared understanding forged in the quiet moments of emotion that words could not capture.

# IV

Recent days passed like a flick of the finger, the more I wanted the days to pass slowly so I could get more time with my family, I could have more conversations, share more laughter, create more memories, but these past days were not exactly 'slow and steady'. Mother and father have been very busy with the svayamvara and the arrangements, and my sisters were also way too excited for the svayamvara so the conversations that we would have would mostly revolve around this topic.

Yesterday's interaction with Mata Gargi gave me some clarity but I didn't get much time to reflect on it. Whenever I would talk about anything with Mata Gargi, I would always take out some time later especially to reflect on it, to let that wisdom seep into myself, to make that understanding clearer. But amidst the joyous preparations in the palace, and with my exuberant sisters, it had been impossible to take that time out. besides, I too wanted to spend as much time as I could with my sisters and family and so I spent the entire evening taking to them, teasing Urmila, since now even we had something to ease her about. However, I slept a little early yesterday so I could wake up before sunrise and got to my favourite stop for that 'reflection', because it was important for me especially now, especially before svayamvara when my mind needed to have the most clarity and my heart needed to be calm.

I never had a problem waking up early, so today as my sleep drifted away and I woke up, it was slightly dark outside, I could tell, by the time I reached where I had to go, the sun would rise. I carefully got dressed up to go making sure I don't wake any of my sisters, especially Urmila, she had always been so full of energy that she didn't 'like to sleep' if I were to say in her words. She would easily get up from her sleep with even a slightest of disturbance.

As I walked out of my room, I passed by my father's meditation room, and as expected, he was meditating. My father always woke up early, but when no one of us knew, he would always be awake before anyone of us. Our palace normally too would not be so quiet this early in the morning because there would be preparation for breakfast and other morning rituals going on, but today because of the big ceremony coming up, it didn't quite feel like early morning since all the helpers of the palace were already up and busy with their tasks, thank God, our rooms were sound proof or Urmila would not be able to get any sleep. I thought to go and see for my mother but then I decided otherwise, I wanted to go and come back on time before my sisters go around the palace looking for me and asking hence informing everyone that I wasn't in the palace.

I strolled out of the palace, heading toward my cherished haven for contemplation. While the meditation room within the palace walls served its purpose, there was an inexplicable purity in sitting amidst nature, a cleansing communion with the elements. My favoured spot for reflection lay atop a nearby hill, affording a panoramic view of the entire Mithila valley. The surrounding mountains cradled our land, creating an idyllic setting of perpetual pleasant weather and lush greenery.

Upon reaching the hill's summit, the familiar fragrance of the forest enveloped me — the earthy scent of green leaves, the lingering moisture from morning dew. Surveying Mithila below, with its sprawling farms and captivating landscapes, I revelled in an affectionate connection to our homeland. Seating myself on a naturally flattened rock that doubled as nature's chair, I closed my eyes and delved into introspection.

Recalling my conversation with Mata Gargi, I sifted through any lingering doubts that had traversed my mind. My father's advice echoed in my thoughts — articulate the problem, identify its root cause, and contemplate potential solutions. Expressing the abstract complexities of my concerns through words became the pivotal first step. Often, the true source of unrest lay not in the trouble itself but in our inability to define it.

*Most times we are not troubled by the trouble but because we don't actually know what the trouble is.*

As I opened my eyes, the gradual ascent of the sun began, casting a warm glow through the mountainous silhouette. The air resonated with the melody of birdsong, each note harmonizing with the others in a rhythmic morning chorus. There was always one bird that seemed to herald the awakening of its companions, initiating a symphony of avian greetings. The cloudless sky overhead allowed the sun's rays to paint the landscape, and a gentle wind tousled my hair, its comforting shiver adding to the serene beauty of the moment. It was, indeed, a breathtaking sight, it was beautiful.

"It's beautiful, isn't it?" A familiar, angelic voice graced the air. Startled, I turned around to find him standing there with a warm smile.

"Greetings, Prince Ram," I managed to utter, my heart fluttering and racing in response. Hastily, I rose from my seat, stealing a quick glance at my attire to ensure everything was in order. As I stood, I brushed off a few leaves that clung to the celestial-coloured saree I had worn for my ascent. Taking a moment to subtly adjust the blush pink dupatta pinned on the top strands of my hair, I used the small actions as an excuse to compose myself. It was an attempt to ward off the overwhelming shyness and startle from this sudden and unexpected interaction.

"Greetings, Princess Maithili." Rarely did people address me by this name, though it was a name I cherished. I loved being called Janaki, Maithili, or Bhumija, feeling a deep connection to my roots and origin. It brought me a sense of warmth and blessing. It was almost surprising to hear him use this name, and I found myself enchanted by the ethereal sensation, particularly when his soothing voice spoke my name.

"I hope I didn't make you uncomfortable," he said, his words revealing my unintentional display of awkwardness. Taking a deliberate deep breath, I acknowledged the need to compose myself for any further conversation.

"Not at all," I replied, meeting his gaze. "I can't even imagine anyone feeling uncomfortable in your presence; the chances are so slim." Pausing to emphasize the sincerity of the compliment, I continued, "I just didn't expect you to be here. I didn't imagine that my first conversation of the day would be with you."

"So, is it a nice thing or a bad thing?" he inquired with a hint of something different than his usual calm, mature smile.

"From the tales I have heard about you, it is my pleasure to meet you." I replied blushing, feeling the intense warmth on my cheeks.

"I am glad," he whispered, his gaze lingering on me for a fleeting moment that set a million butterflies aflutter within me.

In unison, we turned our attention towards the ascending sun. The backdrop of chirping birds and the gentle caress of the wind formed an unspoken connection. In the ensuing quietude, a serene comfort enveloped us, not awkward but akin to the warmth of home.

***In the embrace of silence, we found a home where words didn't disturb, and familiarity spoke volumes without utterance.***

However, a sudden thought bubbled up in my head, so breaking this beautiful silence, I said, "May I ask you a question?"

"I don't think we should hesitate to clear the fog of our mind. I will be more than happy if I can be the medium to clear that fog" he replied. His responses bore the mark of careful consideration, each word was imbued not merely for the sake of conversation but carrying the weight of profound wisdom. As he turned his attention from the scenery before us to me, a subtle gesture encouraged me to pose my question.

"Why did you release the curse of Mata Ahalya?" I asked the question that has been in my head since the day I heard about this news that a prince of Raghu clan released the curse of Ahalya Mata.

"I thought the empathetic Princess Janaki would be happy about it."

A flush of warmth painted my cheeks at his words. His varied ways of addressing me hinted at a certain closeness, as though he was gradually uncovering layers of familiarity. The way he said, 'I thought the empathetic Janaki would be happy about it', this acknowledgment that he had pondered upon my perspective left me elated.

"Of course, I was immensely happy when I heard about it, being a daughter, being a woman, I was ecstatic. But I also know that it was highly debatable in the society, many people questioned it. Besides, in these many years no one dared to even question the curse, everyone thought it was a justified action by Gautam rishi because you know..." I hesitated a little and then said, "she made the mistake of believing Indra dev to be Gautam rishi when he came disguised as Gautam rishi."

After a thoughtful pause, he posed a question, "Do you believe that what's a matter of debate in society is necessarily wrong?"

"Absolutely not," I responded with conviction. "Debatability implies the existence of differing perspectives, and it is only prudent not to adhere rigidly to one viewpoint. Instead, one should ponder and, based on their individual wisdom, choose a stance."

He remained silent, a knowing smile on his face, prompting me to further inquire, "And that's precisely why I wish to understand your perspective. Why did you choose to act as you did?"

"The answer lies within your own question, Sita," he replied. Detecting my puzzled expression, he continued, "You mentioned that Mata Ahalya was mistaken when she took Indra Dev for Gautam Rishi, when he was disguised as Gautam Rishi himself. That was an innocent mistake, not a crime or sin. It exemplifies the importance of discerning which actions warrant forgiveness and which are beyond redemption."

He looked at me pondering and then continued again, ""In the cradle of innocence, a baby's hand may inadvertently graze the father's face—a tender dance of curiosity. Yet, as the same hand matures and then uses that hand against the father, its touch morphs into an unforgivable symphony, echoing the profound shift from a harmless mistake to the haunting notes of sin." After a pause he continued, "Mistakes are like pebbles on the path, tripping us for a moment, but not diverting us from the journey. Sins are like chasms swallowing the road whole, leaving no way back to light."

He put it so beautifully, I always thought of many replies I would get if ever I got a chance to meet Raghunandan and ask this question, but he would put it so beautifully was beyond my imagination. I looked at hi again, mesmerised, the amount of wisdom he carried. And then a gush of wind landed a leaf from the tree on his broad round shoulders. Shoulders that were also grazed by his thick dark brown hair. I motioned to remove that leaf but then held back as it was inappropriate and this sudden realisation made me feel so shy.

he might have saw this and the evident sudden shy in my expression as his lips curved into a smile as he coughed to hide it and said, "what do you think about it?"

Confused what he was referring to, I looked at the leaf on his shoulder. Though I hadn't said anything about it but there are things you know you didn't say but they heard.

He followed my gaze and dusted off the leaf and said, "I meant about my incident with Mata Ahalya. I mean I know personally you were happy about it, but what do you really *think* about it socially; I am sure there has to be something more."

Oh, this is what he was talking about. He wanted to know my opinion on this. So I thought about it for a moment and said what I felt,

"Kausalyanandan" Sita began, her voice shimmering with quiet awe, "your decision in Ahalya's case wasn't a mere stroke of compassion; it was akin to the pole star, illuminating the path for generations to follow. You didn't simply release a curse; you liberated the very spirit of womanhood. You declared, with thunderous clarity, that the victim shall not be branded the culprit."

I took a pause, there were so many thoughts I wanted to deliver about this and I wanted just the right words to do justice to my thoughts about this sensitive talk. As I saw him still looking at me to continue, I continued,

"Yes, the world sees your act as forgiveness, but I see an even deeper brilliance – the profound acknowledgment of her innocence. Her suffering, born of a cruel twist of fate, not guilt. Her error, as you rightly said, a wisp of misunderstanding, not a stain of sin. You did not just lift a curse; you bestowed upon her the most precious gift – freedom, not as a boon, but as her birthright. In doing so, you have sown the seeds of justice for countless daughters yet unborn, weaving hope with every thread of your righteousness"

I paused for a moment; I couldn't help but deeply connect to this. I don't know why but I have always been deeply touched with this incident, and today he himself was here to ask me abut this. And so I said again,

"No matter how long the gold is kept in filth, it never loses its purity.

Similarly, Mata Ahalya, no matter in what circumstances was surrounded, she didn't lose her purity. She has always been pure, so the suffering that she had to face was very unfortunate." After I uttered my words, I looked at him.

*He looked at me, as if I was a book and he was a fascinated reader.*

His gaze found mine, not with the unsettling feeling that I would have anticipated, but with a curious warmth that unfurled a smile on my lips.

*My knees, instead of buckling under the weight of his presence, rooted me deeper into the earth, like an ancient oak basking in sunlight.*

A confidence bloomed within me, anchoring me like a ship finding safe harbour. My heart, instead of acting like a timid rabbit in the undergrowth of emotions, surprised me with its newfound rhythm, a hummingbird's wings on a sugar rush. Though my heart raced with an unfamiliar cadence and tingles danced through my being, an inexplicable ease and comfort accompanied these sensations. It was as if a surge of vibrant energy animated my spirit, infusing me with a profound sense of vitality, all while maintaining a serene composure that whispered tranquillity to my soul.

Very rare had been the feeling of calm left me, but whenever it did, I could feel its absence in my unsettled mind. So, either it would be gush of feelings entirely or the feel of calm but never both at the same time, I would have even said before today that it was not possible. But it was, I was feeling it.

"I heard that daughters of Mithila were very learned, wise and well educated. Today I feel honoured to witness it with this interaction." Raghunandan said leaving me speechless.

In my father's view, the prosperity of a kingdom hinges on the empowerment of its women, who must be afforded equal access to education and training in all areas traditionally reserved for men. Consequently, my sisters and I were not only instructed in the teachings of scriptures but also in the arts of weapons.

As much as it is important for a woman to be as humble as Gauri, it is also crucial to realise the Durga within.

However, many kingdoms still didn't resonate with my father's beliefs, and my father never even tried to force someone to follow what he believed. I didn't say what to say to this, or rather I decided to not say anything.

*Sometimes you don't say anything not because you have nothing to say but because you know the words can ruin the beauty of it.*

So, after a beautiful pause, Raghunandan said again, "Do you come here daily?"

"On days when I need some time to reflect" I replied.

"So, what is it?"

"What?"

"So, what is it today that is troubling you or you think you need that time for reflection."

I had so many thoughts that needed reflection, some were about him, some were about svayamvara, some revolved around the sorrow f leaving my home Mithila, some were filled with hope about the new family, there were so many thoughts that didn't let my mind rest, so what should I say to him, I was confused.

"Is it about the svayamvara?" Raghunandan asked leaving me by surprise.

"How do you know?" I asked

"For any woman, this juncture marks the pinnacle of confusion and uncertainty, a moment fraught with conflicting emotions. Departing from the familiar embrace of one's family, rich with cherished memories, to embrace an unknown future with open arms isn't a decision taken lightly. Considering your upcoming svayamvara, I couldn't help but wonder if this weighs heavily on your mind," Raghunandan responded, his tone carrying a weight of solemnity and contemplation.

"Yes, that's true" is all I said with a heavy heart because again all those mixed thoughts clouded my head.

"As far as I have had the opportunity to know about Rajrishi Janak, I don't think he imposed this decision on you, about your svayamvara.

"Not at all. My father never imposes anything on us. He asked me if this svayamvara had my consent and only then he sent the invitations for it. But, it's just that..." I again stopped abruptly, I didn't want to say anything negative, I was confused, but I didn't want anyone to think I was unhappy, because that would straightaway question my father, if he imposed his will on us, and that was not the case.

Raghunandan's gaze lingered on me for a fleeting moment, his eyes seemingly probing the depths of my own. Then, with a solemnity that bespoke his understanding, he began, "I recognize the arduous journey that women undertake. They navigate through countless challenges, emerging from each trial stronger and more resilient. Amongst these trials, the svayamvara and marriage stand as formidable tests. While families jubilate at the prospect of a new union, there is a heart that beats with both anticipation and trepidation. She stands on the precipice of choosing a partner, weighed down by questions of whether her decision will prove right. Amidst the festivities of joining a new family, she grapples with the sorrow of leaving behind the familiar embrace of her childhood home. In these moments, she experiences a whirlwind of emotions, each one pulling her in different directions."

I could see how he was not saying just for the sake of saying, but I could see how he meant each and every word, how much respect he carried in his voice when he talked about this, the depth, the compassion that was so evident in his eyes was not easy to neglect.

This time he completely turned towards me and said, "there lies a very big decision in front of you princess Sita, and your heart might be restless. However, knowing and acknowledging your restless heart will only give you the way to a clear mind."

I let those deep words sink in, it was indeed very valuable especially at this point. He didn't have to explain any further, he didn't have to say anymore, it just sank deep in my heart, it was as if his words transcended from his mouth and landed straight to my very soul giving me a clear understanding.

By now, the first blush of dawn had surrendered to a symphony of morning. In the east, the canvas of the sky shifted from soft lilac to fiery apricot, bleeding into a cerulean expanse dotted with wispy clouds like cotton candy ships adrift on a celestial sea. The sun, a benevolent monarch ascending its throne, bathed the world in a golden caress, coaxing shadows into retreat. From slumbering boughs, a feathered chorus erupted. Birds, their voices imbued with an avian glee, wove a tapestry of chirps and whistles, a merry serenade welcoming the newborn day. Dewdrops, clinging to leaves like glistening pearls, caught the sun's first kiss, transforming into fleeting diamonds that winked and sparkled before surrendering to the warmth. A gentle breeze, whispered by the awakening earth, stirred the emerald cloak of the forest, sending leaves shivering in a dance of dappled light and shadow. Fragrant tendrils of honeysuckle and wild rose unfurled, releasing their sweet secrets to the air, creating a perfume as intoxicating as the first sip of sunlight.

"I should get going. My family might be looking for me" I said and looked at his eyes, wishing my eyes could tell him how nice this conversation for me. He looked at me in the same way as if he too was trying to reciprocate the same. After a considerate eye contact that conveyed something beyond words, he said,

"Have a good day princess Janaki" he bowed and turned to walk. The path leading to our current location wound through dense foliage, and dotted with clusters of shrubs. With a deft movement, he forged ahead, parting the thickets to create a clearer passage. His actions, though subtle, conveyed a silent invitation, as if to signal that he was paving the way for me to follow.

I trailed behind him, watching his sturdy figure lead the way. His broad back, straight and broad, exuded an air of confidence symbolising his strong personality. With each step, the muscles on his back flexed subtly, emphasizing his athletic build. As he effortlessly cleared the path ahead, the defined contours of his shoulder blades caught my attention, momentarily drawing my gaze. Quickly refocusing, I shifted my eyes downward, returning my focus to the ground beneath my feet. I had to be considerate about the thoughts and even the observations that crossed my mind in these delicate days.

So, focusing on the ground, paying close attention at every step, the path finally came to a point where we parted our ways to our respected destinations.

# V

*You don't realize how much a person can impact you until you feel the lingering emotions even in his absence.*

Sometimes you meet someone and you feel all your energy to be drained and sometimes after one single conversation you feel so much more empowered so much more positive towards life, almost like you arc living again with a bright new refreshing start. The interaction with Raghunandan left me with this same impact,

that conversation with him was like a balm on my heart that I didn't even knew I needed.

After returning that day went by like a fluttering butterfly, beautifully, cheerfully but before you realise it fluttered away. All these days, we would use words like, my svayamvara is around the corner or it is in some day, but today we would say, 'svayamvara is tomorrow', "tomorrow", such a strange feeling, just the thought of it twisted the inside of my stomach in knots. Never in my life, I felt such a mix of emotions with contrasting feelings all at once, I was happy, excited but also confused and anxious. I was optimistic for a new life ahead, but also my heart wrenched for leaving my paternal home, my Mithila. These recent days, though both my parents were busy, I still got to spend some quality time with my mother, but it was not the case with my father, I didn't get a second's time to spend with him alone, in silence, to have that deep conversation with him, the conversation where he would say some wise words, some motivating words, some words to uplift me. I didn't get a chance to have those conversations with him, especially when it was much needed. And now I would under no circumstances let the chance of having a conversation with him fly past me. But of course, I also had to be considerate about the guests, he might be surrounded by them, and it will rude if I just barge in and demand his company. Well then what should I do...what!! Oh yes, I'll ask *chaacha shri* to help me out, he will find the right moment to convey my message to father. Now all I need to do is look for him.

After making my way through the crowd of working people in the palace, the hustle bustle of preparations, and very cautiously excusing myself from my sisters, I finally spot chaacha shri asking the helpers to escort the guests to the guest rooms.

"Pranaam Chaacha shri"

"God bless you, my child. Tomorrow is a big day; you should be taking some rest" he replied.

To this I said nothing but my tensed brows and distressed eyes wandering on the ground gave him the signal that I wanted to say something.

"Won't you tell your chaacha shri what is it that is troubling you?" he asked.

"I need a little favour" I said but to this I witnessed an unexpected change of expressions, rather than smiling empathetically and asking what it was, his expressions changed to angry, and after a pause he said,

"So, you are this grown up now? Asking me for favours? It breaks my heart."

I stood there clueless not sure what to say, but then a giggle escaped his lips and he said, "remember when you were a little girl, how you would command me to get you extra sweets. Well, that was my Sita. No matter how grown up you think you are or the society thinks you are, but for your parents and me, all you sisters will always be those tiny little mischief makers. Now tell me what is it."

I smiled at him at those words, my eyes filled with tears. What he said brought back the nostalgia and again that feeling of twisted knot in the stomach that now all this will change, it will be left behind, it will only be in my memories. A pat on my shoulder brought me back from my worries, it was chaacha shri, gesturing me to say something.

"Could you please let Pita Shri now that I have been meaning to meet him" I said hesitatingly.

"Just this much? Why don't you ask him yourself, I am sure he won't say no" chaacha shri asked.

"I know he won't say no but it won't look nice if I go in front of guests and say I want to meet you. I know there are prestigious guests who are here to attend my svayamvara so I don't want to be a reason for anyone's inconvenience. You will be with pia shri most part of the day so whenever you think it is appropriate you could deliver my message and whenever the time is right, he cold grace me with his presence."

To this he said nothing, he just looked at me smiling for a while, kept his hand on my head and said,

"I always thought I was the most blessed to have Rajrishi Janak as my brother, but today I feel Rajrishi Janak is the most blessed one to have a daughter like you."

"Well now that breaks my heart, am I not your daughter too?" I replied.

He patted his eyes and said "well of course you are. I will let your father know that you want to meet him." He smiled and then walked away after a nod.

I made my way back to my room admiring and feeling grateful for the people of Mithila, everyone was celebrating the preparations for h upcoming ceremony. The helpers of the castle worked merrily as if it was their own family's celebration, when I looked from the balcony, I could see the streets covered in flowers, people joyously doing the preparations. Anyone would think it was because they loved me so much, but I liked to think it was because of the way my father had inculcated the love and affection in Mithila, he never let the people feel that they were the people of Mithila but instead Mithila was for them, the king, the royal family was there for them, the entire Mithila was one big family. There was so much to learn from my father, and I couldn't help but see similar colours in Raghunandan and maybe that is one those reasons I respected Raghunandan even without knowing him closely.

"Where have you been, didi?" Urmila's voice rang out from behind me, bringing a smile to my face. I turned around to see the three of them approaching with mischief dancing in their eyes. As Urmila, Mandavi, and Shrutkirti approached me, their playful banter filled the air.

"Well, well, all three of you together! Who's in trouble?" I teased, raising an eyebrow in mock suspicion.

"You are?" Shrutkirti chimed in mischievously, her playful grin widening.

"Shrutkirti!" Mandavi scolded, though I could see the hint of a smile tugging at the corners of her lips. They always had a way of lightening the mood, even in the most mundane situations.

"Alright, alright. What I mean is..." Shrutkirti began, but before she could finish, Urmila interjected with a mischievous twinkle in her eye.

"What we mean is we were looking for you, Sita didi. Today, you will spend every single moment of the day with us," Urmila declared with a grin, her enthusiasm contagious.

I couldn't help but chuckle at their antics. "Every moment? That sounds like quite the adventure," I replied, playing along with their enthusiasm.

"Absolutely!" Mandavi agreed, her eyes sparkling with excitement. "We have a whole day of fun planned out for you."

Shrutkirti nodded eagerly. "You won't regret it, didi. It's going to be epic."

I couldn't resist their infectious energy. "Well then, lead the way, my adventurous companions. I'm ready for whatever the day has in store for us," I said with a laugh, falling into step beside them. Though I knew anytime I might receive a message from my father to meet him but I didn't want to break my sisters' heart or ruin their enthusiastic energy. Any which way I am sure I will receive the message or rather the message will find me, all I had to make sure was not to go too far away from the palace premises.

Shrutkirti, Mandavi, and Urmila flitted around me; their excitement palpable in the air. They pampered me with meticulous care, tending to every detail of my appearance as if it were a sacred ritual. My hair was lavished with fragrant oils and gently massaged, each strand treated to a luxurious treatment. Rosewater mist enveloped me, leaving a delicate floral scent lingering in the air. Amidst the bustle of preparations, we stumbled upon a trunk filled with childhood treasures, evoking memories of simpler times and shared laughter. As we sifted through the nostalgic relics of our past, a sense of warmth and camaraderie filled the room, grounding me amidst the whirlwind of anticipation for the day ahead. With each loving gesture and shared moment, my sisters infused the day with an undeniable magic, transforming the preparations into a cherished memory to be treasured for a lifetime.

The evening crept in slowly, the sky ablaze with vibrant colours as the sun prepared to dip below the horizon. Time slips away so fast when you are surrounded by your loved ones or maybe it is there love that you forget about the factor of time. I felt like it was just moments ago when I walked in the hall with my sisters in the bright sunny morning. But now when I stepped out of the hall.

"What is the hurry didi? Wait for us" Mandavi called from behind.

"Oh, I thought you and Urmila had more squabbling to do that's why I walked out" I said with an obvious smile escaping my lips.

"Absolutely, and every time it is me that gets stuck between their fights" shrutkirti said walking out of the hall with a pouty face.

"Oh, you surely are no innocent one, always trying to be the victim in front of Sita didi" Urmila walked by her pulling her braid.

I was about to say something as the hall keeper came, bowed, and said,

"Greeting princess Sita, king Janak wishes to meet you in the second room in the second floor".

"Okay. Sure" I replied and he walked away after a bow.

"The second room in the second floor, your secret room?" Urmila exclaimed.

"Well, that wasn't my secret room" I replied.

"Surely not secret but magical" Mandavi said.

"Oh yeah I remember whenever Sita didi would be distressed or worried or anxious, which was by the way very are, but whenever she would be, she would go to that room, and then bade papa would have some conversation with you and you would be alright." Shrutkirti said pondering which was evidently an exaggerated expression of her going deep down the memory lane.

"Oh, does that mean you are worried again. Is there something troubling you. What is it?" Urmila asked with a rush of questions.

"She would say something if you would stop. Come on Urmila let didi answer." Mandavi said to Urmila.

Before they begin their fight again, it was only right for me to say something. "Okay how about we take a break. So don't worry nothing is troubling me. All other rooms might be occupied and that's the reason he asked me to come that specific room, there's nothing to be worried about. I am really glad to have such sweet and caring siters like you now no more fighting, okay!"
"okay so didi let us escort you to that room, shall we?" Manavi said.

I knew she wouldn't give up so I said yes.

We then walked down to the room I was expected in, and as we reached that entrance to that room my sisters very gracefully said goodbye and left.

I waited patiently for my father to come, he had sent me that message to meet him so he might be here any moment now, I was not sure what I had to ask him, I just wanted to spend some time with him. In this moment of waiting,

I thought why did he specifically call me to this room, did he know that I was worried and anxious or what I said to my sisters was right that there was no other room maybe that's the reason he picked up this room in particular sine this room was not that big like other room for it to solve any purpose. But I also knew that my father would aways know whenever I was anxious or if something was troubling me, I never had to tell him, he would just know and then come and discuss it with me. But this time I was not very sure because he was surrounded with so many works, so many preparations, so many things to think about. I was in fact a little surprised that he could get some time for me, because it was not just a father who was busy with his daughter's svayamvara preparations, but also a king who had hosted so many guests from various kingdoms.

As I stepped into the room, memories flooded my mind, washing over me like a gentle wave. My gaze swept across the familiar surroundings, taking in the sight of the little chairs arranged neatly in a row. Each one held a cherished memory of laughter and play, reminding me of the days when we, sisters, would gather here, lost in our own world of imagination and innocence. I was overwhelmed to see that everything that belonged to our childhood was kept here safely, event he things that we forgot about. They were preserved. It had been years since I cam to this room, and today when I did, it proved a surprise for me.

The room held a timeless charm, preserving fragments of our childhood within its walls. The wooden horses stood proudly in one corner, silent witnesses to countless adventures and make-believe journeys. Nearby, shelves adorned with tiny faded manuscripts that the four of us sisters used to make and then would use those to mimic my father's scripture reading. A subtle laugh escaped my lips thinking of those notorious little activities.

A soft smile tugged at the corners of my lips as I traced the familiar contours of our childhood relics. These simple yet precious treasures were more than just objects; they were fragments of our shared history, symbols of the bond that bound us together as sisters.

Tears welled up in my eyes, a bittersweet reminder of the passage of time. Emotions swirled within me, a blend of nostalgia and gratitude for the moments we had shared in this room.

*Smiling through tears. That's what beautiful memories do. You smile because it was amazing, but your heart aches because you know it's gone forever, you can never relive them.*

*The ache in your heart and the smile on your face, maybe that's the price you pay for cherishing beautiful memories you can never repeat.*

As I sat in the room, surrounded by the echoes of cherished memories, my thoughts drifted back to the countless lessons my father had imparted to me over the years. He was more than just a father; he was my mentor, my guide, and my staunch supporter in a world where women's voices were often silenced.

I remembered how he had always encouraged my thirst for knowledge, tirelessly answering my endless stream of questions and nurturing my curiosity. In a time when many kingdoms denied women the right to an education, my father had insisted on providing us, his daughters, with the same opportunities as the male counterparts.

His teachings went beyond the realm of academics; he instilled in us values of courage, compassion, and integrity. He taught us to stand up for what we believed in, to never compromise our principles, and to always strive for excellence in everything we did.

I recalled the countless hours we had spent together, poring over scriptures and discussing the nuances of philosophy. He had never treated me differently because of my gender, always valuing my opinions and insights as equal. As I reflected on these memories, a pang of sadness crept into my heart. The impending departure loomed over me like a shadow, casting a pall of gloom over the room. The thought of leaving my father, the one constant presence in my life, filled me with a sense of loss and longing.

But just as the weight of melancholy threatened to engulf me, a gentle knock on the door interrupted my reverie. With a deep breath, I composed myself and rose to greet my father, knowing that his reassuring presence would provide solace in the face of impending change.

"There is my daughter" my father said as he entered the room and patted my head as a gesture of blessing. I could see a different spark in his eyes today, his eyes sparkled with what felt like pride.

"You seem very happy Pita shri" I said.

"a father who has a daughter like you can only be happy" he replied.

"I am really glad you think that way, but did something special happen today?" I still wanted to ask not that I didn't like him raising me but just that I wanted to know what it was.

"Enough about me, you tell me how have you been feeling lately?" he changed the subject, so I didn't push it further now, and considered his recent question.

"Me? I am feeling just fine. Why do you ask?"

My father paused and then said, "sometimes Sita,

**Our words dance around the truth, like fireflies flitting in the night. They create a beautiful show, but leave the darkness mostly hidden.**

You are answering all my questions with questions, and one does that when there are emotions to hide within, and those emotions are trying to conceal themselves beneath the questions. Before someone even gets to observe what you are feeling, you first ask question about the other."

The fact that he was precisely right made me feel a little embarrassed and a little astonished. This mix of emotions have been my companion lately, which surprisingly was very unusual for me, I have always been the one who has been clear with emotions. But now I have come in term with it, instead of resisting these, I have accepted it and don't fight them away because maybe that is how a woman feels in the days when she is about to get married or even some days after that.

Sita, my dear, your melancholy is palpable. I see the weight of sorrow in your eyes, and it pains me to witness your distress. Please, share your thoughts with me. What troubles your heart?" My father's voice was a soothing balm, a melody that resonated with understanding.

"Father, why must I leave? Why should a daughter bid farewell to the only home she has ever known, the haven where her heart finds solace? I want to be by your side, to serve you, to spend countless moments with you and Mother. Why does the prospect of marriage demand such a sacrifice?" My voice trembled with the emotions that had welled up within me.

His gaze, filled with a blend of empathy and wisdom, met mine. "My beloved Sita, the pain you feel is a reflection of the deep bond we share. A father's love is boundless, and I understand the sorrow that accompanies the prospect of separation. But, my dear, life is a series of transitions, and each transition brings forth new opportunities for growth and learning."

He continued, "Marriage is not merely a departure but an entry into a new chapter, a union that expands the tapestry of your experiences. It's a journey where you'll discover new facets of yourself, forge new bonds, and contribute to the harmony of a new family. As a daughter, your love for us remains unwavering, and no distance can diminish the connection we hold in our hearts."

"But, Father, why must love be synonymous with separation? Why must my happiness come at the cost of leaving behind the warmth of my childhood, the security of my home?" I implored, my eyes reflecting the turmoil within.

He clasped my hands tenderly and replied, "Love, my child, is not diminished by distance. It transcends the boundaries of physical presence. Your journey is not a farewell but an expansion of the love you carry within you. Embrace this change with an open heart, for in doing so, you not only honour your destiny but also contribute to the eternal cycle of life and love."

He paused and then began again, **"Though a vine may stretch towards the sun, its roots remain firmly planted in the earth. So too, your love for us, my dear Sita, will endure, even as you bloom in another's garden."**

As the echoes of our heartfelt conversation lingered in the room, my father gazed at me with affection. "Sita, my dear, if you believe your childhood here was beautiful, then let those cherished memories be the lantern that guides you through the path of separation."

A mischievous glint sparkled in his eyes as he reminisced about a particular childhood incident. "Do you remember the time you convinced the palace guards that you were a royal inspector sent to evaluate their duty? Your audacity brought laughter to the entire palace, and even the sternest of guards couldn't help but smile."

As we reminisced about cherished memories, laughter echoed through the room, weaving a tapestry of joyous moments shared among siblings. My father regaled me with anecdotes of our childhood adventures, recalling the mischief of my sisters with fondness and affection. Together, we revelled in the warmth of nostalgia, finding solace in the bonds that tethered us together.

However, our reverie was interrupted by a discreet knock on the door, signalling an unexpected intrusion. "Forgive the interruption, Your Majesty," a solemn voice intoned from beyond the threshold. "There is a matter of urgency requiring your attention—a representative of King Ravan of Lanka awaits your audience."

My father's brows furrowed in mild concern as he turned to me, a silent query lingering in his gaze. Without hesitation, I nodded in understanding, offering a reassuring smile to assuage his apprehension. Though a part of me yearned for more time in his comforting presence, I recognized the weight of his responsibilities and the demands of his station.

"I understand, Father," I murmured, my voice imbued with a sense of gratitude and acceptance. "Our conversation has really been a balm to my soul, dispelling the shadows of uncertainty that lingered within."

My father returned my smile with a gentle nod, a silent acknowledgment of our unspoken bond. With a final glance filled with paternal affection, he bid me farewell, his steps echoing the grace of a king burdened with the weight of his kingdom's destiny.

As he departed, I lingered for a moment, savouring the remnants of our shared communion before making my way towards the bustling main hall, where preparations for the impending svayamvara were underway. Though our time together had been brief, I carried with me the reassurance of my father's love and wisdom, a beacon to guide me through the uncertainties that lay ahead.

# VI

Eager to make the most of our last evening together before the svayamvara, I was determined to cherish every moment with my sisters. With the weight of our impending separation looming over us, I longed to immerse myself in their company, seeking solace and strength in our bond.

Having found reassurance in my heartfelt conversation with Father, I felt a newfound sense of calm wash over me. With Mother preoccupied with the myriad preparations for the ceremony, I seized the opportunity to steal away and seek out my sisters.

Knowing that tomorrow's svayamvara would usher in a whirlwind of ceremonies and responsibilities, I was acutely aware of the fleeting nature of this evening. It was a precious window of time, a chance to indulge in heartfelt conversations and laughter before the solemnity of the occasion took hold. Because anyway after the svayamvara ceremony tomorrow, there will be other ceremonies, and we all will be involved in that and before I know, I will be having the *vidai* ceremony. It was only today evening that we could talk properly as much as wanted to. Looking for them I finally reached the Urmila's room where the three of them were sitting.

Stepping into Urmila's room, the glances of my sisters briefly acknowledged my presence before returning their gaze back on the floor. The room, though of a decent size, exuded a distinct personality, much like Urmila herself. Large windows framed in silk curtains of a rich purple hue adorned the space, their height nearly reaching the ceiling. A sizable round bed served as a central gathering spot for the three of them, its crimson bedsheet adding a touch of warmth. In one corner, a dartboard stood, a testament to Urmila's leisure pursuits. Unlike Mandavi, who found solace in dance during her free moments, Urmila found joy in the precision of dart throwing. The room carried a sweet scent of roses, a fragrance that defined Urmila's personal space. Personally accustomed to the soothing fragrance of sandalwood in my own room, the overpowering sweetness of roses felt slightly unfamiliar.

When I noticed their expressions, I saw Urmila and Manavi in furious expressions and shrutkirti with tensed brows. I took the usual guess that they might have had a fight, sighed aloud for them to hear, walked towards the bed and sat. then after a moment of silence, when none of them said anything, I broke the silence saying, "don't tell me you fought again. What was it about this time?"

Urmila and Mandavi looked at me their expressions changing from angry to disappointed as they exchanged glances. So, they didn't fight, so what was it, I looked at shrutkirti but even she had nothing to say. To lighten up the mood I said, "oh so Urmila met Prince Lakshman again, and they both had an arrangement again?" I smiled and looked at them, and yet no change of expressions.

"Okay now, what is it, you are really scaring me. Shrut, you tell me" I asked shrutkirti this time.

"Didi, you know one of the invitations for the svayamvara was also sent to the kingdom of Lanka?" shrutkirti began with a question.

"Yes, I know that..." I replied waiting for her to say further.

"And those so-called guests have arrived and it appears the rumours of that kingdom and that king ae all true" Urmila burst out in anger, her tone was rude and anger was evident in her eyes.

Mandavi rested her hand on Urmila's shoulder to cam her down and then she began, "so they brought a Pushpak Viman with them..."

"Pushpak Viman?" I interrupted.

"Yes didi, Pushpak Viman, it is a very giant thing which takes that king from one place to another. It flies in the sky. It is very huge, almost the size of many farmer's fields."

"Okay, and..." I asked.

Urmila began, her tone edged with frustration, "That's exactly what happened. They chose to land their Pushpak Viman right in the midst of Mithila's fields, destroying all the hard work our people had put in. What's worse, there was plenty of space available on the outskirts, but they deliberately disregarded it out of what they called 'respect' concerns."

"Pita Shri even mentioned that if they had informed us earlier, we could have arranged a more suitable mode of transport for them. But Malyavan decided to argue with Pita Shri, justifying their actions. And to make matters worse, this enormous Pushpak Vimana was solely for Malyavan, the king, and a few of their aides. It's not like the entire kingdom of Lanka had to descend upon us, yet they chose to bring this monstrosity and wreak havoc on our people's hard work," Mandavi added with evident dismay.

It pained me deeply and ignited a surge of anger within me to witness such disregard for the toil of our people in Mithila. The destruction caused by their mere flying machine was unfathomable. However, I understood that displaying my anger would only exacerbate the situation. So, in an attempt to soothe their agitation, I remarked, "Now I understand why they sought Pita Shri's counsel. I have confidence in his ability to handle this situation with wisdom and tact. Let us trust in him. Everything will be resolved."

"Of course, we know that didi," Urmila continued, her voice tinged with concern. "But what troubles us is the thought of him effortlessly lifting the Shiv Dhanush. The mere notion sends shivers down my spine, dear sister. That is our greatest fear."

Her words jolted me out of my reverie. Lost in the enchantment of Raghunandan's presence, I had overlooked the potential outcomes of the svayamvara. Deep down, I harboured a quiet confidence in Raghunandan's strength and abilities, believing that he would undoubtedly emerge victorious. However, Urmila's reminder brought to light the reality of the situation - that there were other participants in the competition, each with their own strengths and aspirations.

And it is not false that there are some very popular tales about Ravana too about how strong he is, but most of those tales reek of negativity where as tales about Raghunandan bloom with positivity. So, considering this I pushed away my fear and said, "Shiv Dhanush not only requires strength but also utmost love and dedication."

As I voiced these thoughts, I anticipated a sense of reassurance to settle upon their expressions. Instead, they exchanged tense glances, their brows furrowed in concern.

After a collective sigh, Shrutkirti spoke up, her tone tinged with apprehension. "Didi, even Ravana is renowned as one of the greatest devotees of Lord Shiva. How then could he possibly fail to lift the Dhanush?"

I could sense their genuine concern, yet their apprehensions only served to exacerbate my own nerves. As my sisters expressed their concerns about Ravana's strength and devotion, a whirlwind of conflicting emotions churned within me. The mere thought of Ravana effortlessly lifting the Shiv Dhanush sent shivers down my spine, igniting a spark of fear in the depths of my heart. His reputation as a devout worshipper of Lord Shiva and his formidable strength painted a daunting picture, one that seemed to overshadow any hopes of a favourable outcome at the svayamvara.

However, amid the tempest of doubt that raged within me, I sought refuge in a glimmer of optimism. I whispered silent assurances to myself, clinging to the belief that Ravana's devotion may have been tainted by the poison of ego, thereby diminishing its potency. In my mind's eye, I envisioned true devotion as a creation of humility, empathy, and selflessness — virtues that I had come to associate with Raghunandan, my beacon of hope.

I took a moment to contemplate their words before responding, although my words were more of a reminder to myself than to them. "Ego, the sense of superiority, these are maladies that corrode devotion from within. A true devotee is characterized by humility, empathy, and inner peace, much like..." I paused abruptly, stopping myself from uttering Raghunandan's name aloud. However, as I glanced at Urmila, a knowing smile spread across her face, indicating that she understood the unspoken sentiment. Well one good thing out of this, at least she smiled.

"Besides I know goddess Gauri will bless me with what is best for me, I have faith in my god. Now don't you want to d something fun before the big day tomorrow, don't you have anything planned for you sister?" I said t lighten up everyone's mood.

"Of course we did, this King Raavan's topic ruined everything, anyways he received more attention than he deserved, he doesn't deserve our time, our talks, or even our thoughts. Now Shrut, get the things that we planned to do." Mandavi replied.

Shrutkirti then brought a scroll of the things they had planned for us to do, which involved her favourite game of charades, where we had to guess the people from our palace. Yet, despite our best efforts to immerse ourselves in the present moment, an undercurrent of fear lingered within me like a shadow, threatening to overshadow our light heartedness.

I desperately tried to conceal my apprehension, burying it beneath layers of forced laughter and casual conversation. I engaged in our usual games, laughed at our inside jokes, and engaged in playful banter with my sisters, all the while struggling to shake off the lingering unease that gnawed at the edges of my consciousness.

However, no matter how fervently I tried to distract myself, the weight of their words hung heavy in the air, casting a pall over our once carefree interactions. Every giggle felt hollow, every jest tinged with a hint of uncertainty. Despite my best efforts to feign normalcy, I couldn't shake the nagging feeling that something was amiss, that the spectre of Ravana's looming presence threatened to disrupt the fragile peace we had cultivated.

With each passing moment, the fear within me grew stronger, its tendrils creeping into the corners of my mind and refusing to be ignored. Despite my attempts to focus on the present, my thoughts kept drifting back to the impending svayamvara and the ominous shadow cast by Ravana's reputation. In that moment, amidst the laughter and camaraderie of my sisters, I found myself grappling with an invisible foe, a silent battle waged in the depths of my soul.

*Like a caged bird, my troubled thoughts fluttered against the bars of denial. The more desperately I tried to silence their song, the louder their chorus became.*

# VII

As I woke with the gentle caress of the morning sun on my face, a rush of emotions swept over me like a tidal wave. Eagerness, anticipation, anxiety, hope—all jumbled together in a tumultuous whirlwind that I couldn't quite untangle. It was the day of the svayamvara, a day I had both longed for and dreaded in equal measure.

Blinking away the remnants of sleep, I sat up in bed, the soft sheets slipping away as I pushed myself upright. The room was bathed in a warm golden glow, the sunlight filtering through the curtains in cascading ribbons of light. Despite the early hour, the palace was already bustling with activity, the sounds of preparation echoing through the corridors.

Yesterday's conversations with my sisters had stretched into the late hours of the night, leaving us all exhausted but content in each other's company. Now, as I glanced around the room, I saw them still sleeping peacefully, their forms wrapped in blankets like delicate cocoons.

Pushing aside the covers, I swung my legs over the edge of the bed and stood up, the cool marble floor sending a shiver up my spine. Moving towards the window, I pulled back the curtains and peered outside. The scene that greeted me was a stark contrast to the quiet tranquility of our chambers.

The palace grounds were alive with activity, servants hurrying to and fro with a sense of purpose, the air buzzing with excitement and anticipation. It didn't feel like the early morning; rather, it felt as though the day was already well underway, the sun high in the sky casting its warm glow over everything it touched.

Taking a deep breath, I tried to steady my racing heart and calm my jumbled thoughts. Today was the day—the day I had been preparing for, the day that would determine the course of my future. And as I stood there at the window, bathed in the soft light of the morning sun, I couldn't help but feel a surge of hope and determination rising within me. Whatever lay ahead, I was ready to face it with courage and grace. I was not just a woman looking for her potential groom, I was a princess of Mithila, I was daughter of Rajrishi Janak, I had weight of many roles and responsibilities resting upon my shoulders.

The sudden knock on the door jolted me from my reverie, and I hurriedly made my way towards it, the anticipation coursing through my veins. As I opened the door, I was met with the sight of my mother standing there, accompanied by a few of her trusted lady helpers.

"Good morning, Mother," I greeted her with a smile, though I couldn't help but notice the tears glistening in her eyes. Despite the tears, there was a radiant smile on her lips, and she enveloped me in a warm embrace that felt tighter and more lingering than usual. Her embrace was filled with a myriad of unspoken emotions, a mixture of pride, love, and perhaps a hint of sadness at the thought of her daughter embarking on a new chapter of her life.

"It's time for you to get ready for the big occasion today," Mother's voice rang with a blend of excitement and tenderness as she entered our room, accompanied by a few lady helpers. Her words carried a wide, affectionate smile, but as her gaze shifted to my sisters, her expression turned somewhat sarcastic.

"Ah, lovely. I am blessed with such early birds," she remarked loudly, her tone dripping with playful sarcasm. However, Mandavi seemed deeply immersed in her slumber, oblivious to Mother's jest, while Shrutkirti and Urmila murmured incoherently in response, still lost in the realm of sleep.

Mother walked over to them; her affectionate smile now replaced by a hint of exasperation. With firm pats on their shoulders, she gently shook them awake. "Your sister's svayamvara is today. Don't you girls have any responsibilities? Wake up, my dears, these girls will drive me insane. Wake up."

They stirred from their slumber, blinking and rubbing their eyes, still caught in the hazy aftermath of sleep. As laughter bubbled up from within me, mingling with the tears that streamed down my cheeks, I couldn't help but be overwhelmed by a mix of emotions. The scene before me, with Mother's gentle scoldings and my sisters' stubbornness, painted a picture of familial love and familiarity that I knew I would dearly miss.

"Ah, didi, you're already up! When did you wake?" Urmila's voice rang out as she noticed me standing beside Mother.

Before I could respond, Mother interjected, "Way before the three of you. She's the responsible one here. Now, enough with the chatter. Get up at once, get ready, and then help your sister in getting ready for the svayamvara. Hurry up now."

After a brief pause, as if lost in thought, Mother muttered to herself, "And where are those flowers I asked her to get... Where is she? I sent her with the..." Her words trailed off as she walked away from the room. I could sense the mounting tension within her as she strived to ensure that everything was perfect for the day.

Amidst thoughts of the significant day ahead, I immersed myself in the process of getting ready. My sisters had already completed their preparations, each looking absolutely stunning in their vibrant dresses. They assisted the lady helpers in adorning me for the occasion. My hair was expertly styled and adorned with intricate hair jewellery. The attire chosen for the day was a striking red saree with a velvet base and delicate net layers cascading over it. A broad golden border adorned with numerous gems added a touch of opulence to the ensemble. To complete the look, an extra layer of clothing was added—a luxurious veil resting gracefully on my head, securely pinned to my hair. The veil boasted the same thread work and gem embellishments as the saree, maintaining a seamless harmony of colour and material. The final result was nothing short of resplendent, befitting the significance of the day.

My hands were delicately adorned with gleaming gold bangles, their weight a comforting reminder of tradition and elegance. The jewellery selected for my neck was a perfect blend of opulence and cultural significance, featuring stunning traditional designs from Mithila. Layers of pearl necklaces adorned my neck, their lustrous sheen adding an ethereal touch to the ensemble. As I admired the intricate designs and shimmering pearls, my gaze shifted to my henna-stained hands, the intricate patterns perfectly complementing the golden bangles. Completing the ensemble, anklets adorned my feet, their soft chimes adding a musical rhythm.

My lips were adorned with a deep red lip tint, adding a touch of boldness and elegance to my appearance. A subtle blush in a matching hue graced my cheeks, adding a flush of warmth and radiance to my complexion. My eyes were accentuated with rich, thick kohl, enhancing their natural beauty and adding an air of mystique to my gaze. Though the attire was not my usual choice, it perfectly complemented the role of a bride, adding an aura of grace and sophistication to my overall look.

"Wow, didi, you look absolutely beautiful," Urmila exclaimed as she delicately adjusted the veil atop my head, her eyes reflecting genuine admiration.

"Indeed, it's surprising that I have to agree with Urmila. You look incredibly graceful," Mandavi chimed in, not leaving any chance to direct a comment towards Urmila as well.

Shrutkirti, always curious and observant, posed a question with her characteristic frankness, "But didi, I'm curious. You usually prefer pastel shades, so why the departure from your usual palette today? I mean, even those colours offer a plethora of beautiful dress designs."

In response to Shrutkirti's question, I offered an explanation with a smile, "It's not just about the colour, Shruti. Red holds significant symbolism. It's considered auspicious, representing love, passion, fertility, and prosperity. What better qualities to manifest on such an auspicious day? Additionally, red is believed to ward off negativity and invite positivity to new beginnings in one's life. Moreover, it's associated with Goddess Parvati herself. So, can you think of a more fitting colour for a bride on this special occasion?"

Shrutkirti nodded, her expression reflecting contentment and satisfaction with my response. "No, not at all," she affirmed with a smile.

I then sighed and finally raised my eyes slowly to look at myself in the mirror, a little shy, a little optimistic. As I gazed at my own reflection, I almost couldn't recognize myself with this different makeover. People have told me that I am a woman now, and especially recently, I believed I had transitioned into a woman. Yet, as I looked at myself in the mirror, I realized that I had indeed become a woman. The little girl within me observed the grown woman standing before her with a sense of admiration, pride, and astonishment. In that moment, I existed as both—a girl and a woman—simultaneously, as I embarked on this pivotal journey of making life-altering decisions.

# VIII

The moment had arrived, the one that had been eagerly anticipated for days, the culmination of excitement that resonated throughout. As I approached the venue of my svayamvara, the grand hall, my heart raced, its beats echoing in my ears. A warmth flushed my cheeks, and though my feet remained firmly planted on the ground, I felt a surge of nervous energy. Walking with my sisters by my side, one might perceive me as confident, resolute in my decisions. However, the truth painted a different picture. Despite the composed exterior, an internal storm of chaos and turbulence raged within me, concealed beneath the facade of composure.

A moment of stillness settled as I stood at the entrance of the hall, the weight of my lineage emphasized by the booming voice of the announcer. "Eldest daughter of Rajrishi Janak, Queen Sunayana, graces us with her presence," echoed the announcement, commanding the attention of all assembled. With each step, I moved forward with deliberate poise, my eyes fixed on the ground yet keenly aware of the guests and participants lining the hall.

The hall itself was a symphony of fragrance, filled with the sweet scent of marigolds and roses meticulously arranged to adorn every corner. As I proceeded, the grandeur of the setting unfolded before me. In the middle of the hall was a yellow curtain drawn to cover a vast table at the centre. It might be the Shiv Dhanush covered by that curtain. A sweeping staircase led to the throne where my father, King Janak, sat in regal splendour. Flanking the throne were seats reserved for esteemed senior rishis, while on the opposite side, elevated and adorned with opulence, were the seats designated for me and my family.

Amidst the magnificence of the scene, my heart fluttered with a whirlwind of emotions. Despite the composed facade I presented to the world, inside, a tumult of feelings swirled within me, a blend of anticipation, nervousness, and a profound sense of duty.

As I gracefully settled into my seat, my father, King Janak, took centre stage, addressing the gathered guests and esteemed rishis. With a deliberate modesty, I kept my eyes lowered, feigning an air of composed detachment. However, beneath the poised exterior, my gaze subtly flitted between the guests, a discreet search for a familiar saffron-clad figure amidst the assembly.

My heart held a silent plea for Raghunandan's presence. He came to Mithila with Maharishi Vishwamitra, not as a participant but as a devoted disciple. I yearned for the reassurance of his familiar presence, a beacon of comfort amid the grandeur of the svayamvara ceremony. Despite the uncertainty, a glimmer of hope danced within me, questioning why he might be present in Mithila if not for the Svayamvara. I tried to surrender myself to fate and hope for the best from it.

As the vibrant yellow curtain descended, its graceful descent snapped me back from the depths of my contemplation. The moment it unfurled, a collective murmur of awe and wonder swept through the assembled guests. Their hushed gasps echoed through the hall, a symphony of reverence as their eyes fell upon the magnificent centrepiece: the grand and resplendent Shiv Dhanush.

In that solemn moment, an unspoken reverence filled the air, palpable in the shared bow of respect from every corner of the hall. The sheer majesty of the divine bow commanded a collective acknowledgment, a humble homage paid by all in its presence.

The svayamvara ceremony unfolded swiftly, with a procession of kings and princes taking their turns to attempt the daunting task of lifting the divine Shiv Dhanush. Each contender grappled with the massive bow; their futile attempts evident in their strained efforts. The bow, seemingly immovable, resisted every attempt to be raised, let alone strung.

Observing this spectacle, a wave of discomfort swept through me. The laughter and mockery that echoed in the hall as one after another failed only deepened my unease. With each scornful comment and derisive chuckle, my heart distanced itself from the participants, questioning their arrogance and insensitivity. In the face of such humiliation, my sympathy leaned towards those struggling, and I found myself detached from the revelry around me.

As the procession of kings and princes continued, my attention wandered, unimpressed by the display of power and privilege. They all seemed to blend into a sea of sameness, their behaviour and demeanour lacking in distinction.

However, amidst the monotony, a single announcement pierced through the air, jolting me from my reverie. It felt as though time momentarily froze, my heart seemed to stop, my stomach tightening into knots, and a dizziness enveloping me. The announcer's voice reverberated through the hall,

"*Lankapati* Raavan will now grace us with his presence as the next eligible candidate for the svayamvara" the announcement declared, the mere mention of his name sending a shared shiver through the entire hall.

As the words reverberated through the hall, a heavy silence descended upon the gathered crowd, each individual's gaze fixed unwaveringly on the entrance. I couldn't help but recall the tales of terror surrounding Lankapati Raavan, and in that moment, those stories seemed all too real. The mere mention of his name cast a chill over the entire hall, enveloping each person in an icy grip of fear. It wasn't merely a prejudice or preconception but rather an undeniable presence of negativity that seemed to permeate the room at the mere mention of his name.

*Like one can see the dark clouds before the rain, before a person comes his aura.*

And then a large figure appeared to enter the hall with thumping steps. He was huge, his face was not very clear at such distance only his bright yellow attire and a big golden crown. As he walked the sound of his jewellery echoed as he walked. He wore too much gold, i felt like as a bride I didn't wear as much gold as he did. I could see how he overdid himself. Some would say his steps were confident, but I had seen Raghunandan walking so I knew what a confident walk was, this was something else, this looked like an arrogant walk of an egoistic king.

Though it was wrong to presume before knowing about him, my initial impressions were confirmed the moment I heard his reply to my father. When my father greeted him with warmth, saying, "Pranam, King Raavan, welcome to Mithila. It seems you just arrived at the svayamvara and missed the inauguration ceremony", Raavan's response was swift and callous.

"Lankapati doesn't wait for anything, let alone a woman. I came when I wanted to, I don't have time to spare on watching people lose" he declared, his voice booming with an air of authority. It was evident that humility was a trait far removed from his usual demeanour.

His words ignited a fierce anger within me. How dare he speak in such a disrespectful manner? In that one sentence, he not only insulted the ceremony but also disrespected me, my father, and all the guests gathered here. His arrogance was palpable, evident in every line etched on his face. While I had always admired dark complexions, finding them attractive, I couldn't say the same for him. With his dark complexion, large moustache, and beard, he stood there with his face tilted slightly upward, exuding an air of superiority that overshadowed everyone else present.

In response, my father attempted to steer the conversation towards a more friendly tone, trying to extend courtesy to our guest. "Well, how do you like our Mithila?" he asked humbly.

To this Raavan burst into laughter at this, then turned to the man standing next to him, saying, "Did you hear that, Naana Sri Malyavan? He's asking how I liked Mithila. As if there's anything to like here! They call this jungle a place. Well, of course, not everyone has had the opportunity to visit Lanka, and that's why they don't understand the enormity of it; otherwise, they wouldn't have asked such a question." The man standing next to him, apparently Malyavan, Raavan's maternal grandfather, also laughed, exhibiting the same ego and attitude reflected in his face.

I had heard my father tell me how a person 'grows' old, he grows into a more humble, wise being, but for the first time I could see a man standing in front of me proving otherwise. Malyavan looked old in appearance but had the ego and arrogance of a man who is far away from wisdom.

From the tales I had heard about him, I had no desire to marry him. However, after witnessing his demeanour firsthand, I was resolute in my decision to refuse any proposal involving him. His actions, words, and mere presence left me feeling repulsed. Never before had I experienced such intense negativity towards another person. I felt compelled to discuss this with my father, to convey my adamant stance against marrying this man. Glancing in my father's direction, I hoped for his reciprocal gaze, and to my relief, he met my eyes. Despite the tension etched on my face, my father responded with a slight smile and an extended blink, conveying reassurance and urging me to trust him. Just as I was reassured by my father's subtle gesture, I felt a comforting hand on my arm. It was Urmila, seated beside me, her expression mirroring my own apprehension. She whispered softly, "Have trust, didi. I'm sure Father will not allow you to marry him, especially after witnessing his behaviour. He must have something planned."

"Then, Lankapati Raavan, kindly grace us all with your calibre and strength that till now we have only heard in tales," Father uttered these words with a tone of formality, yet I could sense the underlying tension in his voice. Clutching Urmila's hand more tightly, I couldn't help but feel a surge of anxiety. Mandavi's voice, though hushed, resonated with anger as she whispered, "Then why is he asking him to pick up the bow? He should just tell this arrogant Raavan to leave the svayamvara. There is no chance he could marry Sita didi."

I could understand Mandavi's anger, and I appreciated her concern for me, but I knew the weight of responsibility that my father carried as a king. So, I explained to her, "Mandavi, Pita Shri might have thought of something. He might be sure that Raavan won't be able to pick up the bow. There can be many reasons. But one thing I know for sure is that he, as a king, can't disrespect a guest, especially when he is as villainous as Raavan."

Even though I tried to reassure Mandavi that Raavan might not be able to lift the bow, my heart trembled with the thought of its possibility.

Raavan's words reverberated through the hall, his voice filled with arrogance. "Absolutely. Who wants to stay in this Mithila any longer? I will just pick up this bow at once and win her. But before that, keep in mind, Princess Sita, that you will never be able to take the place of my dear Mandodari, my first wife. She will always have the first place that she deserves, and you will never be my top priority."

His words cut through the air like a sharp blade, leaving an uncomfortable tension in the hall. I felt a chill run down my spine as his disdainful gaze fell upon me, and I couldn't help but feel a surge of anger and indignation at his audacity. How dare he speak to me in such a disrespectful manner, as if I were nothing more than a mere pawn in his game of ego and power? But despite the fire burning within me, I remained composed, determined not to let his words shake me.

As tears welled up in my eyes, I looked at my father, feeling a mixture of anger and frustration coursing through me. This was the first time I had experienced such intense negative emotions, and it was overwhelming. My gaze met my father's, and I could see the suppressed anger reflected in his eyes. Despite his efforts to maintain composure, I could sense the boiling rage beneath the surface, evident in his pursed lips and tightly clenched hands.

The silence that followed Raavan's words weighed heavily in the air, the tension palpable as we all awaited the outcome of his attempt. In that moment, I fervently hoped that Raavan would fail in his arrogant endeavour. The thought of him succeeding, of being bound to such a man for eternity, filled me with dread and despair.

As Raavan reached for the bow, my heart pounded with fear, each beat echoing in my ears. I watched anxiously as he grasped the bow, his expression shifting from pride to tension as he attempted to lift it. Despite his efforts, the bow remained unmoved, as if anchored to the ground. A wave of relief washed over me as it became evident that Raavan was unable to even budge the bow.

Glancing at my sisters, I saw Urmila and Mandavi sporting broad smiles, their eyes sparkling with amusement. Even Shrutkirti, usually composed, couldn't contain her laughter, her hand pressed against her mouth in a failed attempt to stifle her giggles. Their joy was infectious, and for the first time since the morning's events unfolded, a smile tugged at the corners of my lips.

As Raavan struggled in vain to move the bow, his efforts met with resounding failure each time. With each futile attempt, a sense of relief washed over me, mingled with a glimmer of hope. I could feel the tension mounting not just in Raavan's expression but also in his grandfather, Malyavan.

After several moments of fruitless endeavour, my father finally spoke up, breaking the tense silence that had enveloped the hall. "It appears, Lankapati, that destiny has a different groom in mind for my daughter. Let us now allow others to try their hand."

I watched in awe as my father maintained his composure and eloquence, even in the face of Raavan's brashness. However, as expected, Raavan responded with characteristic arrogance, his voice echoing through the hall with a roar. "If not me, then who? Don't you know I am the greatest devotee of Lord Shiva? Only I possess the strength to lift this bow, and no one else."

Before anyone could interject, Raavan closed his eyes and joined his hands in prayer, his demeanour shifting from fury to tranquillity in an instant. As he chanted fervently, a sense of unease settled over the hall, contrasting sharply with the calm expression on Raavan's face. It was strange to see how a person who was roaring in arrogance till now was so calmly chanting his prayers.

He then slowly opened his eyes and touched the bow with both hands and he tried to pick it up. As Raavan touched the bow and attempted to lift it, a sense of dread washed over me. The bow responded to his efforts, rising slightly in his hands, causing my heart to race with fear. I watched anxiously as Raavan continued to exert force, the bow moving inch by inch, still only a fraction of the way off the table, but still it was the most anyone did so far. Despite the slight progress, Raavan's expression shifted once more, his calm demeanour replaced by a self-satisfied grin that oozed with ego and arrogance.

However, as quickly as the grin appeared, it vanished, replaced by a scowl of frustration as the bow slipped from his grasp and clattered back onto the table. Enraged, Raavan made another attempt, using both hands to lift the bow, but it remained immovable, mocking his efforts. Rage bloomed on Ravana's face, his voice echoing through the hall like a tempest. "Treachery!" he boomed, his words vibrating with fury. "King Janak seeks to make fools of us all! He parades this so-called Shiva Dhanush, a mere mockery, and expects us to believe it real!"

A collective gasp rippled through the assemblage. Ravana, the mighty demon king, known for his unparalleled strength and devotion to Shiva, had failed. Now, he questioned the very legitimacy of the divine bow, casting a shadow of doubt upon the entire Svayamvara.

My father, the Rajarishi Janak, rose from his throne, his regal bearing radiating a quiet power that contrasted sharply with Ravana's bluster. His voice, though firm, held a note of steely resolve. "Choose your words carefully, King Ravana," he declared. "To question the integrity of the Dhanush is an insult not only to me, but to this sacred Dhanush. If your vaunted devotion cannot overcome this challenge, then perhaps your faith is not as unwavering as you claim."

Ravana's roar echoed anew, tinged with a wounded pride. "If it were indeed the true Dhanush, wielded by Shiva himself, I would have lifted it with ease!" he bellowed. "But this? This is a pale imitation, a mockery! The greatest devotee of Shiva stands defeated, not by the bow, but by a sham!"

"Lankapati Ravan, mind your words before I forget that you are a guest and should be treated with respect." This time my father's words echoed loud, for the first time I saw my father use this tone, but I wouldn't blame him for this, in fact I was surprised on witnessing the amount of patience he had.

But as he said this Ravan roared, as Raavan's roar echoed through the hall, sending shivers down our spines, the entire assembly fell into an eerie silence. Only the lingering echo of his furious bellow hung in the air, a haunting reminder of the terror that gripped us all.

And then, in a moment that seemed to defy all logic and reason, the tales we had only heard in whispers and legends unfolded before our very eyes. The ten heads. Before us was a gruesome scene, before us stood Raavan, his form grotesque, his eyes burning with rage, and atop his shoulders, not one, but ten heads.

The sight was gruesome, horrifying, and utterly surreal. The entire assembly, myself included, stood frozen in shock and disbelief, rendered speechless by the nightmarish spectacle before us. It was as if the boundaries of reality had been shattered, plunging us into a realm of darkness and terror that we could scarcely comprehend.

In that moment, I closed my eyes tightly, hoping against hope that when I opened them again, it would all be nothing more than a dreadful illusion. But as I reluctantly opened my eyes, the ghastly truth remained unchanged, and I found myself forced to confront the horrifying reality unfolding before me.

Fury contorted Ravana's face, his ten heads seeming to pulsate with a dangerous red glow. "A pathetic display!" he roared, his voice scraping against the ornately carved ceiling. "This kingdom, this Mithila, is a mere speck compared to the grandeur of Lanka! And the princess, is she truly worthy of such a spectacle? Whispers follow her like shadows, whispers of an unorthodox birth. Perhaps that's the real reason behind this sham of a Svayamvara, a desperate attempt to pawn her off on some unsuspecting fool!"

A gasp escaped my lips, and I felt the blood drain from my face. My sisters, their faces flushed with anger, started to rise, but a hand on my arm stopped them. It was I who should respond, but my voice seemed to have deserted me.

My father, however, remained unfazed. His gaze met Ravana's with unwavering steel. "King Ravan," he said, his voice low but powerful, "your words are unbecoming of a king. The Dhanush is no mere prop, and the princess's lineage is beyond reproach. If your strength and devotion fail you, perhaps it's time to look inward for the true source of your shortcomings."

Ravana's roar was deafening this time. He hurled insults at the assembled guests, mocking their weakness and questioning the very purpose of the Svayamvara. With a final, scathing glance at my father, he stormed out of the hall, his loyal companion, Malyavan, scurrying after him.

An unsettling silence descended upon the room. The guests, a moment ago enthralled by the drama, now buzzed with nervous whispers. "Can no one lift the Dhanush?" "What happens to the Svayamvara now?" "Was it all a sham?" Their questions hung heavy in the air, a storm brewing beneath the previously festive atmosphere.

I felt a surge of anger, hot and fierce. My palms clenched into fists, the fabric of my sari digging into my skin. Shame burned in my throat, fuelled by Ravan's malicious words. Yet, a sense of calm settled over me as I looked at my sisters, their faces mirroring my own outrage. We exchanged a silent understanding.

"Stay seated," I whispered, my voice firm despite the tremor within. They might want to lash out, to defend me and our family's honour, but pride wouldn't answer these accusations. Father would handle this.

My father, his back ramrod straight, surveyed the murmuring crowd. He raised a hand, and the hall fell silent once more. "The Svayamvara may have taken an unexpected turn," he began, his voice steady, "but the

Dhanush remains. The challenge stands. Let those who possess the strength and devotion continue to try their hand."

His words held a quiet authority that quelled the rising tide of chaos. The guests exchanged uncertain glances, some looking at the formidable bow with renewed trepidation, others seemingly reevaluating their chances.

# IX

"Absolutely right Rajrishi Janak. The shiv Dhanush is here, and so stands the svayamvara, and so does the potential groom for princess Sita" a calm yet strong voice appeared before the man who said it. As the words echoed through the hall, a hush fell over the assembly, and all eyes turned towards the source of the calm yet resolute voice. It was a familiar voice, and soon we recognised the man who said it as he walked into the hall for everyone to see followed by two figures in the back. It was none other than sage Vishwamitra, his esteemed presence commanding attention and respect.

My heart skipped a beat as I recognized the figure walking beside the sage, and a surge of hope coursed through me. Could it be? Was it truly him? Before my mind could fully comprehend the possibility, reality swiftly intervened, dispelling any lingering doubts as my gaze fell upon Raghunandan, walking with purpose behind Sage Vishwamitra.

In that moment, a rush of emotions flooded my being — relief, joy, and an overwhelming sense of anticipation. With Raghunandan's arrival, a newfound optimism enveloped the hall, casting aside the lingering shadows of doubt and fear.

My heart, a frantic bird trapped in my chest, fluttered its wings against my ribs. Tears welled in my eyes, hot and unexpected, a mixture of overwhelming happiness and a hope that dared to bloom. Raghunandan's presence, a beacon amidst the storm, chased away the gnawing anxiety that had shadowed me all day. My gaze locked onto him as he walked with a grace that spoke volumes. Confidence radiated from him, yet he was grounded, unassuming. A subtle smile graced his lips – not a forced gesture, but one that seemed to emanate from a wellspring of inner peace. It had the power to disarm even the tensest soul, and in that moment, it was as if the stale air of the hall, poisoned by Ravana's venomous words, was purified.

He stopped his walk, his eyes lifting ever so slightly in my direction. My heart, in that instant, felt like it dispersed into million tiny butterflies. I would have bartered every possession I owned, every future hope, to make time stand still. Just to recapture that exhilarating skip in my heartbeat as his gaze met mine. There was a language in those eyes, a silent conversation that transcended words. Stories untold, emotions unspoken, yet a familiarity bloomed between us, a comfort as deep as an ancient well. They were eyes, I felt, that had known mine for lifetimes, even if our conscious minds remained oblivious.

I felt like his eyes asked me to calm down, as if his eyes knew I have been restless all this while, I felt like his eyes said, have faith,

*I felt like his eyes did a million talkings which lips were too shy to say.*

My eyes broke contact with his as Urmila tightly clenched my hand in excitement, the joy on her face was very evident as she smiled and whispered, "well now I already know who is about to be our brother-in-law"

Her words made me blush, but I quickly composed myself realising once again I was an unbiased princess here.

"Welcome, welcome Rajrishi Vishwamitra. It is our honour to have you here, this assembly is blessed to have your presence here." My father said.

"Pleasure is all mine; you can trust me on that King Janak" maharishi Vishwamitra said with a smile as if something was going on in his mind.

"Welcome prince Ram, Prince Lakshman" my father added as they both bowed to my father in pranam. After they bowed to my father I pranam, Raghunandan looked at my direction, with a smile a little extended than the constant one on his face, and then hi nodded slightly. This brought a smile on my face that was very difficult to hie, and I knew anyone looking at me would have seen this but I couldn't help the smile that came straight from my heart.

"I heard the people raising questions about the shiv Dhanush, about this svayamvara, but why? The assembly which had no problem suddenly doubts and expresses rage when just one-person expresses his discontent? Is it so easy to manipulate you people, does your wisdom carry only this much of gravity?"

Silence fell upon the entire assembly; I could see the kings and princes lowering their heads feeling embarrassed for how they just reacted losing all their patience. the assembly which had become all chaotic was now completely silent,

silent not in terror but it a silence of ponder.

After a moment of silence, Rajrishi Vishwamitra began again, "still, since you 'great' kings have raised questions and queries about the svayamvara, about this Dhanush, I proudly introduce you to my absolutely extraordinary student, eldest son of king Dashrath and queen Kausalya, who has defeated many demons, brought back safety, security and peace on many lands, this is Prince Ram of Ayodhya."

Even after such a proud introduction by sage Vishwamitra I saw Raghunandan just standing there with that subtle smile, no change in body language, no sign of ego or superiority, and that there I found the difference, the difference between real great men and ones who just claim to be.

Great men like Raghunandan are praised by others whereas men like Ravan seem to feel the need to not just praise themselves but boast about themselves.

All eyes in the hall converged on one figure—Raghunandan. With purposeful strides, he approached the revered bow, his gaze steady as he addressed my father. "I seek your permission, Rajrishi Janak, to participate in the Svayamvara and test my fate, if I am fortunate enough to be graced by the presence of your daughter, Princess Sita, in my life."

His words stirred a flurry of emotions within me—blushes tinted my cheeks, nervousness danced in my stomach, and a sense of being truly cherished enveloped me. I lowered my gaze, my lashes forming a protective curtain over my eyes as I revelled in the warmth of his words. I felt special, treasured, and deeply moved by the sincerity in his request. Slowly, I raised my lashes, mustering the courage to meet his gaze once more.

His earnest gaze locked with mine as he spoke again, his words a gentle caress upon my soul. "Princess Sita, I seek your permission to participate in this Svayamvara. Allow me the chance to test my abilities and perhaps, if fate permits, to be blessed with your presence in my life. Any man would count himself fortunate to have you as his wife—a princess known for her empathy, wisdom, and knowledge not only of scriptures but also of weaponry. You possess the love of Gauri and the strength of Durga. Oh, Princess of Mithila, Princess Vaidehi, I stand before you humbly, ready to partake in this Svayamvara."

His words, laden with reverence and admiration, painted a smile across my lips. I offered a slight nod in acknowledgment, though even that simple gesture felt like a monumental effort. My heart swelled with shyness and gratitude, overwhelmed by the depth of his respect and the warmth of his words. In that moment, I realized how deeply he had touched my soul, already winning me over with his words and reverence.

In the midst of the grandeur of the hall, amidst the kings, princes, and revered sages, it felt as though the entire world had faded away, leaving only him and me in a cocoon of anticipation. Despite being surrounded by my sisters and the gathered assembly; my focus was solely on him. Every word, every gesture seemed to carry immense weight, as if the fate of my future hung delicately in the balance.

Nervousness fluttered on the surface of my being, threatening to overwhelm me with its intensity. Yet, beneath that veil of apprehension, lay a profound sense of trust. It was a trust that ran deep, like an unspoken bond that tethered our souls together. In that moment, I felt a certainty, a quiet assurance that whispered to me from the depths of my heart. I knew, somehow, that he would succeed. It was as though destiny itself had ordained this moment, weaving our lives together in the intricate tapestry of fate. With every beat of my heart, with every breath I took, I held onto that unwavering belief—that he would lift the Dhanush, that he would emerge victorious, and that our destinies were intertwined in ways beyond our understanding.

As Raghunandan's hand extended toward the sacred Dhanush, my heart mirrored the rapid pace of his action. With bated breath, I watched as his fingers wrapped around the bow, a silent prayer echoing in the depths of my soul. In a seamless motion, he effortlessly hoisted the once-immovable object, as if it were a feather-light token.

A wave of disbelief washed over the assembly, mingled with awe and reverence. It was a sight to behold, one that defied the bounds of rationality and ventured into the realm of legend. In mere moments, Raghunandan had achieved what seemed impossible, shattering the boundaries of doubt with his unwavering resolve.

Yet, amidst the collective gasp that rippled through the hall, there was an unexpected twist of fate. As Raghunandan sought to secure the bowstring, a sudden crack split the air, sending shockwaves through the silent chamber. The sacred Dhanush, once revered as a symbol of divine might, now lay broken in two, a testament to the unforeseen turn of events.

Despite the unexpected outcome, there was no trace of dismay on Raghunandan's countenance. With a demeanour as tranquil as a placid lake, he remained poised and composed, his gaze still steady and composed.

# X

What now? What next? A vast cloud of such questions covered the entire assembly. No one was prepared for this, everyone was already in such shock on witnessing someone to be able to pick up the bow, but this, this was something no one could have ever possibly imagined.

Maybe this is why we don't like unexpected things to happen, we are left vulnerable, all our planned thoughts and actions abandon us.

This was exactly the situation in the hall right now, no one knew what now. Usually, we think of all the possibilities that might happen, the pros the cons, the things that might go right, the things that might go wrong, but in this situation, even our capability of our mind to think the farthest of possibilities betrayed us, we knew not what even the very next moment would look like.

The stunned silence, thick and heavy, was then sliced by a voice.

"This is an insult!" boomed a king, rising from his seat with a fury that mirrored the crimson blooming on his face. "What is happening in this assembly, King Janak?" His voice held a dangerous edge, and a tremor of fear snaked down my spine.

"Such a disastrous act!" another prince chimed in, his voice echoing the sentiment. Disbelief morphed into outrage, and soon the hall was filled with a cacophony of angry voices. Accusations flew like poisoned arrows, aimed at Rama and my father.

"Absolutely! Since you were too specific to choose your groom, oh King," another voice sneered, laced with malicious glee, "now what will you do? Will you still marry your daughter to this man who has insulted the Dhanush?"

Amidst the rising chaos, I saw my father and uncles try to restore order, their voices lost in the rising tide of outrage. Shame burned hot in my cheeks. This wasn't how the Svayamvara was supposed to end. My dream, the anticipation I had nurtured for so long, was crumbling before my very eyes.

"Please, I request you all. It's my humble request to kindly maintain the integrity of the svayamvara" my father said trying to calm down the chaos, with evident tension on his brows.

"Don't question our integrity, King Janak!" a particularly pompous king roared, his voice dripping with disdain. "Yours is questionable now! What decision will you make? Will you marry your daughter to this man?"

My father stood there, his face an unreadable mask. A tight knot formed in my stomach. The silence that followed his stillness felt deafening, pregnant with unspoken tension and repressed anger.

Then, a voice, calm yet strong, cut through the din. It was Raghunandan, his gaze sweeping across the agitated crowd. "Perhaps," he said, his voice carrying a quiet authority, "the question should be asked to the person involved. The question should be asked not to King Janak, but to Princess Sita."

A hush fell over the hall once more, surprise momentarily silencing the outrage. Raghunandan's words, simple yet profound, shifted the focus. All eyes turned towards me, a sea of faces reflecting a sudden curiosity. Relief washed over me, cool and soothing, chasing away the fear that had threatened to consume me.

A small smile played on my lips as I met my father's gaze. I saw the content on his face as if he was himself waiting to say these words.

My father's voice, steady amidst the turmoil, echoed in the hall. "Indeed. My daughter's happiness is paramount. Sita, what is your decision?"

I raised my chin, taking a deep breath. "I have made my decision," I declared, my voice carrying through the silent hall. "But before I announce it to this esteemed court," I continued, my eyes locking with Raghunandan's, "I have a question for him."

I knew from the very start from the moment I met Raghunandan, what my decision would be if I was asked, if no requirements of svayamvara were considered, if it was my sole wish to choose, then I would and will choose him. But I knew this was about to be a new start, a new beginning, I didn't want it to begin with questions or any bad energy, I knew people had questions and doubts, I knew my reason to get married to Ram but I wanted to let them know that the man I chose was for a reason, I had a reason, that Raghunandan was indeed the perfect match for me.

"Why, Kausalyanandan Prince Ram," I asked, my voice soft yet firm, "did you break the Dhanush?"

Rama, his eyes locked with mine, considered the question for a moment. A hint of a smile, almost imperceptible to anyone else, played on his lips. "Honestly," he admitted, "It just... happened. Things always happen on their own."

A murmur rippled through the crowd. Was this the answer they were expecting?

"We do things, sometimes," he continued, his voice taking on a more philosophical tone, "and only later do we understand the true reason behind them. Actions come first, then our minds scramble to find meaning."

I nodded, my gaze. He was right. In the whirlwind of emotions, sometimes the heart acted before the mind could catch up.

"So, what does your mind tell you now?" I asked. "Why do you think this happened?"

His gaze swept across the hall, taking in the faces of the assembled princes, their expressions now a mixture of confusion and apprehension. "Perhaps," he said, his voice rising slightly, "because this entire assembly had taken a wrong turn. King Janak sought a worthy husband for his daughter, someone who could stand as her equal. Yet, what transpired here was not a test of character, but a grotesque display of competition."

A proud smile appeared on my lips. My eyes still fixed on Raghunandan; my posture straightened with proud. I knew his words would clear any clouds of confusion. After this no one could question ram or my father, or my decision

"You, the assembled princes," Rama continued, his voice unwavering, "did not strive to prove yourselves worthy of Sita; you sought only to claim her as a prize, a trophy to be won. And in doing so, you failed to see her as the extraordinary woman she truly is you all saw her as a prize, who would then become a mere a symbol of your strength. But she is no commodity, she is a human, she is not someone to be kept as a mere symbol of your own victory, she is a woman to be respected, to be shown affection to."

A gasp resonated through the hall. Rama's words, infused with truth, struck a chord with many. I saw shame flicker across some faces, while others remained defiant.

Relief washed over me, warm and reassuring. He understood. He saw me, not just a princess to be won, but a woman deserving of respect and love.

He then continued again, "The breaking of the Dhanush, was needed to break the illusion, to shatter the foundation of this misguided competition. It was a necessary disruption, a chance to start anew."

He then looked at me and smiled, my heart fluttered but my feet confident on the ground, proud of my decision, proud of my fate, my lips wide in smile, not shying away to express the happiness that I felt at the moment, my eyes filed with tears, tears of witnessing the best thing getting fulfilled.

*sometimes you don't know what you wish for until you witness it getting fulfilled.*

# XI

Then, a voice. A thundering roar that shook the very foundations of the building, shattering the stunned silence. The air itself crackled with raw tension. "What on earth is happening here? Such a disaster in the very presence of Rajarishi Janak and Sage Vishwamitra?" The mere volume of the words made it impossible to mistake the speaker. It was none other than *Bhagwan Parashurama* himself, his arrival a storm cloud unleashing fury.

All eyes turned towards the entrance, where the mighty Parashuram stood, his form radiating an aura of barely contained rage. His gaze, sharp as a honed blade, swept across the hall, taking in the scene before him. The fractured two remains of the divine Dhanush lay in front of him, a stark reminder of the unthinkable event that had transpired.

"Rajan Janak," Parashurama boomed, his voice dripping with icy disapproval, "explain yourselves! This bow, a gift from Lord Shiva himself, has remained unyielding for millennia. How is it that such a sacred relic lies desecrated within your sacred halls?"

A tremor of fear rippled through the assembly. Even the most valiant warriors cowered under the intensity of

Parashurama's wrath. His question hung heavy in the air, demanding an answer.

He waited for a moment, and then began again, "I asked who had the audacity to commit such a sinful act. He must be in a hurry to get punished; he must be the most unaware person of Parashuram's rage. Whoever did this, I challenge you to come in front of me, if you have gathered any courage from your father, if you have any love ever received from your mother, I challenge you to stand here in front of me, confess your sin and I might be a little lenient with your permission otherwise it will only get worse. King Janak, ask that unaware man to stand before me."

Before Pita shri could respond, a voice, surprisingly defiant, cut through the tense silence. It was Prince Lakshman, his youthful face etched with a fiery determination that mirrored his brother's unwavering spirit. "We owe you no explanation, Bhagwan," he declared, his voice ringing clear despite the palpable fear in the room. "The bow was broken by a worthy contender, one chosen by destiny itself."

Parashurama's eyes narrowed dangerously. "A worthy contender, you say? A contender so brazen they'd dare defile a divine weapon?" He turned his withering gaze upon the assembled crowd. "Who is this fool who dared to break the bow of Shiva?"

A collective silence descended once more. No one dared meet Parashurama's gaze. The act of breaking the bow, however unintentional, was a transgression of epic proportions.

Lakshmana, emboldened by a righteous anger, continued his defiance. "You call yourself a sage, Bhagwan," he countered, his voice shaking slightly with barely suppressed emotion. "But true sages possess wisdom and control, not anger. Your rage clouds your judgment."

Parashurama's face contorted in fury. The veins on his forehead throbbed, reflecting his barely contained rage. "How dare you, mere boy, lecture me on the ways of a sage! Do you even know who I am?" he roared, his voice a thunderclap.

"Of course, I know who you are. Your anger and all the deeds your anger made you do are all very popular tales."

"I am the biggest shiv devotee, you naïve child, you don't know who you are talking to." Sage Parashuram replied in anger.

Pita shri and Sage Vishwamitra exchanged a worried glance. The situation was quickly escalating. While the heated exchange dominated the hall, I watched with rising fear, my heart pounding a frantic rhythm against my ribs. My gaze, however, remained fixed on Raghunandan. Unlike everyone else who trembled under Bhagwan Parashuram's fury, Raghunandan stood unflinching, his posture betraying no fear. A faint smile, almost imperceptible to anyone else, played upon his lips, a sign of his inner strength. Despite the chaos unfolding around him, he looked calm.

"You have already talked enough about yourself, I think we need no more introduction, you yourself are contended talking about yourself. Besides, we have broken many bows and arrows when we were young kids, no one said anything, now I don't see a reason for the exaggerated reaction" Lakshman said instigating Bhagwan Parashuram.

"Exaggerated reaction you say! Has no one given you any education, any wisdom? It's no ordinary Dhanush. That's it you are getting on my veins now, I challenge you, I will use all my weapons against you, try whatever you can to protect yourself."

"Who doesn't get on your nerves Bhagwan. And with your little weapons who think you can defeat me, trying to move mountains with a blow of air are you? Besides, why do you even need your weapons, your words are enough of a substitution"

"This is the limit" Bhagwan Parashuram roared loudly and raised his weapon.

There was fear spread in the hall, I too stood there frozen, not sure what the very next moment will make us witness.

"Forgive him, o mighty sage. Consider him a child and forgive his mistake." Raghunandan's calm words proved to be ice on a burning bruise.

"I just want my answer, who broke this Dhanush, and this young man here is trying to bring himself in the face of rage." Bhagwan Parashuram replied directing his eyes back at prince Lakshman.

"Bhagwan, a person who can not only lift the Dhanush but also break it must be your devotee." Ram's calm words brought back Bhagwan Parashuram's attention.

"Oh no, a devotee's entire personality is about surrender and respect, this si no sign of a devote, this deed is done by an enemy." Bhagwan Parashuram roared.

"I can never imagine to be standing against you Bhagwan, then how ca I be your enemy, I m your devotee. This is done by me, I stand before you, if you think if I have committed a mistake then I am ready for any punishments that you want to give." Ram's words somewhere calmed Bhagwan Parashuram's anger, slight change in expression was very obvious.

"Who are you?" Bhagwan Parashuram asked.

"He is King Dashrath's eldest son, Prince ram. He is the one who defeated tadka and eradicated the fear of demons from society, he is the one who released Mata Ahalya's curse. And now he won the svayamvara and is to marry my daughter, we seek your blessings, Bhagwan." My father intervened, introducing Raghunandan to Bhagwan Parashuram.

Bhagwan Parashuram's expressions were now difficult to define, anger was definitely vanished, but also there was no sign of smile, he just looked at Raghunandan as if trying to look for a meaning. After a moment of silence he said, "it appears that I have recognized you but I want you to hold this Vishnu Dhanush and aim an arrow."

Raghunandan did as he was told, and before anyone knew what exactly happened, tears welled up in Bhagwan Parashuram's eyes with a smile on his lips, he said, "ow I know who you are, I exactly know who you are." Bhagwan hen asked Raghunandan to shoot the arrows in specific directions where all the fruits of his good deeds and victories were stores, so that the very reason that developed ego and hence his anger can be destroyed.

A wave of relief washed over me as I witnessed, once again, the power of Raghunandan's words. Like sandalwood paste soothing a burning wound, his calm and insightful explanation had diffused the tense situation before it could escalate further. The air in the hall seemed lighter, the hostility replaced by a cautious curiosity.

A slow smile, genuine and almost reluctant, graced Bhagwan Parashuram's lips. He stepped forward, his gaze settling on Raghunandan and me. We both bowed our heads in respect.

"Ram," he said, his voice no longer a thunderclap but a deep rumble, "your actions were unorthodox, to say the least. But your explanation holds merit." He paused, his eyes searching Rama's face. "You possess not only strength, but also wisdom and a deep respect for tradition, qualities befitting a true warrior and a prince. Your union with Princess Sita will prove to be a blessing for the entire humankind."

A flicker of warmth lit up Raghunandan's eyes. "Your blessings are an honour, Bhagwan," he replied, his voice respectful yet firm.

My father, his face etched with a smile of gratitude, approached the mighty warrior god.

"Thank you, Bhagwan Parashurama," he declared, his voice ringing with sincerity, "for blessing the children." His words held a deeper meaning now, a recognition of the unexpected turn of events and Raghunandan's role in diffusing the tension.

My father, his eyes twinkling with renewed hope, then turned to Raghunandan. "Prince Rama," he began, his voice warm and inviting, "we would be honoured to send messengers to Ayodhya, seeking your family's blessings for the union. Once we receive their consent, preparations for the grand wedding will commence. Until then, consider yourselves esteemed guests here. Every comfort will be arranged for your stay."

Rama, ever respectful, bowed his head in acknowledgment. "Your hospitality is deeply appreciated, Rajrishi Janak. However," he continued, his voice firm yet polite, "we are currently under the tutelage of the esteemed Rajrishi Vishwamitra. It would be most appropriate for us to reside with him during our stay."

A flicker of pride danced across Rajrishi Vishwamitra's face as Raghunandan voiced his decision. My father, always being the wise man looking into the matter with great understanding, readily understood. He exchanged a subtle nod with my mother, who stood by his side. With a gentle smile, she reached for my hand, her touch a silent communication, a reminder for u to leave the hall.

Together, me and my sisters along with my mother moved to exit the hall, my sisters flanking me. As I walked past Raghunandan, my heart raced fast, I managed to raise my lashes and meet his eyes with mine despite the already fast heartbeat. He too then looked at me, and at that very moment time seemed to stop, everything around us in that very moment felt invisible, as if it was only him and me. But then quickly I lowered my eyes again, trying to hide my smile of lush and I slowly walked past him and could hear my sisters giggle, it was evident that the world around was just invisible to me, I was not to them!

As the grand doors closed behind us, the joyful sounds of the ongoing celebration drifted down the corridors, a melody that echoed the newfound hope blossoming in my heart.

# XII

The dust of the Svayamvara had barely settled when Mithila burst into vibrant colours of celebration. It felt like waking from a dream, one filled with uncertainty and a touch of fear, only to find yourself in a world painted in hues of sunshine and laughter.

Every corner of the kingdom hummed with activity. Skilled artisans, their faces etched with concentration, transformed swathes of raw silk into shimmering bridal garments. Jewellers, their fingers nimble and precise, weaved magic with precious stones, crafting ornaments that would dance along my skin. The fragrance of exotic flowers filled the air, a constant reminder of the joyous occasion they were preparing for. It seemed even the trees, their leaves rustling in the gentle breeze, whispered secrets of the impending wedding.

News of Ayodhya's royal consent arrived like a warm summer breeze, carrying with it the promise of a grand reunion. Soon, whispers morphed into excited pronouncements as word of King Dasharatha's impending arrival, accompanied by Rama's two brothers, spread through the kingdom. Mithila was abuzz with preparations to welcome the esteemed guests.

Everywhere you looked, there was a flurry of activity. Skilled cooks, their faces flushed with the heat of the ovens, conjured up culinary masterpieces, their aromas a symphony of spices and exotic ingredients. Musicians practiced their melodies, the rhythmic beats of drums and the soulful twang of string instruments blending into a joyous harmony. Decorators, their imaginations running wild, transformed the palace grounds into a wonderland of vibrant colours and fragrant blooms.

For me, it felt like living in a constant state of wonder. Each day unfolded like a vibrant festival, every corner of Mithila celebrating the happiness blooming in my heart. The joy wasn't confined to the palace walls; it spilled out onto the streets, infecting every citizen with its infectious cheer. Young girls, their smiles wide and eyes sparkling with excitement, practiced intricate dance routines, their laughter a joyous melody that filled the air. Elderly women, their wrinkles etched with the wisdom of years, shared stories of love and marriage, their voices a soothing balm amidst the joyful chaos.

This wasn't just a wedding, it was a celebration of new beginnings, a joyous event that united two kingdoms and two families. And as I walked through the bustling marketplace, adorned with vibrant decorations and filled with the rhythmic clamour of happy vendors, a profound sense of gratitude swelled within me. I felt a proud feeling to be the daughter of Mithila, ow they celebrated their daughters, I still remember when the letter for consent of this union was sent to Ayodhya, as per Mithila's traditions, foremost the daughter's consent and tilak was required on that letter. I felt blessed to be a part of this grand spectacle, a daughter of Mithila on the cusp of a new life, a life filled with love, laughter, and the promise of a good future, it was so overwhelming to see the entire Mithila rejoicing for me, for my new life.

All these days we had different ceremonies and rituals that made me so occupied that I got no chance to go any further than our palace premises, so it has been days since I saw Raghunandan.

I wished to see him again, this time I would meet him with no guilt, I would meet him knowing that now my destiny was intertwined with his. But then what even if I get a chance to meet him, it would only be for a moment and then again, we would have to wait for next meeting till the day we will finally be together.

Though Urmila being Urmila would do her best and make excuses to mother just for us to go and make the possibility of meeting Raghunandan, but mother saw through her talks, and would be firm in her decision of not letting us go.

But I had this content in my heart that after all my destiny lies wit is, so no matter what we will meet, so I can anytime let go off these brief interactions to spend the lifetime with him. And that content of spending the lifetime with him calmed my gloom of not getting to meet him or see him.

Finally, it was the day, the day when King Dashrath was to arrive along with his two other sons. All preparations were done, a sense of perfection with celebration swung in the air of Mithila. People of Mithila have always been more creative, free spirited, but for the first time in air of Mithila a certain sense of seriousness along with happiness could be sensed. Afterall in-laws of Mithila's daughters were to arrive from Ayodhya! That is how Mandavi liked to put it.

The first tendrils of dawn had barely crept across the horizon when a flurry of activity erupted in our chambers.

Unlike her usual serene mornings, Mother awoke with a vibrant energy, her eyes sparkling with a secret excitement. The air crackled with a nervous anticipation that echoed in my own heart.

Breaking from her usual routine, Mother took charge, personally attending to each of us. With meticulous care, she selected our attire for the day. I found myself draped in a breathtakingly beautiful saree of deep red; its richness accentuated by delicate embroidery in shimmering gold. My sisters, too, were adorned with an unusual level of detail, mother made Urmila wear a bright yellow saree, Mandavi a beautiful sea green saree and Shrutkirti a rose pink. It was a clear sign of the significance Mother attached to this day, and a hint of the grand occasion that awaited us. But there was something else, something more, she was excited for me definitely, but it felt like she also had something else in mind as well, something more that maybe she was planning or she had planned, but I was not worried because whatever it was, evidently it was something nice, and when the time would be right it would unfold itself.

After I was perfectly ready as per my mother's contentment, my stomach twisted in knots, anticipating my interaction with Raghunandan's father, King Dashrath, though he has already sent the consent letter for the union of Raghunandan and me, but still the thought of interacting with him for the first time made me nervous. And my sisters were definitely not helping with it, together they were on the mission to make me more nervous with the thoughts of what might go wrong on my interaction with Raghunandan's father. They were enjoying every it of my nervousness, but their laughter only made me happier, their laughter was the only thing that brought certain sense was ease in me.

A tense silence blanketed our chambers, broken only by the nervous flutter of our breaths. Each passing moment stretched into an eternity, anticipation gnawing at my insides. My sisters, unable to contain their excitement, flitted around the room like butterflies caught in a gentle breeze. They pressed their ears against the ornately carved doors, straining to catch any whispers of the approaching arrival.

Suddenly, the air vibrated with the rhythmic pounding of drums. A collective roar erupted outside, a wave of joyous sound that washed over the palace walls. It was the unmistakable sound of conch shells and trumpets, a grand symphony heralding the arrival of King Dashrath.

My sisters, their faces alight with excitement, rushed towards the grand window overlooking the royal courtyard. They squealed with delight as they caught glimpses of the approaching procession – a dazzling display of colourful flags snapping in the wind, proud warriors on horseback, and elaborately decorated elephants bearing the weight of royalty.

I, however, remained rooted to my spot, a knot of nerves twisting in my stomach. The joyous commotion outside served only to heighten my own trepidation. Every drumbeat echoed in my chest, every celebratory shout a reminder of the imminent encounter with King Dashrath. The very thought of facing the esteemed king, the father of the man who held my heart captive, filled me with a mixture of apprehension and fluttering hope. I closed my eyes, taking a deep, calming breath.

We waited in our room patiently for any message to come. Though, it would be more appropriate to say I waited patiently, because Urmila, Mandavi and shrutkirti had no association with patience today whatsoever.

"Didi how are you feeling exactly?" Urmila sat next to me, back straight in excitement.

I sighed, looked t her for a moment and said, "Urmila how many times have you asked this question today, and how many times are you going to ask?"

Urmila pouted at my reply but Mandavi burst out laughing and said, "absolutely didi. Urmila just doesn't get what anyone says the first time." She then looked at Urmila and continued, "Urmila can't you see our didi is nervous today, it's not everyday you get to meet your father-in-law for the first time, don't you know how things can go wrong. Besides w have heard tales about how disciplined Ayodhya is, too many rules, rituals, and regulations, and..."

Mandavi was about to say something else as I puled her braid sightly and said, "you are no less, enjoying every bit of my nervousness...." Mandavi made a pretentious cry and then laughed.

"Didi this proves I am your dearest sister, see I don't tease you at all, I am always there to comfort you" shrutkirti said smiling and patting herself on the back, this made me giggle and I was about to say something as we saw our mother enter the room. We all stood up, I could not really read her expressions, happy? Nervous? Worried? Tense?

As she walked in, she stood for a moment, then placed her hand on my shoulder and said, "Sita, King Dashrath is here, but..."

"But what mother"

"But you can't meet him"

Confused I looked at her for an explanation, I knew I didn't have to ask this in words, I could sense the same shared questions amongst my sisters too...why? and so mother continued after a pause,

"It is the ritual of Ayodhya. They don't see their daughter-in-law before marriage. and their queens don't attend the marriage"

Now we too had the same expression as our mother, we didn't know what to react to this. For the first tie we heard of such a rule in Mithila, women are always given the first importance in any decision or occasion, there are no such rules for us. But then a question clouded my head but before I could say it, Mandavi said it and tuned out she was having the same question as me.

"But wat about the rituals, like today evening you said there is a ritual where didi and King ram have to light the diya together and then seek blessings from both parents. Then King Dashrath will have to meet didi." Mandavi asked.

"Sita will not look directly in direction of King Dashrath and slightly hide her face with her saree when she will face him to seek blessings."

"but" Urmila interjected.

"But nothing. It's their ritual we can't say anything against it." Mothe replied leaving us all speechless. She then turned to leave but then stopped at the doorstep and said,

"Sita today you have to prepare the sweet for king Dashrath and the guests from Ayodhya, Urmila, Mandavi, and Shrutkirti, you'll then come with me to help serve the guests." She said and after I gave her a slight nod in agreement, she left.

There was a brief silence after mother left, this ritual particularly contained to women was new for us, it felt slightly uncomfortable, but the that is what happens when you walk into a new life, you might get to see and experience and adapt to some things that might be new, and that newness might seem uncomfortable.

Afterall like Gargi Mata says,

*comfort is just another trap lined with rose petals*

newness is always discomforting, but that shouldn't stop one from experiencing the new.

"don't envy us didi" Mandavi's words brought me back from my thoughts. A smile appeared on my lips, I know where she was going with this but I play along and said, "and why would I envy you?"

"You know because we will get to meet and talk to your in-laws but you won't" Mandavi answered and then gave a slight budge on Shrutkirti shoulder.

Shrutkirti laughed masking her mouth with her hands.

"Shrut you too!" I said.

"This Mandavi is responsible in making this sweet little Shrut notorious." Urmila intervened and we all shared a hearty laugh. I could see how my sisters sensed the tension in the air and made this into a light atmosphere just so I don't worry too much about it.

Following the age-old tradition of Mithila, I found myself drawn to the familiar warmth of the kitchen. The air hung heavy with the comforting aroma of spices and simmering delicacies. I did as I was told by my mother, the task at hand was a simple one – to prepare a sweet dish for the guests from Ayodhya.

My sisters accompanied me! No, not with the cooking, but with the talking! They continuously talked about the guests from Ayodhya. Every now and then, they'd rush to the window, catching fleeting glimpses of the Ayodhya princes as they settled into their quarters. Upon their return, their chatter filled the air as they dissected every detail they could glean from their brief observations.

Their lively exchange, though a touch distracting, brought a smile to my lips. It was a relief that Mandavia and Shrutkirti had good things to talk about Prince Bharat and Prince Shatrughan, the two other younger brothers of Raghunandan. Unlike the animosity that had brewed between Lakshmana and Urmila, here was a possibility of friendship, a hope that Rama's brothers would find common ground with my sisters.

As the sweet dish reached the perfect consistency, a warm wave of satisfaction washed over me. It was a small gesture, but one imbued with the love and hospitality of Mithila. With a final flourish, I set the dish aside, leaving my sisters to join Mother in presenting it to the guests.

Alone in the quiet kitchen, I turned my attention towards my own preparations. The evening light filtered through the window, casting long shadows across the room. Taking a deep breath, I walked towards my chamber, a nervous anticipation fluttering in my chest. The day was drawing to a close, and with the setting sun came the promise of the evening ritual, though not a formal "introduction" to King Dashrath, but still an interaction. And mostly my heart fluttered at the thought of meeting Raghunandan once again after such a long time, I would not only see him, I would light the diya with him.

As the fiery orb of the sun dipped below the horizon, painting the sky in a canvas of fiery oranges and blushing pinks, my room bathed in a soft, golden light. The room, adorned with fresh flowers and fragrant incense, seemed to hum with an expectant energy. I stood before the ornately carved mirror, my reflection a vision of nervous anticipation.

Dressed in the saree of the deepest crimson, its hue mirroring the setting sun, I felt a surge of emotions. Images of Raghunandan danced in my head – the stolen glances during the Svayamvara, the quiet understanding that bloomed between us. But today was different. Today, we were not just a princess and a prince drawn together by fate. Today, we stood on the precipice of a new life, a life intertwined.

A tremor of nerves ran down my spine as I envisioned our upcoming encounter. How would I look? How would I react? This was the first time we would meet as a bride and groom, a couple seeking the blessings of our parents before embarking on the sacred journey of marriage.

Before I could dwell further on these churning thoughts, my sisters, their faces beaming with a mixture of excitement and pride, materialized at my side. One on each arm, they flanked me as we made our way towards the temple. My mother, her face a serene mask that barely hid her own maternal anxieties, walked a few steps ahead.

The rhythmic clatter of our anklets resonated against the polished stone floor, a melody that echoed my pounding heart. With each step, the nervous flutter in my stomach intensified. As we approached the temple, the murmur of a large gathering reached my ears. A surge of certainty washed over me – Raghunandan was already there. It wasn't just a feeling; it was an undeniable knowledge that resonated deep within my soul, I just knew it.

*Sometimes you feel so deeply connected with someone that you don't need eyes to know their presence you just need their presence to know their presence.*

As I walked, the crowd made way for us. As we reached at the heart of the crowd, which was the main entrance of the temple, I lowered my head holding the edge of the saree *pallu* on my head, I stopped as my mother in front of me stopped. I knew everyone was around, my father, chaacha shri, King Dhritrashtra, his three sons, and, Raghunandan.

I kept my face lowered, my eyes lowered, my heart beating so fast. After exchange of formal greetings between our families, my mother motioned me in the direction of King Dhritarashtra, I walked a few steps towards him, and bowed to touch his feet, with half my face still hidden with pallu.

"You have my blessing child. I am the happiest man on earth to have you as a blessing in my family, to have you as my daughter-in-law." King Dashrath's words were so warm, so fatherly. In my head, I had thought of his tone as a firm one, one that is expected from a king, but here I heard not a king but a father giving blessing.

"God bless you son. You are a gem, I know you might have heard it a lot, but it is only true, ad one should be reminded again and again of how good of a person he is. So, my child, I feel immense happiness that my daughter is marrying a gem, a person who is not just a great prince, but a humble, empathetic human." I heard my father's voice, which was a sign that Raghunandan might have touched his feet when I sought his father's blessings.

Then after a few more, exchange of greetings between our family, we were asked to walk into the temple for the ritual. Raghunandan came and stood next to me, though my eyes were still lowered I could feel, I sense, I could even see all his presence next to me. All my anxiety, all my tension, all my thoughts just vanished away.

*Its strange how someone's mere presence can make you feel like home and sometimes the entire home without that person can feel so foreign.*

*Our bodies didn't touch each other yet I felt completely, safely enveloped by his presence.*

We didn't talk, yet we somehow knew what we had to do.

As one, we moved forward, our steps echoing softly on the polished floor. A sense of calm settled over me, replacing the earlier flutter of nerves. Here, in the hallowed sanctum of the temple, surrounded by the soft glow of flickering diyas and the comforting scent of incense, the weight of the world seemed to melt away.

Together, we bowed before the deity, our heads reverently bent in respect. The priest, his voice a soothing murmur, guided us through the rituals of prayer and chanting. As I repeated the sacred mantras, each syllable resonated with a profound sense of purpose. This wasn't just a formality; it was a solemn vow, a commitment we were making not just to each other, but to the divine forces that would guide us on our journey together.

With each shared offering to the flames, a silent promise flickered between us. In that sacred space, with the blessings of the divine echoing in our ears, the bond that tied us together strengthened, transforming from a budding hope to an unshakeable promise.

As we emerged from the temple, a warm wave of laughter washed over us. Though I kept my eyes downcast, a shy smile played on my lips, savouring the shared joy in the air. King Dashrath's voice, booming with happiness, reached our ears.

"When I left Ayodhya," he declared, each word brimming with contentment, "I knew I was blessed to have a daughter-in-law like Sita. But I never imagined the gods would shower me with such immense fortune in a single day!"

My father, his face mirroring the King's elation, replied, "King Dashrath, as a father of these precious daughters, nothing could bring me greater joy than this moment."

A spark of curiosity ignited within me. What news could have brought about such unexpected jubilation? I longed to be a part of this shared happiness, to understand the cause of this joyous celebration. My sisters, usually the first to erupt in infectious laughter, stood beside me, strangely silent. Unlike their usual lively presence, they seemed subdued, their excitement held in check.

King Dashrath, oblivious to my internal turmoil, continued with a flourish, "Indeed! And witnessing the grace and virtue instilled in all your daughters, I can't help but feel truly blessed. Thanks to the divine intervention of Sage Vishwamitra, I am not getting one, but three daughters of Mithila – each a gem in her own right – raised with such admirable values, knowledge, and grace. I couldn't have wished for a better match for my sons!"

A gasp escaped my lips as the weight of his words settled in. Could it be what I was thinking? Before I could formulate a coherent thought, King Dashrath himself confirmed my unspoken question.

"Sita-Ram, Urmila-Lakshmana, Mandavi-Bharat, and Shrutkirti-Shatrughna," he announced, his voice resonating with joy, "seek blessings from Sage Vishwamitra, as pairs!"

Never did I think a single day could hold so much happiness. This unexpected turn of events sent a wave of pure elation crashing over me. My sisters, too, were getting married! And not just anywhere, but into the same family, ensuring we would never be separated. In fraction of seconds, millions of happy thoughts about our shared future danced in my heads.

# XIII

I did observe how Mandavi and Shrutkirti giggled when they would catch glances of the two young princes Bharat and Shatrughan. It was evident in their smiles that they had no objection from the two princes. I only heard praises about them from their mouth and from the tales they heard about the princes and how they respected them from listening to their tales. Shrutkirti and Mandavi always had something nice to say about them, and a little hidden smile and blush would always create shades on their face when they would talk about them.

But the only worry I had was about Urmila. She was asked to marry none other than Prince Lakshman, the prince she had so many fights with, the two of them never agreed upon anything, I had always seen them squabbling. So, I could never jut be quiet and see not just Urmila but any woman being married against her will, so I wanted to talk to my father about this, but before that I thought it would only be right if I talk to Urmila, and make her talk everything out about what she really wants.

Searching through the hallways and rooms I looked for Urmila. And as expected I saw her chatting with Shrutkirti and Mandavi, I could see the inner happiness reflecting on

Mandavi's and Shrutkirti's face. How they were shy and happy.

*It beautiful how one glows differently on the mere thought of being loved by that one person.*

But the strange thing was I saw Urmila with the same expression, of happiness and shy. I wanted to believe what I saw but I also didn't want in no way that she was pretending in any way. So, I simply look at her and give a slight nod to give hr the signal that I wanted to have a little conversation with her in private, and as expected she understood what I was trying to say without me having to say a word, and she simply excused herself from us. Then t the perfect moment, I excused myself saying now they should go and meet their mother, because after all even that was important, their mother would want to spend every second from now till marriage to spend with her daughters.

I then looked for Urmila and there she was, standing and witing for me, with that subtle shy smile on her face. I walked to her, paced an empathetic hand on her shoulder. She looked at me and said,

"What is it didi? You look worried? You wanted to talk about something?" Urmila asked, now her expressions changing from a shy smile to a concerned one.

"Urmila, I want you to be honest with me. Completely honest, you have never hidden any truth from me, told me everything and anything that has ever bothered you. So even today I expect the same from you. Be honest with me, okay?" I asked.

"Well, of course didi. But please tell me what is it?"

"I know you had certain grudges with prince Lakshman, and everything happened so suddenly, and ow you are getting married to him. But we can talk to father about it, no one can force you Urmila, your wish, your choice is of prior importance. Come with me lets talk to father about it." I said as I held her hand to walk with me, but he didn't move, she stood where she was, she placed her hand on mine and smiled. When I looked at her, she blushed and turned away. I walked beside her and asked, "what is it?"

"I have no objection to our union didi. I am in fact happy with this marriage proposal." Urmila's words stunned me. She looked at me and my obvious expressions, she busted out laughing and she again nodded suggesting what she said was actually true.

"When did this happen? Where was i. the last time I checked, you two were at loggerheads with each other."

"Well, didi, after your svayamvara I had many interactions with prince Laxman, and..."

"And...?"

"and though we squabble a lot, deep down we both respect each other. The day of your svayamvara when he took stand for his brother, he was willing t stand up against even sage Parashuram, stand up for what he believed for, stand up for his family, that was when my thoughts and perception about him began to change."

She then paused, and smiled, so I said,

"Okay, I am listening..."

And then she continued again, "then later when we had the opportunity to interact more, I realised how different he is than what I first thought he was...

Sometimes the initial interactions deceive you into perceiving someone as someone they are not

*A smile's first light can be deceiving; beneath may lie a heart unforeseen.*

Like now I get it what you used to say, I get it now, that quote, true essence..."

*"True essence, like a blossoming flower, takes time to reveal its full spectrum of colours. So, judge not by the first brushstroke, but wait for the masterpiece to unfold."*

I completed what she was about to say, it was something I used to tell her all the tie, because Urmila ahs always been the one to make presumptions about someone too quickly, so every time she would do this, I would tell her this.

I was relieved to know this but still I wanted a reassurance, this was a big decision for her, I wanted her to be completely sure, and not wanted her to make herself believe into something that she didn't actually feel, and was just feeling out of pressure.

So, I asked her again, "are you sure about this Urmila? I want you to feel no pressure about this."

"Absolutely didi. I love how prince Lakshman loves her brother, respects him, the same way I feel about you. So, I am sure about it. I am sure about us." Urmila's words held emotions that needed no more explanation.

Now I was truly contended and happy that everything was into place, that this was all meant to be.

The following days flew by in a whirlwind of activity. Mithila buzzed with preparations for not just one, but four grand weddings. Skilled artisans toiled tirelessly, transforming the palace grounds into a wonderland of vibrant colours and fragrant blooms. The air thrummed with the rhythmic clatter of looms weaving intricate fabrics, the rhythmic clanging of metal as jewellers crafted exquisite ornaments, and the joyous melodies of musicians practicing for the grand ceremonies.

My heart overflowed with a happiness so profound it felt like a tangible entity within me. Yet, a tinge of melancholy shadowed my joy. As the days dwindled, the reality of leaving Mithila, the place I called home, began to sink in.

The thought of bidding farewell to my parents, the familiar comfort of my chambers, and the playful banter with my sisters, brought a lump to my throat.

But amidst the bittersweet emotions, the joy of the impending union with Raghunandan eclipsed all else. The day dawned bright and clear, the sky a canvas of pristine blue. The air vibrated with an electric anticipation as we, the brides-to-be, began our preparations.

Bathed in fragrant oils and adorned with intricate henna designs, we sat before our reflection, each of us a vision of radiant beauty. My crimson silk saree, adorned with shimmering gold embroidery, felt heavy with tradition and the promise of a new life.

The nervous flutter in my stomach intensified as the ceremony drew closer. The weight of the rituals, each steeped in ancient tradition and symbolic meaning, settled upon me. The garlanding ceremony, the circling of the sacred fire, the exchange of vows – each step held the power to bind our destinies together.

As I stood beside Raghunandan, his hand warm and reassuring in mine, I met his gaze. A silent conversation passed between us, a shared understanding that transcended words. In his eyes, I saw not just love, but a reflection of my own bittersweet emotions – the joy of union intertwined with the sorrow of leaving behind what was familiar.

The chanting of the priests filled the air, a rhythmic tapestry woven with the blessings of the divine. With trembling hands, we exchanged garlands, the fragrant blossoms symbolizing the start of our new life together. As I circled the sacred fire, the warmth against my skin echoed the warmth of the love that bloomed within me.

With each step, I recited the sacred vows, my voice filled with a quiet determination. I pledged my love, my respect, and my unwavering support to Raghunandan. The weight of tradition, the promise of forever, settled upon my shoulders, not as a burden, but as a badge of honour.

The ceremony culminated in the joyous pronouncement of our union. As husband and wife, Raghunandan and I stood hand-in-hand, our hearts overflowing with a love that promised a lifetime of happiness. A bittersweet ache lingered in my heart, a farewell to the life I knew, but it was overshadowed by the radiant joy of the new chapter unfolding before me.

Together, with our sisters and their newfound husbands, we embarked on a new journey. We left behind the familiar embrace of Mithila, but we carried with us the love of our family, the blessings of the gods, and the promise of a future filled with love, laughter, and a lifetime spent side by side.

# XIV

The vibrant echoes of the wedding rituals faded into a bittersweet silence. The joyous chaos of celebrations had settled, leaving behind a poignant stillness that held the weight of endings and beginnings. As a newly married woman, adorned in the crimson silk that now marked my marital status, I approached my father, his kind eyes reflecting a storm of emotions that mirrored my own.

"Pita shri," I choked out, my voice thick with unshed tears. The word, once so simple, now felt heavy with the weight of impending separation.

He knelt before me, his weathered hand gently cupping my cheek. "Sita," he whispered, his voice rough with emotion, "My little Sita, my flower child."

Tears finally spilled over, tracing warm paths down my cheeks. All the years of shared laughter, comforting embraces after nightmares, and the quiet wisdom he imparted, washed over me in a tidal wave of memories. How could I, in a single day, be expected to sever this deep bond, to walk away from the life I knew for a new one, exciting yet unknown?

"I... I won't be able to see you every day, won't be able to take care of you anymore, Pita shri." The words tumbled out, a torrent of unspoken anxieties.

He held me close, his embrace a silent promise of unwavering love. "My child," he murmured, "your happiness is my happiness. Prince Ram is a good man, a man worthy of your love. You will build a beautiful life together, filled with laughter and love. But know this," he continued, his voice firm yet gentle, "the bonds of family transcend distance. You will always be my daughter, my Sita. And whenever you need me, I will be here, a single message away."

His words offered a balm to my wounded heart, a flicker of hope amidst the overwhelming sense of loss. A choked sob escaped me as I clung to him, seeking the comfort of his familiar embrace but still that feeling clung to my heart that from today on everything changes, I won't be able to take care of my father, I won't be able to have those chats with my mother, I won't be able to play and live on this land of my Mithila, everything will change, has changed.

Life often presents us with wounds that refuse to heal, yet in the midst of their persistent ache, we find the courage to carry on.

*Like delicate beautiful petals embracing the thorns, we learn to focus on the beauty that surrounds us, letting it guide us through the pain of thorns.*

Across the room, similar scenes unfolded. My sisters, each in their own way, grappled with the bittersweet reality of their new lives. Urmila, usually the most composed, found solace in Lakshmana's gentle reassurance. Mandavi, her eyes shimmering with unshed tears, held onto Bharat's hand, her touch expressing the unspoken fear of leaving her familiar world behind. Even Shrutkirti, her youthful demeanour masking a deeper vulnerability, leaned into Shatrughna's comforting presence.

Raghunandan, ever perceptive, witnessed our silent anguish. He knelt beside me, his touch a warm anchor in the storm brewing inside me. "Sita," he murmured, his voice a soothing balm, "I understand your pain. Leaving loved ones is never easy. But know this, I will be your family. We will build a life together, filled with love and respect. And your parents," he continued, his gaze holding a quiet sincerity, "will always hold a special place in our hearts. We will return often, and you can visit them whenever you wish."

*In the dance of life, some souls become our entire universe in a single moment. They are the solace we seek, the hands that wipe our tears, the very essence of home for our wandering souls. And yet, amidst the familiarity of long acquaintance, some hearts remain as distant as strangers in the crowded corridors of fate.*

His words, filled with empathy and understanding, offered a ray of light in my darkened world. He was right. This wasn't a goodbye, but a new beginning, a chapter filled with the promise of a shared future. Yet, the thought of not seeing my parents every day, of missing their familiar presence in my life, continued to gnaw at my heart.

As the final goodbyes were exchanged, the air thrummed with a raw mix of emotions. Hugs were delivered, promises whispered, and tears freely shed. The world seemed to blur as I climbed into the chariot, Raghunandan's comforting hand clasped tightly in mine. We were leaving Mithila, the place that had cradled my childhood, the place I called home. But as the chariot pulled away, carrying us towards a new life, I knew that the love and memories forged here would forever remain a cherished part of me. And who knows, perhaps, someday soon, I would return, not only as a daughter leaving, but also as a happy wife returning, with stories to share and a lifetime of love to build with Rama by my side.

# XV

The rhythmic clatter of chariot wheels against the dusty path served as a melancholic counterpoint to the joyous farewells that echoed in my ears. Mithila, the land of my birth, the cradle of my childhood memories, receded into the distance with every passing moment. A kaleidoscope of emotions swirled within me – a bittersweet cocktail of excitement for the new life that awaited me in Ayodhya, a pang of loss for the familiar comfort of my parents' embrace, and a quiet apprehension about the unknown that stretched before me.

Glancing out the ornately carved window of the chariot, I saw my sisters, each in their own chariot, following a similar path. Mandavi, a faint tremor in her hand betraying the silent turmoil within. Urmila, ever the adventurer, leaned out of her chariot, a wistful smile playing on her lips as she exchanged farewell gestures with a group of departing Mithilan nobles. Even the usually vivacious Shrutkirti, her gaze fixed on the horizon, seemed lost in her own thoughts.

The weight of a thousand unspoken questions pressed down upon me. How would we, women raised in the nurturing embrace of Mithila, adapt to the customs and traditions of Ayodhya? Would we find acceptance within the royal household? More importantly, could we create a home, a haven of love and laughter, within the unfamiliar walls of the Ayodhya palace?

These anxieties weren't new. The impending transition from daughter to wife, from a life of carefree joy to one of wifely duties, had been a recurring theme in conversations with my mother and aunts. They had spoken of sacrifice, of leaving behind the familiar and embracing the unknown, all for the sake of love and marital harmony.

Yet, despite the trepidation gnawing at the edges of my heart, a spark of determination flickered within me. This was a choice I had made, a path I had willingly embarked upon. The love I shared with Rama, a love nurtured through stolen glances and shared dreams, was a beacon guiding me through the uncertainty.

As the day wore on, the familiar landscape of Mithila gave way to rolling hills and verdant meadows. The setting sun cast long shadows across the land, painting the sky with hues of orange and pink. A sense of weariness settled over me, a physical manifestation of the emotional turmoil of the day. Our charioteer, sensing our fatigue, announced it was time to make camp for the night.

The bustle of activity that followed was a welcome distraction. Servants, skilled in their craft, erected tents with practiced ease. Fires were lit, casting a warm glow against the gathering darkness. The aroma of spices and roasting meat filled the air, a comforting reminder of the normalcy that awaited us, even amidst the transition.

As I settled within the confines of my tent, a wave of loneliness washed over me. I knew they were around, but with their husbands now. The absence of my sisters, usually just a playful banter away, felt particularly acute. But before

I could succumb to self-pity, the familiar tinkle of approaching jewellery announced a visitor. A smile bloomed on my lips as I saw Rama enter, his face etched with concern.

"Janaki, how are you feeling" Raghunandan's voice carrying a hint of concern, but majority compassion and calm.

I got up from my seat, eyes still lowered, "I am fine Raghunandan"

"It has been overwhelming for you, I know, and I am sorry I couldn't' come sooner to be here for you, but as a prince I needed to make sure everything was at place." A kaleidoscope of emotions swirled within me as Rama spoke. His words, simple yet profound, resonated deep within my soul. It was a feeling I had never experienced before – a sense of belonging so profound it felt like a homecoming; a surge of pride that intertwined with his own; and a blossoming appreciation for the life we were about to embark on together.

I remained silent, unable to articulate the depth of emotion his words evoked. A blush crept up my cheeks, a silent testament to the warmth radiating within me. Then, I saw his hand outstretched before me, palm open in a silent invitation. My gaze met his, a silent conversation passing between us. With a hesitant smile, I placed my hand gently in his.

It may have seemed like a simple gesture, a mere touch of fingertips. But in that fleeting moment, a universe of unspoken emotions unfolded. My hand, warm against his cool touch, sent a tremor through me – a fluttering in my stomach, a rush of warmth across my cheeks.

He offered a gentle smile, a silent request that I couldn't refuse. With a silent nod, I allowed him to lead me out of the tent. We walked side-by-side, a comfortable silence settling between us. Leaving the bustling camp behind, we ventured further, seeking a moment of solitude amidst the unfamiliar landscape.

The night sky was a breathtaking canvas, a tapestry of twinkling stars woven against the inky blackness. A cool breeze whispered through the leaves of the surrounding trees, carrying with it the sweet fragrance of night-blooming flowers. The gentle rustle served as a soothing background melody to the rapid rhythm of my heart.

We stopped at a secluded spot, a distance away from the sounds of the camp. Here, amidst the quiet serenity, bathed in the soft glow of the moon, I could finally steal a proper glance at his face. Its familiar features, etched with a newfound softness, held a captivating charm under the moon's ethereal light.

A shy smile graced his lips as he met my gaze. The unspoken emotions swirling within me, the nervous excitement, the sense of belonging, the budding affection – I longed to share them all, to find the words to bridge the silent space between us. But in that quiet moment, under the watchful gaze of the moon, words seemed superfluous. All that remained was the comfortable silence, the gentle touch of our hands, and the promise of a future we would build together, one step and one stolen glance at a time.

"I know it is not easy for you Sita to lave your parents, to leave your mother land." Raghunandan said in a whispering sound.

After a pause, feeling the tears welled up in my yes, I replied,

"Bhumija, that is what they called me because of my land, because of my mother. A daughter found after digging the very land of Mithila. I was born from the very womb of this Bhoomi, so yeah it is not easy to let go off that pain of detachment, but then I think I am the daughter of this *bhumi* and so my mother is everywhere with me, it just that..."

I fell silent, a pause hanging heavy in the air. Raghunandan's gaze lingered on my face, his eyes searching mine as if deciphering an intricate code. He seemed to sense the turmoil brewing within me, the unspoken anxieties that threatened to spill forth.

"It's just that..." I began, my voice laced with a hint of trepidation. The words tumbled forth, hesitant at first, then gaining momentum as the dam of emotion threatened to break. "It's just that my father... now he is far away. His teachings, his wisdom, his love..." The sentence trailed off, choked by an unshed tear that glistened in the moonlight.

Raghunandan remained silent, allowing me the space to express the torrent of emotions that washed over me. He understood, without me needing to elaborate, the profound sense of loss that gnawed at my heart.

A soft sigh escaped his lips as he finally spoke, his voice gentle, understanding. "Sita," he murmured, "I know that anything I say can never truly resonate with you. No matter how hard a man tries," he continued, his gaze holding a quiet sincerity, "we can never fully experience the depth of pain, the sacrifices, the unwavering love that a woman feels throughout her life. It's a strength, a resilience that goes beyond our comprehension."

He paused for a moment, his hand reaching out to gently squeeze mine. "But," he continued, his voice firm yet filled with empathy, "even though my words may not erase the pain of separation, I can offer you solace, a balm for your wounded heart. Understand this, Sita," he said, his gaze meeting mine with unwavering conviction, "the love, wisdom, and teachings of your father are treasures that can never be lost or stolen. They are a part of you, woven into the very fabric of your being. And don't you think," he added, a slight smile gracing his lips, "that these very elements, these principles that guide you, carry the essence of your father himself? In that sense, he is always with you, a guiding light on your path."

The weight of his words settled upon me, a soothing balm to the raw ache in my heart. Each syllable rang true, dispelling the doubts that had clouded my mind. In that moment, I felt a profound sense of gratitude wash over me. Gratitude for the man standing beside me, a man whose unwavering support and empathetic nature were a source of immense solace. He wasn't just my husband, he was a confidant, a friend, a pillar of strength in the face of my anxieties.

The cool night breeze whispered through the trees, carrying with it a newfound sense of peace. The anxieties that had threatened to consume me earlier began to recede, replaced by a quiet determination. Raghunandan's words had served as a gentle reminder – my father's love, his teachings, would forever be a part of me. And with that knowledge as my compass, I was ready to face the unknown, hand-in-hand with the man who promised to be my partner, my anchor, in this new chapter of my life.

A wave of realization washed over me. I wasn't just leaving behind my old life, my cherished family in Mithila, but also embarking on a new journey, one that involved weaving myself into the fabric of a new family. A family I knew little about. With a determined sigh, I wiped away the stray tears that clung to my lashes. Steeling myself, I turned to Raghunandan, a flicker of a smile gracing my lips for a fleeting moment before I looked down again.

"Kausalyanandan," I began, my voice barely above a whisper. "Tell me about Mata". The very mention of his mother's name seemed to ignite a spark within him. A radiant smile spread across his face, his eyes twinkling with a warmth that mirrored the emotions budding within me.

"Mata Kausalya," Raghunandan began, his voice filled with a reverence that tugged at my heartstrings, "is one of the strongest women I have ever known. She is my pillar, my source of inspiration. Yes," he continued, a hint of amusement dancing in his eyes, "she can be firm at times, her demeanour reflecting the weight of responsibility that rests upon her shoulders as the eldest queen. But beneath that seemingly stern exterior lies a heart brimming with love and compassion."

A pang of curiosity coursed through me. This glimpse into his mother's personality painted a fascinating picture – a woman of strength and unwavering resolve, yet possessing a wellspring of love for her son. I yearned to meet this remarkable woman, to experience her grace and wisdom firsthand.

"And I can't wait for you to meet her," Raghunandan concluded, his gaze holding a warmth that sent a tremor of anticipation through me. "And especially Mata Kaikeyi," he added, a slight hesitation momentarily flickering across his features.

But it was the immense love and respect that resonated in his voice as he uttered her name that truly captured my attention. It was a stark contrast to the whispers and veiled glances that had shrouded Kaikeyi's name back in Mithila.

Raghunandan continued, his voice weaving a tapestry of his childhood memories. "Though she is the biological mother of Bharat," he explained, "her love extends far beyond blood ties. Her affection for me is unparalleled. She has nurtured me like her own son, showered me with a love that transcended even that of a mother. I spent most of my childhood basking in her warmth and care. I know she will be overjoyed to meet you, Sita."

"Tell me more Raghunandan," I pressed gently, a flicker of nervousness dancing in my stomach. "What are they like?"

Raghunandan chuckled softly, the sound warm and reassuring. "Ah," he began, a wistful smile gracing his lips, "our family is woven with love and respect. Mata Sumitra, Lakshmana and Shatrughna's mother, is the epitome of kindness. She is like a playful friend to us all, often joining our games and sharing our laughter. There's never a dull moment when she's around. She becomes one of us to understand us."

"And Mata Kaikeyi?" I prodded, the name still holding a slight air of mystery because I knew how much pleased he seemed the first time he mentioned her.

"Mata Kaikeyi," he said, his voice filled with an almost reverent affection, "is the most demonstrative of her love. She never hesitates to show her feelings, showering us with affection. It's no secret," he added with a playful grin, "that she often declares me her favourite son." This was the first time I observed this playful expression on Raghunandan's face, almost like a child's.

A flicker of amusement danced in my eyes. "Favourite, huh?" I teased, a playful smile blooming on my lips.

I know relationships mean understanding ach other, being mature to handle the difficult of situations, but it also means to laugh together, to be like children together, to bring out the inner child, to make each other feel alive again.

"Perhaps," he conceded with a chuckle, "but her love extends equally to all of us. You'll see, Sita, how all three mothers live in harmony, w brothers were fortunate enough to b raised by not one but three mothers. They say greatest heaven is a mother's lap, ow imagine receiving the warmth of not one but three."

His words painted a heartwarming picture of a family bound by love and respect. The conversation flowed effortlessly from there. We spoke of our siblings, their quirks and dreams, of the stories whispered within the palace walls of Ayodhya. We shared our hopes for the future, a future we would now build together, brick by loving brick. As the moon climbed higher in the sky, casting its silvery light upon the tranquil scene, we drifted back towards our tents.

A gentle breeze whispered through the leaves, carrying with it the soft melody of crickets chirping. As I settled into my bedroll, a feeling of contentment washed over me. The anxieties that had gnawed at me earlier had dissipated, replaced by a quiet confidence and a newfound sense of belonging. Here, under the vast expanse of the night sky, with Raghunandan by my side, the unknown future no longer seemed so daunting. In fact, it brimmed with the promise of new experiences, shared laughter, and a love that promised to blossom with each passing day. With a contented sigh, I surrendered to the gentle embrace of sleep, the anticipation of a new life a comforting presence in my dreams.

# XVI

The rhythmic clatter of chariot wheels against the dusty path served as a melancholic counterpoint to the joyous farewells that echoed in my ears. Leaving Mithila, the land of my birth, the cradle of my childhood memories, was a bittersweet experience. Each passing day etched a new vista onto the canvas of my memory.

Rugged hills that rose from the earth like slumbering giants, their peaks adorned with a diadem of pine trees were now replaced by the rolling plains, with their verdant meadows and emerald rice paddies, the route to Ayodhya had given way to a more dramatic landscape. The air, once heavy with the crisp, sharp scent of pine needles and damp earth, now held the sweet fragrance of jasmine and mango blossoms.

Just as the landscape transitioned, so too did I sense a shift within myself. The carefree laughter and playful banter that had been the hallmark of my life in Mithila were replaced by a quiet contemplation. Like the changing terrain, I too was on the cusp of transformation. My life as a daughter, cherished and protected within the loving embrace of my family, was drawing to a close. A new life, as wife and daughter-in-law, awaited me in Ayodhya.

This realization wasn't a source of apprehension, but rather a recognition of the natural order of things. A woman's life, like the seasons, was cyclical – a time for carefree joy, a time for blossoming love, and a time for nurturing a family of her own. Just as springtime with its vibrant colours held a unique beauty, so too did the prospect of becoming a wife and bearing the responsibilities that came with it.

The journey continued, the landscape evolving with each passing mile. Dense forests, teeming with unseen life, replaced the rolling hills. Mighty rivers like the Ganges, their broad, sun-dappled surfaces shimmering like liquid gold, snaked through the plains. We crossed vast stretches of fertile land, where farmers toiled under the relentless sun, their faces etched with the lines of hard work and quiet satisfaction.

Each new vista mirrored a facet of the complex emotions swirling within me. The raw, untamed beauty of the forests resonated with the burgeoning love I felt for Raghunandan. The serene flow of the rivers mirrored the quiet acceptance of my new life. The fertile fields, with their promise of bountiful harvests, spoke of the family we would build together.

The journey itself became a metaphor for the transformation I was undergoing. Just as we travelled from the familiar plains of Mithila to the unknown terrain of Ayodhya, so too would I traverse the uncharted territory of married life. It was a journey filled with both trepidation and excitement, a journey I was ready to embark upon, hand-in-hand with the man who now held my heart.

Finally, after days on the dusty road, a new vista unfolded before our weary eyes. In the distance, bathed in the golden glow of the setting sun, rose the majestic city of Ayodhya – our new home. The sight sent a tremor of anticipation through me. This was it. The beginning of a new chapter, a chapter brimming with the promise of love, duty, and a life intertwined with the man I loved.

As our chariot rolled through the bustling streets of Ayodhya, a stark contrast to the serene countryside we'd just traversed, my senses were overwhelmed in the best way possible. Unlike the sprawling openness of Mithila, Ayodhya was a city that hummed with life. Grand buildings lined the well-paved streets, adorned with intricate carvings depicting tales of gods and heroes. Shops overflowed with vibrant silks, gleaming jewels, and exotic spices, a testament to the city's prosperity.

The most striking sight, however, was the sheer elation etched on the faces of the people. Houses and shops were adorned with colourful garlands and vibrant tapestries. As our chariot passed, joyous cheers erupted from the crowd, a shower of fragrant flowers raining down upon us.

A pang of nostalgia struck me, a yearning for the familiar warmth of the people of Mithila. People of Mithila and Ayodhya felt so familiar in love and respect for the royal family and yet so different. They, too, cherished the royal family, their love as raw and untamed as the vibrant festivals celebrated in our homeland. But here, in Ayodhya, the love and respect for the royal family seemed imbued with a certain sophistication, a well-ordered elegance. It was as if their affection was woven with a thread of reverence, a feeling of unwavering loyalty.

The closer we drew to the imposing palace gates, the more frantic the excitement became. The rhythmic beat of drums filled the air, punctuated by the sonorous blasts of conch shells. A troupe of dancers, their movements as graceful as swaying lilies, twirled before us, casting colourful shadows in the late afternoon sun. My heart hammered a frantic tattoo against my ribs, a potent blend of nervousness and exhilaration. This was it – the threshold to my new life.

With a dramatic flourish, the massive palace gates creaked open, revealing a scene straight out of a celestial dream. The courtyard bustled with activity – soldiers in gleaming armour, attendants bearing garlands and trays brimming with exotic fruits, and a sea of smiling faces, their eyes sparkling with welcoming curiosity.

As our chariot crossed the threshold, a sense of overwhelming responsibility settled upon me. This was no longer just a visit; this was my home now. These were the people I would rule alongside Rama, the subjects whose well-being would be a part of my daily life.

A mixture of emotions – excitement, trepidation, and a flicker of fear – swirled within me. Yet, as I stepped out of the chariot, the setting sun casting a warm glow over the bustling scene, a single thought crystallized in my mind: this was my future, and here, amidst the vibrant chaos of Ayodhya, with Raghunandan by my side, I was ready to write my new story.

# XVII

As my three sisters and I made our way towards the awaiting mothers, each step felt heavier than the last. The weight of anticipation hung thick in the air, wrapping around me like a suffocating shroud. With my head tilted low and my eyes cast downward, I walked slowly, almost hesitantly, my heart pounding with nervous energy. Every footfall echoed the uncertainty swirling within me.

Beside me, Raghunandan's presence offered a soothing anchor amidst the whirlwind of emotions. His steady stride beside mine infused me with a sense of calm, a reassurance that I desperately clung to in this moment of uncertainty.

As we approached the mothers, who stood with large *pooja thaalis* in their hands, my breath caught in my throat. The weight of their expectations felt palpable, their eyes like scrutinizing flames that threatened to consume me whole.

Then, like a beacon of warmth in the midst of the cold uncertainty, the eldest mother, Mata Kausalya, stepped forward. Her presence seemed to command the space around her, radiating an aura of maternal authority and love that enveloped me like a protective embrace.

In that moment, as Mata Kausalya drew near, I found myself enveloped in a haze of introspection. These were the first steps of a journey that would forever alter the course of my life. And as I stood there, my heart a tumultuous tempest of emotions, I braced myself for the unknown that lay ahead, guided by the reassuring presence of Raghunandan by my side.

As she approached closer, Raghunandan and I together bowed to seek her blessings and as we stood up, my eyes were still lowered and she said, "God bless you my children, my daughter Sita, welcome to Ayodhya. May you both always live happily, but at times when things are rough, don't forget to look after one another. Marriage is not just about the happy moments, it is about those monotonous moments, those moments when you are burdened under certain responsibilities, those moments when life seems too tough, in those moments, you have to be each other's anchor."

Raghunandan was right about her, she was a very strong woman, a true queen, I every action of her, in every word she said, she had the essence of a mother and also a queen. She was so composed and her mere presence echoed of power and strength. I couldn't contain myself, so I slowly raised my lashed to have a look at her.

And there she was, just as I imagined, the reflection of her strength, her dignity, her strong personae was evident on her face. The charm, the grace on her face was something very attractive. But she had the kind for beauty that a person couldn't look long at, for that beauty was so pure that it could remind a person of their weakness, her strength was so reflective on her face, that anyone who would look at her would have to lower their eyes in respect.

After seeking her blessings, Mata Sumitra came towards us, my eyes were still lowered, so Raghunandan whispered slowly that it was Mata Sumitra. We again bowed to touch her feet and seek her blessings. She then said, "I can't believe my children are so grown up, Ram is here with his wife. Welcome both of you, may you God bless you with pure joy and bliss. may your life always echo with laughter. Oh, my children are so grown up, it's so overwhelming for me, how fast time passes. And Sita I have heard a lot about you, can't wait to sit and spend time with you."

Words of Mata Sumitra brought a smile on my face, Raghunandan was rally so accurate in his description about the mothers. Mata Sumitra's voice had this certain liveliness, the kind for liveliness that no matter what she says, it will only bring joy to the person listening. The excitement and liveliness in her voice, in her presence, in her aura was so refreshing. When I looked at her, all I saw was sparkling eyes and a wide smile, and so I quickly lowered my lashes back again with a smile on my face, since her smile was so infectious.

Now it was time for Mata Kaikeyi, whom Raghunandan talked about so dearly, who I knew Raghunandan shared a very special ad close bond with. So, my nervousness was at it's peak, what would I say, how would I react, will she like me. While all these questions were clouding my mind, she was already here. Her mesmerising perfume already felt so warm.

We bowed tot ouch her feet and as we stood straight, she wrapped her arms around Raghunandan and me into a tight embrace. I could ear her little happy sobs. And after she released her form her embrace, this time I didn't have to steal a glance to look at her, she herself placed her hand on my chin and raised my face for me to face her.

As my eyes met hers, I felt what Raghunandan was saying, about her immense love. She needs no words; the love and warmth were evident in her eyes. She looked absolutely beautiful.

*It was as if her face was draw by the lines of love, the kind of face that makes you think of nothing but unconditional love.*

Love, warmth, and affection in her eyes, the nurture in her subtle smile, everything spoke nothing but the adoration she had for Raghunandan. Tears in her eyes, she looked at us both for some time and then finally said, "may the love between you two never vanish. No matter how stormy life gets, if you are holding each other's hand, you can cross any disaster. Trust, faith, and love, these are the things that makes any relation strong. And Sita, you are not her as a daughter-in-law, you are my daughter, and so I want you to feel just like you felt in Mithila. My ram here, he is very special, I have faith in him, he will keep you immensely happy, *with love that can cross any boundaries for you no matter how tough or thorny they are.*"

Sometimes how you meet certain people for the first time and they feel so warm like you have known them for ages, sometimes the laces so new can feel like home. Sometimes the new changes can still feel like familiar old paradigms.

There was just one person who for me didn't fit into the harmonious colours of the family and I somewhere felt wrong for feeling this way about her, but it was a feeling, some sort of intuition that I couldn't not ignore. She was Manthara. She was the most special attendant of Mata Kaikeyi, almost like a mother figure. She would always stay close to mother Kaikeyi at all times. Though she welcomed me warmly, said some sweet things, but it just didn't resonate to my heart.

*Sometimes some people say nothing and yet the unsaid words carry so much love and sometimes some people use a million sweet words which still lack the fragrance of affection.*

Mothers were so warm towards us all sisters. Mothers were so warm towards us all, sisters. Soon as the welcome aarti concluded, the air thick with the sweet fragrance of sandalwood and incense, a sense of relief washed over me. It wasn't the blind acceptance I had anticipated, but a genuine welcome, a promise of a bond waiting to be nurtured. With a newfound sense of belonging, I followed Raghunandan and the others, stepping through the ornately carved doorway into the grand palace.

# XVIII

After all the ceremonies, Raghunandan and I went to our room. It's felt a little different, saying our room! Now from today on, thing will not be mine, but ours.

The room was huge, and just the way I liked it, the room fragranced with sandalwood. This brought a smile on my face, how did Raghunandan knew this, how did he arrange this, he might have talked to Urmila about this. Because I saw every little detail in the room exactly the way I liked.

I walked towards the large window to take in the fresh air, I was exhausted from he long journey, happy and overwhelmed from all the love and warmth I received here, felt enveloped by the air of Ayodhya, so much new was happening, had happened, was about o happened, I felt so many things, so in that moment only the gentle caress of air was what I needed,

*When you feel too much the best thing to do is simply think nothing at all.*

As I took in a large breath of cool fresh night air, I heard Raghunandan's footsteps approaching closer. He came and stood next to me.

"So how did you like Ayodhya?" he asked.

I smiled, almost blushed, thought for a moment and replied, "it's warm"

He gave a slight laugh to this and said, "I expected nothing less from you Janaki. Now of course people from mountains will find Ayodhya warm"

I smiled turned towards him and looked at him. His ocean deep pools of ocean, as if I could dive deeper into is eyes with my entire existence, and still see no end to it. Looking at his eyes, I could feel no presence of mine own, it was only those eyes filled with so much of love, empathy, care. No one could feel any emotion other than love when looking into those eyes, it was him, entirely him,

*his eyes were not only his but even mine entire existence at that moment.*

He raised his eyebrows, and that brought me back to reality, it was the first time when I had spent so much time to look into his eyes, no fear of judgement, no guilt, no hesitation, I knew it was my right to look into his eyes, no one could stop me. I felt like I had all the time in the world, I could dive deeper into his eyes until my heart's contentment. But then he raised his brows again and that made me chuckle.

I recalled the conversation we were having and then I said, "well what I meant is, I like this new warmth, the warmth is not just in Ayodhya's air, but people's heart, their gestures, their expressions."

"And what about the family?" Raghunandan sked again, still looking at me, into my eyes.

I smiled and said, "I think the smile on my face says it all. I had this fear deep inside me, how will I adjust with the longing for my home at Mithila, how will I be completely happy while still thinking about my old family, how will I adopt to my new family knowing I have left my old one for this new one. But today I realised something that made my heart so happy."

"And what is that?'

"I always thought after marriage a girl leaves, he home for a new one. But what she actually experiences when the now family is so ice s that, she is actually becoming a very fortunate one on the day of her marriage,

She is not leaving her old home to come to a new one she is about to create two homes for her. She is not leaving her old family for a new one but rather she is being a part of two, now she has two families to love her, to care for her. In all now, the amount of love and warmth in her life has only increased, she ahs only received more in this, and not lost a bit."

After saying this I looked at Raghunandan and I could see the proud in the smile on his face when he looked at me.

He began, "I usually have something to say about things, but today, Janaki, you have truly left me speechless, your wisdom, your calm, your understanding had left me with no words, only proud. I am blessed to have you I my life."

I just smiled at this and again faced towards the window, looking straight. A comfortable silence settled between us, broken only by the soft chirping of crickets outside our tent. After a while, Raghunandan spoke, his voice thoughtful.

"The assistants mentioned the mothers were incredibly enthusiastic," he said, "personally overseeing every detail to ensure everything was perfect for your arrival."

Then after a pause I said. "People often focus on the pain the bride's family experiences during a wedding. It's a loss unlike any other. But in all the commotion, we tend to overlook the anxieties and pressures faced by the groom's family as well. They feel this immense responsibility to create a welcoming environment, a new home where the bride feels comfortable and loved. They want her to feel happy and not miss her old life as she embarks on this new chapter."

Raghunandan's gaze found mine. A slow smile spread across my face as he reached out, gently wrapping his fingers around my arm to turn me towards him. His eyes, glistening with a mixture of pride and concern, held mine captive.

*He wanted me not to listen to what he felt, but look at how he felt.*

A comfortable silence settled between us once more, the quiet hum of crickets weaving itself into the tapestry of the night. We stood by the window for what felt like hours, the cool night breeze carrying with it the sweet fragrance of jasmine flowers from the palace gardens. The conversation flowed effortlessly, touching upon everything from childhood memories to our hopes for the future. In that moment, bathed in the soft glow of the moon and enveloped by the gentle breeze, Ayodhya didn't just feel like a new city; it felt like a new home.

Looking up at Raghunandan, I saw a reflection of my own emotions in his eyes – a blend of hope, anticipation, and a quiet joy. With a gentle squeeze of my hand, he spoke no words, but the sentiment resonated loud and clear: here, in each other's arms, we found solace and belonging.

As I drifted off to sleep, a sense of contentment washed over me. Today, my first day in Ayodhya, had been an experience unlike any other. It wasn't just the opulence of the palace or the elaborate ceremonies; it was the warmth I felt emanating from every corner, the genuine affection radiating from the royal mothers, and the unwavering love shining in Raghunandan's eyes. All of it combined to create a feeling of being enveloped in a cocoon of care and love –

a feeling that promised a future brighter than any I could have ever imagined.

# XIX

Exhaustion had draped itself over me like a heavy cloak during the journey from Mithila to Ayodhya. The constant motion, the unfamiliar sights and sounds, all conspired to leave me yearning for a deep sleep. But yesterday's fatigue couldn't compete with the thrill that bubbled within me. This was my first day in Ayodhya, my first day as part of a new family. The anticipation gnawed at the edges of sleep, rousing me earlier than usual.

Instead of the familiar routine of my life in Mithila, a sense of purpose guided my actions. I carefully draped a beautiful brick-red saree around my form, its colour vibrant against the beige base adorned with a delicate border of shimmering pearls. As I adorned myself with the ornaments of a married woman, the weight of each piece settled not just upon my body, but upon my heart. The crimson sindoor, a symbol of my union with Raghunandan, felt warm against my skin – a tangible reminder of the love that bound us. It was a strange sensation, this weight that wasn't a burden, but a recognition of the responsibilities and joys that awaited me. It filled me with a sense of awe, a realization that something so small could hold such immense power, evoking a kaleidoscope of emotions within me.

The thrill of the new day lingered as I finished dressing. With a deep breath, I stepped out of my quarters, eager to seek the blessings of the mothers and begin this new chapter. The hallways bustled with activity, servants scurrying about in preparation for the day ahead. As I rounded a corner, a familiar sight brought a smile to my lips – my sisters, Urmila, Mandavi, and Shrutkirti. Dressed in their finest sarees, adorned with the emblems of married women, they looked radiant. Yet, a tinge of melancholy flickered in their eyes, a silent acknowledgment of the life we had left behind in Mithila. We were no longer simply daughters; we were now daughters-in-law of Ayodhya, with new roles and responsibilities to navigate. The realization tugged at my heartstrings, a wave of nostalgia washing over me.

The morning unfolded in a flurry of activity. As tradition dictated, today was the day we, the new brides, would cook a special dish for the family. Stepping into the bustling kitchen, the familiar warmth of the hearth filled me with a sense of comfort. Under the watchful eyes of the experienced cooks, we kneaded dough, chopped vegetables, and stirred simmering pots. The rhythmic clanging of utensils and the fragrant aroma of spices filled the air, a symphony of culinary creation.

The days in Ayodhya unfolded like a dream, each one slipping seamlessly into the next. Time seemed to lose its grip, the hours melting away in a cascade of laughter and newfound connections. We, the newly arrived brides, spent our days revelling in the simple joys of our new life.

Shared laughter echoed through the palace as we bonded with the mothers, their regal demeanours softening as they regaled us with tales of Raghunandan and his brothers' childhood escapades. As the day drew to a close, we found solace in the comforting presence of our husbands. Each evening, nestled in our chambers, we exchanged whispers and dreams, weaving the delicate threads of intimacy that bind a marriage.

However, a shadow of concern lingered in my heart for my sisters, Shrutkirti and Mandavi. Their husbands, Shatrughna and Bharata, had been called away to the kingdom of Kekaya due to the sudden illness of their grandfather, King Ashvapati. The mere thought of being separated from Raghunandan, especially in the tender first days of our marriage, filled me with a pang of sympathy for them. The joyful rhythm of our days seemed incomplete without the partner's presence. However, Urmila and I, and also the mothers tried our best to keep Shrutkirti and Mandavi happy as much we could.

Like any other day, after greeting mothers, spending some time with them, we sisters went to Kitchen to ensure everything was running smoothly. However, today, an undercurrent of tension crackled beneath the surface of the bustling activity in the palace. Though we had just arrived in Ayodhya, it had only been a few days and one would say that we were not very familiar with the usualness of Ayodhya, but this difference in the air of Ayodhya was very evident to us all. King Dasharatha had been sequestered in the main hall for hours, locked in a long discussion with his ministers. Messengers flitted back and forth between the hall and the quarters of the mothers, their hurried movements and hushed whispers hinting at a matter of great importance.

We, the newly arrived brides, couldn't help but feel a prickle of apprehension. Despite the joyous welcome we had received, there was a sense of something looming, a decision of great weight about to be made. However, determined not to let the unknown anxieties cast a shadow over our first day, we immersed ourselves in the task at hand. The rhythmic clanging of utensils and the fragrant steam rising from the pots served as a soothing counterpoint to the undercurrent of disquiet. We focused on perfecting the dishes, on fulfilling our newfound roles, a silent show of unity and resilience amidst the swirling uncertainties. I loved how Urmila, Mandavi, and Shrutkirti talked about their husbands, shying but also trying to share so much with so much energy. Especially Urmila, I never could have thought that she out of all the people would have so much sweet things to talk about Lakshman.

"Don't you think it's a little strange didi?" Urmila said as we walked towards the sitting room.
"What?" I asked.

She exchanged a glance with shrutkirti and Mandavi as if they already had a talk about what they were going to ask or rather tell me. When they looked a little hesitant, I asked again,

"What is it?"

After a hesitant pause, Urmila said, "didi, don't you think something is going on. I mean our husbands, we haven't seen them since morning, mothers though so loving and welcoming to us, we can still feel something beneath that surface, that they are worried abut something, sending the messengers to the main hall where the meeting is taking place."

I got what they said because the same thing was recurring in my mind as well, and I knew not what to tell them, so I said,

"Ayodhya is a big kingdom, there are usually big decisions taking place. Well, I think all we can do is, have patience and make sure to create comforting atmosphere for mothers."

Urmila and Mandvi smiled to this but said nothing and then suddenly shrutkirti squealed, "oh wait, did I show you the sarees mothers gifted me. They are so beautiful. Ome I'll show"

This brought a genuine smile on our faces. She was still the same, our little old shrutkirti, even after marriage, getting happy for little things, and always knowing how to lighten up the mood. So, we had no other option but to agree to her, we had done all our work, spent time with the mothers, and so we now we sisters decided to send some time together, and so we went to Shrut's room.

As were sitting, joining in to Shrut's excitement about her new sarees, we heard loud drum rolls, sounds of conch shells, trumpets, and then a little faded sound of announcer walking by the streets of Ayodhya.

Apparently, some big decision had been made. We looked at each other with confused expressions, and before we could exchange any words, a messenger knocked at our door.

"*Rani* Sita, Rani Mandavi, Rani Urmila, and Rani Shrutkirti, greetings! With all due respect, I am here with the message from the King, you are all summoned in the grand hall. *Maharanis* will be there as well."

After delivering this message, he sought permission and walked away. Still the clouds of our confusing didn't go away, they only grew denser, so we thought it was only best to reach the grand hall as soon as possible.

Our hearts pounded a frantic rhythm against our ribs as we, Sita, Urmila, Mandavi, and Shrutkirti, entered the grand hall. The air, thick with a mixture of anticipation and unspoken tension, crackled around us. The mothers, already assembled, wore expressions that mirrored our own – a veil of confusion draped over their regal composure.

King Dasharatha, however, presented a stark contrast. Seated upon his throne, adorned in his royal finery, a radiant smile illuminated his face. A celebratory garland, hung loosely around Raghunandan's neck. His expressions were the same, a calm, humble smile. Lakshman however looked the most happy and excited of all the people gathered in the hall. The incongruity of these elements – the celebratory atmosphere amidst the mothers' furrowed brows – only served to heighten the sense of mystery hanging heavy in the air.

We, the newly arrived brides, instinctively huddled closer together, seeking silent comfort in each other's presence. All eyes were turned towards King Dasharatha, waiting for him to break the silence and unveil the reason behind this enigmatic gathering. What momentous event had transpired? What news, joyful or fraught, had prompted such a display of contrasting emotions? We held our breath, anticipation tightening its grip on our hearts, as the king cleared his throat and began to speak.

"An announcement has been made today, a decision that can be marked as the best decision to have been ever made in the history of Ayodhya. Today, I King Dashrath, son of King Aja scion of Suryansha dynasty, declares Ram, my eldest son as the heir of my throne. The preparations of Raj Tilak shall begin soon."

As he made this announcement, the entire hall cheered I joy, all the faces beamed with happiness. With King Dashrath's proclamation of Ram's raj tilak, a wave of jubilation swept through the entire hall like wildfire. Cheers erupted, echoing off the grand walls, as joy painted every face with radiant hues. Proud smiles danced upon lips, a testament to the collective happiness that permeated the assembly.

As my gaze swept across the room, I caught sight of Mata Kausalya, her eyes shimmering with unshed tears of pride. A serene smile graced her lips, reflecting the depth of her emotions. Beside her, Mata Kaikeyi and Mata Sumitra wore expressions of immense joy, their eyes alight with excitement.

But it was the look on Lakshman's face that truly captured the essence of the moment. His features were aglow with unbridled happiness, a reflection of the profound significance of Ram's impending coronation.

In the midst of the jubilant celebrations, my sisters enveloped me in warm embraces, offering their heartfelt congratulations. Their eyes sparkled with happiness, mirroring the joy that filled the air, while their smiles conveyed a depth of sisterly love that transcended words.

But amongst all these smiles, all this harmonious pallet ether was one smile that didn't blend with the rest of smiles, that smile came from behind Mata Kaikeyi, it was Manthara, though she was smiling, still her smile didn't resonate with anyone, it was as if something else but happiness was hidden beneath that smile, as if the smile carried something else, it tried to hide something else. Usually, her every actin all her appearance felt to hide something, like the hunch on her back, it felt like she has been carrying something through ages through births, as if her hunch was symbolic of something, she was carrying some ambitions, some hopes, some fear on her back, hard to tell. And just like that it was hard to tell what she was feeling right ow.

*As much as eyes are the windows to the soul since they never lie, smiles are the curtains to the mind, they might deceive.*

# XX

The joyous pandemonium that erupted within the palace walls after the announcement of Raghunandan's Raj Tilak was intoxicating. Laughter echoed through the corridors, servants scurried about with a renewed spring in their steps, and the distant strains of celebratory music filtered in from the courtyards below. I stood by the window, a silent observer to the unfolding spectacle, yet a participant in the whirlwind of emotions that swirled within me.

A surge of pride, so potent it threatened to burst from my chest, threatened to steal my breath away. Raghunandan, the man I loved with every fibre of my being, was to be crowned the next king of Ayodhya. The weight of this news settled upon me not as a burden, but as a testament to the extraordinary man I had chosen to share my life with. His wisdom, his compassion, his unwavering strength – these qualities, long admired in private, were now being recognized by the entire kingdom.

A gentle hand brushed against mine, grounding me in the present. Raghunandan stood beside me, his eyes reflecting the same joyous light that danced in the palace courtyard. A warmth spread through me as I leaned into him, seeking solace in his familiar presence.

"The news has spread like wildfire," he said, his voice laced with a barely contained excitement. "The entire kingdom is abuzz with preparations for your soon-to-be King."

I turned to face him, my heart overflowing with a love as vast as the sky. "Raghunandan," I whispered, the weight of the title settling on my tongue, "I am so incredibly proud of you. You have always possessed the qualities of a great leader – your wisdom is unmatched, your compassion boundless, your strength unwavering. But today, the entire kingdom sees it too."

His gaze softened, and a gentle smile tugged at the corners of his lips. He cupped my face in his hands, his touch a silent promise of love and support. "This honour, Sita," he said, his voice dropping to a husky murmur, "is ours to share. As I ascend the throne, your responsibilities will grow alongside mine. The people of Ayodhya will look up to you, not just as their queen, but as a mother figure pillar of strength, a figure of empathy and love. A other has to be empathetic and filled with love care and nurture but also firm at times when needed. Remember Janaki, neither mere rain can help the plants grow, neither mere sunlight, it needs a combination of both to grow beautifully."

A flicker of apprehension danced in my eyes. "Will I be able to fulfil their expectations, Raghunandan?" I confessed, a tremor of uncertainty lacing my voice.

His thumb brushed away the worry line forming on my forehead. "You have everything within you, Janaki," he reassured me, his eyes conveying a confidence that mirrored his words. "Your unwavering kindness, your sharp intellect, your unwavering support for me – these are the qualities that will make you a queen worthy of Ayodhya's devotion. You will be the embodiment of a mother's love,

Sita, offering both the firmness needed for guidance and the compassion that fosters growth."

His words ignited a spark of understanding within me. I envisioned myself not just as a wife standing by his side, but as a queen in her own right, her role as crucial as his. A queen who would stand beside him during joyous celebrations, but also offer unwavering support during times of hardship. A queen who would use her voice not for personal gain, but for the well-being of her people.

I met his gaze, my own filled with newfound determination. "I will learn, Raghunandan," I pledged, my voice firm with resolve. "I will learn alongside you, and together, we will usher in a golden age for Ayodhya. A kingdom not just prosperous, but filled with compassion, justice, and the unwavering love of its people."

Raghunandan's smile widened, brighter than the sunlight streaming through the window. In that shared look, a silent promise bloomed between us. We were not just lovers, but partners, destined to walk this path together. We would face the challenges that lay ahead hand-in-hand, weaving a tapestry of love, responsibility, and devotion that would forever bind us to the kingdom of Ayodhya. The weight of the future, once daunting, now felt like a shared burden, a purpose that intertwined our destinies and ignited a fire of excitement within me. As Raghunandan pulled me into a warm embrace, the joyous sounds of the palace seemed to fade away, replaced by the comforting beat of his heart – a rhythm that promised a future filled with love, duty, and the unwavering support of the man I loved.

# XXI

The entire Ayodhya was in celebration, each and everyone seemed to rejoice from young little kids to elderly, everyone rejoiced. The joy on everyone's fae made it evident how much they loved Raghunandan, how much respect they had for him. It had been a few days since the announcement for Raj Tilak and entire Ayodhya was involved in preparations. Everywhere there was just environment of celebrations.
the night before, Raghunandan had told me that today we would go and meet the people of Ayodhya, we would walk into their streets, meet them, talk to them, to know about their pain, to know about them, to really listen to what they had to say and not what the ministers and messengers had to say. Raghunandan said one can never truly understand a story until heard from the person living it, and I completely agree to it,

*Though whispers may paint the portrait of events, only the brushstrokes of the heart reveal the truest image.*

Today, sunshine seemed woven into the very fabric of my sari. I chose a vibrant yellow, its colour shimmering with gold thread works and a cascade of delicate pearls. The colour, like a burst of summer warmth, felt innately welcoming, a perfect choice for meeting the people of

Ayodhya.

As we emerged from the palace gates, Raghunandan's hand resting gently on the small of my back, a hush fell over the gathered crowd. A thousand eyes turned towards us, and in their depths, I saw a kaleidoscope of emotions. For Raghunandan, it was a wave of pure adoration – the love and respect a son receives from his own people. The gazes that lingered on me, however, were a revelation. Despite having arrived only a few days ago, a sense of warmth and recognition emanated from their depths. It was as if, in their eyes, I wasn't just a foreign princess, but a part of their own story, a thread woven into the rich tapestry of Ayodhya.

Raghunandan moved through the throng with the grace of a seasoned leader. He greeted each person with a genuine smile, a warmth that resonated in his voice as he inquired about their well-being. He listened patiently to their concerns, his brow furrowing in concentration as he pondered their problems. It wasn't just the solutions he offered, but the way he offered them – with an empathy and understanding that spoke volumes about his character. Witnessing his interactions, a quiet pride bloomed within me. This was the Raghunandan I knew and loved – a leader who ruled not just with power, but with compassion, a man who saw the faces not of subjects, but of his people.

After we came back to the palace, the air of the palace felt a bit off, the preparations for Raghunandan's raj tilak felt to be on a halt. Everything seemed to stand still. There was something I didn't want to admit, but the trees, the flowers of palace garden, and the air inside palace sent the signals of something gloomy, something stressful. But I tried to ignore it, I could see the similar concerned observation on Raghunandan's face but neither of us exchanged any words regarding this.

"Sita, you must be tired after the long walks, you may go to your room and take some rest. I shall come late." Raghunandan looked at me and spoke.

I knew where he had to go, to look for the answer that even I was looking for, 'what exactly was going on inside these walls of the palace'

So I nodded in agreement and walked to my room.

The walk back to my chambers felt like an eternity. Each step echoed hollowly on the polished marble floor, a stark contrast to the joyous din that had filled the palace earlier. My gaze remained stubbornly fixed on the intricate mosaic patterns beneath my feet, a desperate attempt to distract myself from the turmoil within. My mind, however, refused to be tethered to the present. It was a tangled web of confusion, snagged on the sudden halt of the festivities. The vibrant energy that had pulsed through the palace just hours ago had been replaced by a suffocating stillness, a heavy weight that pressed down on my chest.

Reaching my quarters, I drifted aimlessly inside, the grand room offering no solace. The luxurious silk cushions on the bed held no invitation to rest, nor did the ornately carved chairs beckon me to sit. My eyes, filled with a desperate yearning for answers, remained fixed on the ornately carved doorway. It was as if I willed Raghunandan's form to materialize, to bring some semblance of clarity to the chaotic swirl of emotions churning within me. Every creak of floorboard, every distant murmur echoed in the oppressive silence, fuelling the growing anxiety gnawing at my insides. The weight of the unknown hung heavy in the air, a relentless companion that demanded an explanation, a resolution to the unsettling turn of events.

The sun was almost set, the twilight mingled with the lighted lamps in my room, and I that warm glow I finally saw Raghunandan entering the room. He had a smile on his face, the usual smile? Not rally. A sad, fake or deceiving smile? Not really?

"WHAT IS IT Raghunandan, you look worried" I asked

no he did not look worried, but I just knew something was off, and now I had to know, not because I wanted to know but because if there was anything concerned with Raghunandan, if there was anything bothering him, I wanted to be a part of it,

*I was desperate to share his pain.*

"Do I really look worried to you Janaki?" he asked with his soothing voice and that subtle smile.

"no" I admitted looking down at floor.

He walked closer, cupped my cheeks, raised my chin and said,

"you can't lower your head Janaki, especially not now. This kingdom needs yu the most now, the people need you the most now, the family needs you the most now." Raghunandan said.

Wait, what did he just say.

"You or us?" I asked.

"What?' Raghunandan asked.

"You said this kingdom needs you, but it should be 'us'. From the first day of marriage, you have promised that it will always be 'us' from now on. And more importantly, what ahs happened, what do you mean by 'now'. I have so many questions and confusions Raghunandan, kindly be more clear."

"Have a seat Janaki, I will answer all your questions." Raghunandan said as he sat with me, net to me.

But he didn't say anything, but neither did I know he had to tell something but he was considering about how to tell me, and I understood and respected that. Then after a long pause he exhaled a long breath of air and then began, "Mother Kaikeyi is a very sweet lady, she is very dear not just to me but everyone, especially to my father. But she is not just sweet but also immensely brave and courageous. Once in a battle, when my father was stuck in a very difficult situation, when his chariot was stuck due to the broken wheel, it was mother Kaikeyi who t just helped him but saved his life. And that day father granted her two boons, but she demanded the boons to be granted to her when she felt the time was right, and...'

Raghunandan then stopped and looked at me, as if someone looking at the child to ensure if the child was ready to learn something new that might be uncomfortable to the child.

"And what...?' I insisted Raghunandan to continue. And then he continued,

"So now she has asked for the two boons."

I knew that the answer to everything, to all my questions, to all my confusion was in these two boons, so I asked, "what are those two boons then?"

Raghunandan darted his eyes back from my face to the floor and then after a moment of pause he said, "the first boon demands father to make Bharat as the heir of his throne."

Listening to this, I did feel different, I felt bad for Raghunandan as his wife but as a part of this family I respected mother Kaikeyi's wish and father Dashrath's promise and decision, I felt happy for Bharat. And I knew the kind of person Raghunandan is, he would not have felt even a tinge of grief upon listening to this, there had to be something else, so I said,

"well I think Bharat will prove to be a great king when he is under the guidance and blessings of his elder brother Raghunandan."

Raghunandan said nothing to this, so I hesitantly I said again, "so what is the second boon?"

"the second boon," began Raghunandan, "is that I should be sent to fourteen years of exile."

A SMILE OF OBIDEIENCE. Now I finally recognized, all this while Raghunandan was carrying the smile of obedience. He had agreed to it. I couldn't believe my own ears, the mother who showered so much love on Raghunandan made this decision, asked for her favourite son's exile for fourteen years?! It was hard to believe, it felt like it was not her asking for this boon, but someone else. But I knew despite me not able to believe, it was the fact in front of me right now, and ow my sole role was to comfort ram, be on his side, since I knew he would not have said no to father maharaja Dashrath, so now I had to respect Raghunandan's acceptance of the decision.

But still before saying anything else I asked, "so what did you say?"

"father's righteousness asked him to agree to mata's boon and my righteousness asked me to help father fulfil that boon and keep his promise. So, I accepted it." Raghunandan replied.

"So, when are we leaving?" I asked with no further need for explanations.

"I will be leaving at dawn" he answered.

My ears heard what he said, but my heart, my soul, my entirety refused to accept it, so I asked again, "when are 'we' leaving" emphasising on we.

"Janaki" Raghunandan stood up and walked across the room slowly and then said with his back facing me, "you are the daughter in law of this family, you are the pride of this family, I can't take you with me."

"but my pride resides in residing with you."

"Janaki, you are unaware about the horrors of the forest. There will be thorns that will hurt your delicate feet, there will be roars of wild animals that might tremble your calm heart, scorching sun that has the capacity to singe your skin. I promised to take care of you Janaki, not trouble you." As Raghunandan said this, he tuned back to face me. Now I stood up and walked towards him, I said,

"you also promised that we will walk on this path of life together, you also promised that we will stay together, you also promised that you will always be there for me, you also promised that you will never leave my side." Tears in my eyes, I didn't realize how fast I was talking compared to my usual steadiness in my tone. I couldn't even bear the thought of Raghunandan leaving without me, I couldn't even bear the thought of imagining him all alone in the forest.

"The family needs you right now Sita. I can't take you with me to face the adversity the forest life has to offer. Stay here Sita" Raghunandan replied.

I just looked at his eyes with mine filled with tears, and then finally when I composed myself enough to utter words, I said, "your advice makes me look so small Raghunandan. After marriage, the husband alone is the refuge of a woman at all times. And so, I shall come with you, I shall walk ahead of you crushing blades of grass and thorns that lie in the way. You are following your righteousness, well mine tells me to some with you to the forest and so let me follow mine. You warn me about the difficulties of the forest, but how can you forget I am Bhumija, how can I be afraid of my own mother, the raw life that he has to offer, you tell me about the thorns that might come on the way, I thin of the flowers that will fragrant our life, you tell me about the roar of wild animals, I think about the chirping of birds, the rare sight of deer that now will not be so rare, you tell me about the scorching sun but I think about the gentle breeze. Difficulties and happiness are everywhere Raghunandan but it is upon us on what to focus."

"but" Raghunandan said, but for the first time I interjected him, "the disadvantages and warnings that have been enumerated by you as accruing from an abode in the forest will become nothing but blessings for me since I am foremost in your affections."

"But Sita being a Raghuvanshi, I can't let you go through the hardships of the forest. Either stay here with the mother or you can go to Mithila back to your father." Raghunandan's replied ignited a certain fire within me, no the fire was not of rage, not of anger, but that fire was of my decision to come along with Raghunandan and his refusal was only intensifying the flames of that fire. And so, I said, "what are you afraid of really? Don't you know a woman disunited from her husband is not able to survive. I know nothing but my sole duty resides in offering my love and car to you. My righteousness asks me to walk every step with you, share very pain with you, wipe every tear of yours, offer you smiles...'

after this I could say no more, I burst into tears covering me face with my palms. And then there it was, I felt his warm hands against mine as he uncovered my face and finally said after looking at me for a moment, "come with me my partner, come with me my Sita. Come with me to make the journey of life a blissful one. Will you accompany me to this

14 years of exile Janaki?'

"I will accompany you till my last breath Raghunandan." I said smiling and wiping away my tears.

"bhaiya, bhaiya" I heard Lakshman's voice calling for Raghunandan, his voice filed with anger, desperation. Raghunandan looked at me and I nodded, I knew even Lakshman would not stay silent upon hearing this news, and hearing his voice it was only best if Raghunandan talked to him right away and calmed is anger.

as I was just reflecting upon everything that happened today, was trying to process it, a messenger came in with the news that father king Dashrath's health is very critical, so I ran towards his room. All my siters and mothers were also present there sitting around father king Dashrath's bed, all crying. As they saw me, my sisters came running towards e and hugged me crying.

Urmila said, "please, please don't go didi."

"Shrutkirti added, "yes didi please don't leave us"

"look even Father King Dashrath can't bear this news, he thought you'll ask *jija shri* to not go but even you have made the decision to go along with him." Mandavi added.

I didn't know what to say to anyone at this very moment, so I simply focused on Father King Dashrath's health who was on his bed unconscious, mothers around him crying.

Doctors were continuous with their efforts to bring him back to good health and soon Raghunandan and Lakshman came in as well to take care of father. Father Dashrath would just wake up from him unconscious state for moments in between and in those moments, he would try his best to convince Raghunandan not to go. And in those exchange of conversations between him, Raghunandan and Lakshman, I came to know even Lakshman would be coming with us for the fourteen years of exile. The moment

I heard this, I looked at Urmila's face who tried her best not to show anyone hoe hurt she was, but I knew how this pain was unbearable for her, but this was the moment where everyone was in pain but no one had anything to say to anyone, no one had anything to say that could wipe away the tears.

*Sometimes the tears don't need wiping they just need to be shed freely.*

*Sometimes your words can't shield their pain so you just take the pain with them.*

# XXII

The oppressive darkness of the previous night clung to me like a shroud. Sleep had been a distant dream, replaced by the haunting sounds of muffled sobs echoing through the palace walls. The mothers, their faces etched with despair, wept openly for the ailing Pita Shri King Dasharatha, his illness casting a long shadow over the entire kingdom. But amidst these tears, another layer of grief unfurled – the impending exile of Raghunandan, Lakshmana, and myself. We were to leave at dawn, banished to the unforgiving wilderness for fourteen long years, a decision meted out for a promise kept.

Throughout the night, frantic pleas filled the air. The mothers, their voices thick with desperation, implored Raghunandan to reconsider. They painted a bleak picture of our future, a life stripped of comfort and filled with hardship. Yet, Raghunandan remained resolute. His voice, though laced with sorrow, held an unwavering commitment to his father's word. He spoke of duty, of the sacredness of a promise made, a vow that could not be broken even in the face of such immense personal sacrifice.

With the first rays of dawn painting streaks of pale gold across the horizon, a heavy finality settled upon us. The once vibrant colours of the palace seemed to have muted, reflecting the sombre mood that hung in the air. It was time to shed the outward symbols of our royal lives. The silks and brocades that adorned our bodies were carefully removed, replaced with simple saffron cotton clothes, a stark reminder of the austere path that lay ahead.

As I donned the rough fabric, a wave of emotions washed over me. Fear, uncertainty, and a deep sadness for the family being left behind intertwined with a fierce sense of loyalty to the man I loved, hope that whatever comes on the way I shall live it smilingly with Raghunandan. Stepping into this exile wasn't just his journey, it was ours – a shared path paved with hardship, yet bound by an unyielding love. In the quiet rustle of the changing clothes, a silent vow was made. We would face whatever challenges awaited us, together.

I stood before the ornately carved mirror, a stranger to the woman reflected within. Gone were the silks and jewels that had marked me as a princess. In their place, a simple saffron saree draped my form, its colour mirroring the rising sun, a symbol of a new beginning, albeit a harsh one. My hair, once adorned with intricate braids and sparkling ornaments, was now gathered in a loose bun, the remaining tresses cascading down my back like a forgotten dream. My hands, accustomed to the weight of gold bangles and rings, now felt different and light, the only adornment was the cool caress of *tulsi* beads, a stark reminder of our new life of devotion.

Across the room, Raghunandan's form mirrored my transformation. The saffron dhoti wrapped around his waist hung with a warrior's grace, while another saffron cloth, rested upon his broad shoulders. His hair, was now tied back in a simple knot, the remaining strands escaping in a way that spoke of the turmoil within of leaving the mothers, ill father, but also following the path of righteousness. The glint of gold had vanished from his neck, replaced by the simple sanctity of tulsi beads, a silent vow of faith in the face of uncertainty. Our eyes met in the reflection, a silent conversation passing between us. Though certain gloom of separation from family flickered in their depths, it was overshadowed by a resolute love, a love that promised to be our guiding star in the wilderness ahead.

We made our way towards the palace entrance, each step heavy with the weight of the unknown. There, a tableau of grief awaited us. The mothers, their regal composure shattered, wept openly, their sobs echoing through the vast hall. Mandavi and Shrutkirti clung to each other, their eyes red-rimmed and voices thick with choked back tears. But it was Urmila who stole my breath away. Her face, once vibrant and full of life, was now a mask of utter desolation. Her eyes, usually sparkling with mischief, were vacant, glazed over with a profound shock that transcended tears. It was as if the world had leached all colour from her, leaving behind a hollow shell. The sight of my once exuberant sister, reduced to this desolate silence, sent a shard of pain through my heart.

Next to her stood Lakshmana, his form etched with a stoic resolve. His gaze, usually filled with warmth, now held an unwavering dedication. It was a dedication that resonated with a love for Raghunandan, a loyalty that would not be swayed even in the face of personal sacrifice. But amidst this unwavering loyalty, a flicker of something else danced in his eyes – a flicker of concern, perhaps, or even a flicker of doubt. Perhaps, like me, he too felt the bitter sting of his decision, the weight of leaving his wife behind.

Though his voice remained silent, the unspoken apology that hung in the air spoke volumes.

In that moment, I was caught in a whirlwind of conflicting emotions. Respect wrestled with sorrow, admiration for Lakshmana's devotion battled with a pang of empathy for Urmila.

Bidding farewell had already been a heart-wrenching affair with Pita Shri King Dasharath. His illness had taken a cruel turn, leaving him in a state of fluctuating consciousness. It was difficult to discern if he truly recognized us as we knelt by his bedside, seeking his blessing. His once-powerful voice was reduced to a raspy whisper, his gaze drifting in and out of focus. Whether the image he saw was of his sons ready to depart or a figment of his fevered mind, we couldn't be sure.

Moving on to the mothers, the air thickened with a palpable grief. Kaushalya Mata, ever the picture of regality, fought valiantly to hold back the tears that threatened to spill. Her blessing came in a voice taut with emotion, each word a testament to the silent storm raging within her. But it was Sumitra Mata's wordless embrace that truly shattered the fragile dam of my composure. Days ago, her hugs had been filled with such joyous warmth, a mother's pride overflowing in her touch. Today, however, her embrace spoke volumes in its quiet desperation. The warmth had been replaced by a chilling emptiness, mirroring the desolate future that stretched before us. The scent of sandalwood that usually clung to her was overpowered by the sting of unshed tears, a poignant reminder of the life we were leaving behind.

Embracing Mandavi and Shrutkirti was a bittersweet symphony of grief and whispered pleas. Their tears flowed freely, staining my saffron robes with silent pleas for me to stay. Their voices, raw with emotion, echoed a desperate plea, "Don't leave, Didi." We both knew, with a heart-wrenching certainty, that defiance was futile. This path, paved with thorns, was one Raghunandan and I had chosen to walk. Yet, the fierce love of sisters refused to acknowledge the bitter truth. I couldn't blame them. How could one simply accept the banishment of a beloved sibling?

A pang of guilt twisted in my gut. Leaving my family behind was a heavy weight to bear, but this path, for all its hardships, was the one I stood by. Regret was a luxury I couldn't afford, nor did I want my sorrow to project a false narrative. To crumble now, to succumb to the overwhelming emotions, would paint a picture of doubt, a flicker of regret that wasn't there. In that moment, amidst the torrent of tears and whispered pleas, I straightened my spine, my resolve hardening like the resolve of the trees that would soon be our companions. My voice, though thick with emotion, remained steady as I offered words of comfort, a silent vow to remain strong, not just for myself, but for them as well. It was a time for steady determination, a time to project not weakness, but the love and loyalty that would guide us through the coming exile.

Then as we emerged from the palace gates, we saw the people of Ayodhya waiting for us, all their eyes set on us. A collective gasp swept through the throng of people gathered beyond. The air, thick with a heavy silence moments ago, now crackled with a raw energy that defied the sombre occasion. A sea of faces turned towards us, each one etched with a mixture of grief and determination. Tears glistened in countless eyes, reflecting the collective pain of the kingdom.

At the forefront stood a wizened old man, his face a map of wrinkles etched by time, yet his posture held a surprising vigour. He spoke, his voice raspy but firm, "*Yuvraj* Ram, *Yuvrani* Sita, we would have pleaded with you to stay, to defy this cruel decree. We know Maharani Kausalya did her utmost, and if she could not sway your heart, how could mere words from us succeed?"

A woman, her voice strong and vibrant, stepped forward, her fiery spirit mirroring the determination in the eyes around her. "Yes! And so, we have decided. If you cannot remain in Ayodhya, then we will come with you!" A wave of agreement rippled through the crowd, a chorus of voices echoing the sentiment.

Raghunandan, his heart heavy but his voice resolute, tried to dissuade them. "My people, your love overwhelms me, but this is a path of hardship. The life in the forest is harsh, unforgiving. It is no place for you. You are my family, how can I let my own family go through suffering and hardships."

I felt a lump form in my throat as I witnessed this outpouring of devotion. Though their words were directed at Raghunandan, the sentiment resonated deeply within my own heart.

A tremor ran through me, a silent plea echoing in my heart. Though their loyalty warmed me, the thought of leading them into a life of hardship gnawed at my conscience. "Kindy try to understand," I began, my voice laced with gentle persuasion, "I respect your love for Raghunandan, it overwhelms me, fills me with joy that the person I love so dearly is loved by so many. But the forest is a harsh reality. There will be little food, scant shelter, and dangers unseen. We wouldn't want you to suffer on our account. Your Raghunandan would not want you to suffer, he would not be happy seeing you all go through difficulties."

A murmur of dissent rippled through the crowd; a sea of faces etched with resolute determination. An elderly woman, her voice steady despite her age, stepped forward. "We understand, Janak Nandini" she said, her gaze unwavering. "The forest may be harsh, but the thought of remaining here, comfortable yet separated from our king, is a far greater hardship."

Her words resonated with a chorus of agreement. Raghunandan stood beside me, his jaw clenched, his eyes filled with a conflict of emotions - gratitude for their unwavering loyalty, yet concern for their well-being.

Taking his hand in mine, I squeezed it gently, offering silent support. "Raghunandan," I whispered, my voice barely audible above the din, "their love is fierce, their loyalty unwavering. They cannot be swayed by logic in the face of such devotion. Perhaps, in their eyes, we are not just members of royal family, but a symbol of hope, a beacon of righteousness that they will not abandon, even into the heart of the unknown. For now, I think it is only right to respect their emotions."

Raghunandan's gaze met mine, a silent conversation passing between us. He saw the truth in my words, the unyielding love that bound these people to him. A flicker of acceptance softened his features. He understood that logic wouldn't suffice in the face of such devotion.

*That's the beauty of love, it is not bounded by logics but freed by emotions.*

These were his people, and they wouldn't be dissuaded.

With a deep breath, he addressed the crowd, his voice heavy but resolute. "The path ahead will be difficult. But if you choose to walk it with us, know that we will face these challenges together. We will protect you, as you have protected us."

Though Raghunandan said theses words, I could sense there was something else beneath it, however I thought this was not the right time to discuss it.

A cheer erupted from the crowd, a wave of joyous energy washing over the gathering. As the first rays of dawn kissed the horizon, we turned from the palace walls, ready to face the unknown, together.

# XXIII

The dust of Ayodhya settled behind us like a fading memory as we ventured deeper into the emerald embrace of the jungle. The transition was instantaneous. One moment we were bathed in the familiar warmth of the palace courtyard, the next we were swallowed by a symphony of unseen creatures and rustling leaves. Sunlight dappled the forest floor, casting intricate patterns on the damp earth. The air, thick with the scent of unknown flora, carried a strange thrill, a whisper of adventure amidst the uncertainty.

People of Ayodhya, loyal to their Kausalyanandan followed us. As the sun dipped below the horizon, casting long shadows across the forest floor, we gathered around a crackling fire. It was a meagre substitute for the grand feasts of the palace, yet it provided a flicker of warmth and camaraderie. Raghunandan, his once-regal features weathered by the day's journey, spoke of his vision for a future kingdom, a kingdom built on the bedrock of justice and compassion. Lakshmana, ever vigilant, his gaze scanning the perimeter of the camp, offered the unwavering loyalty of a brother and protector. And I, nestled beside Raghunandan, found solace in weaving stories of our past life – tales of palace gardens and bustling marketplaces – a flicker of nostalgia warming the loneliness that occasionally gnawed at my heart.

As the fire dwindled to embers and the camp settled into a murmur of slumber, a disquietude stirred within me. The sight of our loyal followers, huddled together for warmth, sparked a pang of guilt in my chest. They had left behind their homes, their families, all out of devotion to their king. We had become, unintentionally, the cause of their displacement.

A gentle nudge from Raghunandan drew my attention. His eyes, usually filled with determination, were clouded with a similar concern. "Sita," he murmured, his voice low, "our people… they have left their lives behind for us."

I reached out, squeezing his hand gently. "I understand your worry, Raghunandan. I was thinking the same, they, their ancestors have spent their lives building homes they have in Ayodhya. Those homes that are made not just by bricks and walls, but by laughter of their children, stories of their elders, love of their family, special notable moments they had. And now all of a sudden, they are leaving all that for us."

He sighed, a heavy sound that spoke volumes. "But surely there must be another way… a way for them to return."

We sat in companionable silence for a while, the crackling embers the only witness to our conversation. My heart ached for a solution, but logic gnawed at the edges of my worry. We couldn't continue down this path, knowing we were a burden on their lives.

Finally, a resolute glint entered Raghunandan's eyes. "Sita," he said, his voice firm, "you are right. Their devotion is a treasure, but we cannot exploit it. They, like us, must make a difficult choice."

I nodded, a bittersweet understanding settling upon me. "Perhaps," I said, my voice barely above a whisper, "it's time for us to let them go."

With a shared look of heavy hearts, a decision was made. We wouldn't wait for the dawn to break, casting its harsh light on our difficult choice. We would act swiftly, before the day's worries could cloud their reason.

Rising quietly, we made our way to the makeshift shelters where our followers slept, their faces peaceful in the moonlight. It was a heartbreaking sight, a confirmation of the sacrifice they had made. With a gentle touch on each shoulder, we awakened a few trusted leaders, explaining our reasoning in hushed tones. Tears welled up in their eyes, but they understood. Their families, their lives, wouldn't wait for our exile to end.

As the first rays of dawn peeked through the dense foliage, we stood at the edge of the camp, watching the remaining people of Ayodhya disappear back into the jungle, their departure a bittersweet symphony of grief and gratitude. We were left alone, a smaller group but with a strengthened resolve. We were no longer just a king and queen in exile; we were survivors, ready to face the unknown depths of the wilderness, together. With Lakshmana by our side, we ventured deeper into the forest, the rising sun painting a hopeful orange on the path ahead.

# XXIV

Sunlight, filtered through a dense canopy of leaves, cast a dappled pattern on the forest floor. Each step I took sent a flurry of dry leaves skittering underfoot, the only sound breaking the unsettling silence of the jungle. Beside me walked Raghunandan, his brow furrowed in worry. Lakshmana, ever vigilant, remained a few paces ahead, his broad form clearing a path through the undergrowth. A pang of longing shot through me. Lakshman's devotion was not only towards Raghunandan btu it was also evident for me; I always saw him as my own brother. Whenever he would talk to me, his eyes would by lowered down, looking at my feet in respect, he would never look straight into my eyes. I yearned for the familiar bustle of Ayodhya, the comforting weight of the palace walls, the warmth of familiar faces. Yet, glancing at Raghunandan's profile, etched with worry against the verdant backdrop, I knew I wouldn't trade this hardship for anything.

Suddenly, a sharp sting jolted me back to the present. I winced, reaching down to find a small, wicked thorn embedded in the soft flesh of my foot. A sigh escaped my lips, a tremor of pain running up my leg.

Raghunandan, his senses perpetually attuned to my every movement, stopped instantly. Concern carved lines across his face as he knelt before me. "Careful, Janaki," he murmured, his voice laced with worry. With practiced ease, he tore a strip of cloth and began to gently remove the thorn.

I suppressed a wince as he prodded at the embedded object.

Taking a deep breath, I squeezed Raghunandan's hand. "It's just a thorn," I said, my voice strong. "That's the reason I didn't want you to come Janaki" Kausalyanandan's said with evident worry and concern in his tone and expressions. I took a pause and then replied, "Raghunandan don't you think this is just like life?'
"what is?'
"This. Just like this thorn, there are moments in life which feel like thorns but that doesn't stop us from living our life or make us regret our decision of living life because we know there are other moments worth living for. Similarly, this path, these 14 years of exile will be filled with thorns but that shouldn't stop us from living the beautiful moments."

Raghunandan looked up at me, his eyes searching mine. A proud smile graced his lips with spark in his eyes. I continued, my gaze unwavering, "There will also be moments of joy, of love, of breathtaking beauty. These fourteen years of exile will test us, but they will not break us."

To this Raghunandan's smile broadened but he said nothing, he didn't have to, the proud he felt was evident in his expressions, then he slowly helped me get up and we resumed our journey. Walking a few miles, we stopped at the Coast of Ganga River. We had t cross it to actually begin our journey, away from Ayodhya. We waited there thinking how to cross it, we could see a boat there but no boatman, and just then moments later we heard a joyous voice, "I am blessed, I am blessed, I am the most fortunate today, gods must be so merciful on me today that I got the glimpse of Sri Ram, Mata Sita, and Lakshman Bhaiya. I am the most fortunate."

I could not only hear the happiness I his voice but also in his actions, the way h took each step it was as if he would start dancing any moment now.

Sometimes one doesn't need words to express their happiness, their actions say it all.

*His happiness looked like a peacock dancing in rain who has been waiting for it for ages.*

As he approached us, I could see soe fine lines on his face which spoke of the years he has lived, many emotions that he has experienced, he looked like a middle-aged man. He had a white cloth wrapped o his head which had mud stains on it. His dhoti with a similar shade of white. But all his appearance was masked by the love in his eyes, the way he looked at Raghunandan, with the love and respect he looked at Raghunandan.

"Pranam Shri Ram, Pranam Mata, Pranam Lakshman Bhaiya" he said as he bowed in Pranam.

We reciprocated his greetings and the Raghunandan said, "is this your boat?"

"Yes, yes, it is mine," the man replied in excitement.

"Can you please help us cross the river?" Raghunandan asked to which he replied, "absolutely, absolutely. It will be an honour. But before that I request you to please pay a visit to my house, it is nearby, and have some meal"

Raghunandan smiled and said, "we understand your emotions, but we can't come. We are in a period of exile now; we can't have food from a settled family's home"

To this his happy expressions switched to gloomy. Raghunandan placed his hand on his shoulder to which he replied, "I understand Shri Ram, I am a ridiculous man, why will people like you form a royal family come to a commoner's house like mine. I apologize."

As he said this, Raghunandan instantly embraced his into a hug and then this made him burst into tears, after a moment when his sobs quietened, Raghunandan asked him, "do you still have any complaints?"
he wiped off his tears after Raghunadndan released him from the hug, and he said, "who am in to complaint, but what you dd todays has defiantly removed all my sins."

Then he again wiped off his tears and said, "please please, come on my boat and bless me."

With practiced ease, the boatman then helped us onto his sturdy vessel. As we settled in, a sense of calm washed over me. The rhythmic lap of water against the hull, the cool breeze carrying the scent of damp earth and unknown flora, it all created a serene symphony. My gaze drifted towards the distant jungle on the opposite bank, a tapestry of green merging with the azure sky. For a fleeting moment, my mind found solace in this simple beauty. It felt like a forgotten part of myself was awakening, a connection with nature that resonated deep within my soul.

Lost in this newfound tranquility, I barely noticed the boatman navigating the gentle current. The sun, a benevolent orb casting its golden light upon the water, seemed to paint the world in warm hues. The journey itself faded away, replaced by a quiet hope, a yearning for a future where peace might find us once again.

Before I realized it, we were approaching the opposite bank, the familiar call of the boatman snapping me out of my reverie. We disembarked, a gentle sigh escaping my lips as my feet touched the solid earth once more.

The boatman, his face etched with a combination of respect and humility, bowed low before us. "Thank you, noble ones, for gracing my humble boat with your presence," he said, his voice raspy from years spent battling the elements.

A pang of sadness shot through me. I had nothing to offer him in return for his service, yet I felt a strong urge to show our gratitude. Reaching into my meagre belongings, I hesitated for a moment before removing a precious ring. It was a simple band, adorned with a single ruby, a treasured memento from my life in Ayodhya.

"Please, kind sir," I said, extending the ring towards him. "Accept this as a token of our appreciation."

The boatman's eyes widened in surprise. He shook his head fervently, his voice laced with sincerity. "No, Mata," he refused. "I didn't do this for any reward. To serve such noble beings is a blessing in itself."

Raghunandan, sensing my disappointment, stepped forward, a gentle smile playing on his lips. "This offering, my friend," he interjected, "is not a return for your service, but a gesture of love. You have addressed Janaki as 'Mata.' Surely, you wouldn't refuse a gift from your own mother, would you?"

The boatman's eyes darted between us, his gaze lingering on the ring for a moment longer. A flicker of understanding dawned upon him. "Yes," I interjected, my voice filled with a newfound resolve, "please take it. It will bring me happiness to know that a part of me travels with you on this river."

The boatman hesitated no longer. With a grateful nod, he accepted the ring, his weathered hand cradling the delicate jewel. He bowed low once more, his voice thick with emotion. "May your path be filled with light, noble ones. You have blessed me far more than I could ever repay."

With a final wave and a silent prayer for his well-being, we turned away from the riverbank. The path ahead beckoned, a ribbon of possibility winding through the dense foliage. Though uncertainty veiled the future, the encounter with the boatman had left a warm ember of hope glowing within me. We were exiles, yes, but we were also human beings, bound by the universal language of kindness and compassion. Perhaps, in this vast wilderness, such encounters would be the guiding stars on our journey.

# XXV

The dense foliage gradually thinned, giving way to a clearing bathed in the golden light of the setting sun. Relief washed over me as we emerged from the oppressive embrace of the jungle. We had been walking for hours, the humid air clinging to us like a second skin.

"This seems like a suitable spot," Raghunandan remarked, his voice hoarse from the day's journey. "We can set up our stay here."

Lakshmana, ever the pragmatist, was already scanning the area for suitable materials. He pointed towards a cluster of tall trees. "Those branches will do for the frame, bhaiya. I'll gather them."

With practiced efficiency, they set about constructing a basic shelter. Lakshmana, wove the branches together, while Raghunandan secured them with vines and fallen leaves. As they worked on the structure, I scoured the clearing for anything that could add a touch of comfort. Colorful pebbles became decorations, vibrant flowers brightened the entrance, and fallen branches were transformed into makeshift furniture.

By the time the last rays of sunlight dipped below the horizon, casting long shadows across the clearing, our makeshift shelter had been transformed. It wasn't a palace, but it was ours.

"Lakshmana," I called out, a hint of pride in my voice, "could you gather some fruit from those trees? We need to find something to eat."

Lakshmana nodded, his usual stoicism momentarily replaced by a flicker of surprise. "Of course," he replied, his voice laced with a newfound respect.

As soon as Lakshmana was out of sight, I turned to Raghunandan, a wide smile gracing my lips. "What do you think?" I asked, gesturing towards the transformed shelter.

Raghunandan's eyes widened in appreciation. "Janaki," he murmured, his voice filled with a quiet awe, "this place feels... warm."

A warmth bloomed in my chest. "We may have left Ayodhya," I said, taking his hand, "but we can still create a home, wherever we may be. A woman can turn any place into a home, with a little love and ingenuity, with her mere presence."

Lakshmana soon returned, a basket overflowing with a bounty of wild berries and tubers. We gathered around a small fire, the flames casting flickering shadows on the walls of our shelter. As we shared our simple meal, a comfortable silence descended upon us. The chirping of crickets and the rustling of leaves formed a natural lullaby, a stark contrast to the sounds of the palace we had left behind.

Nightfall drew a curtain over the clearing, ushering in a blanket of stars. Exhausted from the day's journey, we retreated to our makeshift beds, the familiar scent of damp earth replacing the opulent silks we were accustomed to.

The morning sun woke us with its gentle kiss. As I stretched and yawned, a strange feeling settled over me. It was a hollowness, a gnawing sense of loss that transcended the physical separation from Ayodhya. As much as I felt hopeful and determined for what was to come, I felt a pang of sorrow, some kind of ache in my soul today. But I tried to ignore this feeling, maybe it will fade away. I practiced the morning chores, and soon morning transitioned to afternoon. I observed a similar gloom in the energy of Raghunandan and Lakshman too.

"Do you feel it too?" I asked Raghunandan, my voice barely a whisper. To which he replied, "yes, as if some flower is being plucked off it's branch, it's every petal screaming in separation.'

Lakshmana, who had been sharpening a branch for some purpose, paused in his task. "It's the silence, perhaps," he offered, his voice thoughtful. "The absence of familiar sounds, familiar faces..."

As Lakshmana was about to complete his sentence, a distant murmur made him stop. Raghunandan's head snapped up, his hand instinctively reaching for the bow. Though his posture remained calm, his eyes flickered with a wary alertness. Lakshmana, however, reacted with raw suspicion. His hand darted to the quiver, an arrow nocked onto his bowstring in a heartbeat. He sprinted towards a nearby rise, his sharp eyes scanning the dense foliage for any sign of a threat.

"There he is," he called out, a tremor of suspicion lacing his voice. "That conniving Bharat! The throne of Ayodhya wasn't enough, it seems. He comes now to claim our lives as well!"

Though Lakshmana's anger was understandable, was he said about Bharat made me upset. He loved Raghunandan too deeply.

"Stay calm, Lakshmana," Raghunandan interjected, his voice firm yet laced with an underlying current of worry.

Just as Lakshmana was about to retort, a figure emerged from the trees. As they drew closer, Lakshmana's voice boomed with a challenge. "Stay where you are, Bharat! My arrows won't hesitate to find their mark!"

A strangled cry pierced the air. The figure stopped abruptly, and a voice, thick with despair, filled the clearing. "Pranam, Bhaiya," it said, the word 'brother' heavy with grief. "Absolutely, kill me right here. I don't deserve to even stand before you. I became the reason for Ram Bhaiya's exile, Sita Bhabhi's hardship, and your pain. I deserve no forgiveness, but please, brother, grant me one last wish. Let me touch your feet, so I may find a shred of peace before I die."

The raw emotion in those words caused Lakshmana's anger to dissipate as quickly as it had risen. The arrow clattered to the ground as his grip loosened, and tears welled up in his eyes. Raghunandan placed a comforting hand on his brother's shoulder, his own eyes glistening with unshed tears.

Overcome with a wave of emotion, I watched the scene unfold. Seeing the love and pain etched on their faces was more than I could bear. As Bharat approached, a group emerged from the trees behind him. Mothers, sisters, even my father – a sea of familiar faces that had haunted my dreams since leaving Ayodhya.

Tears streamed down my cheeks, a mixture of relief and sorrow. Tears flowed freely, a mixture of relief at seeing familiar faces and a gnawing anxiety that I couldn't quite place. I was so overwhelmed with the sheer joy of seeing my family that I hadn't noticed the details of their attire in those initial moments. Then, as if struck by a bolt of lightning, my focus sharpened. The white cloths draped over the mothers, the somber beige of my newly-wed sisters‘ clothes – a stark contrast to the vibrant colors they usually favored.

Dread curdled in my stomach. I didn't dare let the thought fully form, the horrifying possibility that these clothes hinted at. But even before I could articulate the fear, Bharat's voice shattered the fragile peace.

"He is no more, Bhaiya," he choked out, tears streaming down his face.

I knew who he was talking about. A part of me, a desperate, illogical part, wanted to shut my ears, to block out the rest of his words. As if by refusing to listen, I could somehow alter reality. But the world seemed to have muted, the sounds of the forest replaced by a deafening silence.

Shatrughan's anguished cry confirmed my worst fears. "Our father, Bhaiya, he is no more."

The world spun. The vibrant colors of the clearing, the comforting presence of my family – everything dissolved into a blurry haze. The world felt silent. Grief, a monstrous entity, rose within me, threatening to consume me whole. Raghunandan needed me, I knew that much. But the news had left me paralyzed, my body a statue carved from cold stone. My mind, overwhelmed with the sudden turn of events, refused to function. I stood there numb, incapable of thought, word, or action, lost in a sea of shock and despair.

Grief hung heavy in the air, a suffocating shroud that choked the my joyous emotions of seeing familiar faces just moments before. A primal instinct spurred me into action. Pushing past the numbness that threatened to engulf me, I rushed to Raghunandan's side. Tears streamed down his face, silent and raw. Words seemed futile in the face of such immense pain. Yet, I knew the weight of his grief needed a silent anchor, a presence that acknowledged his suffering. I stood beside him, offering a silent understanding, a hand resting gently on his arm.

*Sometimes the words fail to comfort, it's only the presence that is the balm.*

Knowing the brothers too needed space for their own private mourning, I gave Raghunandan a gentle squeeze before stepping back. The knowledge of their father's passing resonated within me, a deep ache settling in my chest. Yet, there were others who needed me too, there were others who needed Raghunandan too. So, I walked to mothers and my sisters, as Raghunandan and his brother along with my father went for Late Pitashri King Dashrath's last rituals.

As they left, my sisters, their youthful faces stained with tears, rushed towards me. Their sobs, a raw expression of grief, were a mirror to the turmoil within me. I embraced them tightly, offering what little comfort I could. Kausalya Mata and Sumitra Mata, their faces etched with sorrow, followed suit, their hugs a warm reminder of the love that still bound us.

But my gaze kept flickering towards Mata Kaikeyi. Unlike the others, she remained at a distance, a lone figure weeping quietly. I couldn't bear my once loving Mata like this, so I walked towards her, I knew she needed us,

"Are you still upset with us, Mata?" my voice emerged a tentative whisper.

The question seemed to shatter the wall she had built around herself. Tears welled up in her eyes, spilling over in a torrent of grief. She rushed towards me, her embrace a desperate plea for forgiveness.

"It's me, Sita," she sobbed, her voice thick with remorse. "It's me who needs forgiveness. What have I done? I seek your forgiveness, Sita. Come home, I have committed a sin."

The pain in her voice broke my heart into pieces. "Mothers don't apologize, Mata," I said, my voice choked with emotion, I tried comforting her. Kaikeyi Mata's repeated pleas for forgiveness were like a knife twisting in my gut. It wasn't forgiveness she needed; it was our understanding, our love. Here we were, a family fractured by circumstance, each of us grappling with the loss of a father, a husband, a king. Yet, Mata Kaikeyi's burden was heavier, weighed down not just by grief but by the guilt that gnawed at her from within.

We surrounded her, a silent circle of compassion. My sisters held her hand, their soft tears mingling with hers. Kausalya Mata and Sumitra Mata offered gentle words of solace, their pain a reflection of hers. She was our mother, and in this moment of profound vulnerability, we, her children, were her anchor.

As moments turned into a comforting silence, her sobs subsided, replaced by shallow breaths that gradually eased with each passing second. A flicker of relief passed through me. It was a small victory, a tiny step on a long road to healing.

Then, from the edge of the clearing, Raghunandan and his brothers emerged, accompanied by my father. We couldn't spot anymore tears on their faces, but the gloom was evident. The tears may have dried, but the pain remained, a heavy weight they carried within.

A wave of emotions crashed over the clearing as Mata Kaikeyi rushed towards Raghunandan. Tears streamed down her face as she pleaded, "Ram, forgive me. Please come back home."

Raghunandan, ever the dutiful son, embraced her tightly. "Mata," he said gently, "mothers don't ask for forgiveness. They guide, they love, they offer unwavering support. There's no room for such words in their vocabulary."

Stepping back, Mata Kaikeyi wiped her tears, a flicker of determination replacing her despair. "Very well then, Ram," she declared, her voice regaining its strength. "Your mother commands you to return to Ayodhya. Come back with us."

Raghunandan's face softened, but his resolve remained firm. "I'm afraid that's not possible, Mata. A decision was made, and as a Raghuvanshi prince, I must fulfill it."

"But I take back my words, Ram!" Mata Kaikeyi cried out, desperation lacing her voice. "I retract everything I said. Don't follow my foolish commands!" The pain in her eyes mirrored the ache in my own heart. Yet, I knew nothing could sway Raghunandan's commitment to his vow.

Raghunandan remained silent, his gaze fixed on his mother's tear-streaked face. Seeing his steadfastness, Mata Kaikeyi turned to my father, King Janaka. "Your daughter, too, is resolute in her choice to stay with Ram," she implored. "For Sita's sake, convince him to return to Ayodhya."

King Janaka sighed deeply. "Son Ram," he began, his voice thick with emotion, "as the eldest son, you now bear the burden of responsibility for our kingdom. Heed your mother's plea and return to Ayodhya. Your people need their rightful king."

Raghunandan listened patiently to my father's words. "Father," he replied, "I have complete faith in Bharat. He was raised with the same values as I, and I know he possesses the wisdom to guide our people. Bharat will be a noble king." He paused, then met my gaze with a silent understanding.

"The doors of Mithila will always be open for my beloved daughter," he continued, addressing me now. "And not just for her, but for you as well. If you choose to leave Ayodhya and your decision is firm, then come to Mithila. Find solace here with us."

"If Sita wishes," he added, his eyes searching mine, "she may certainly accompany you. However, my vow demands that I spend these fourteen years in the forest. Sita, what is your choice?"

His question caused a furrow in my brow. We had already discussed this, but he must have sensed my internal conflict. He clarified, "I ask this again, not just as your husband, but on behalf of your father, King Janaka."

"Father," I addressed him directly, "do you trust me? Do you have faith in your daughter's strength?"

A smile broke across his face. "You are my Bhumija, Sita," he said with pride. "I know the depths of your strength and resilience. Wherever you choose to go, you will only bring strength with you. I have no doubt."

"Then," I declared, my voice firm, "allow me to be with Raghunandan. My place is by his side. You know, Father, that I will face these fourteen years with courage and find growth, not hardship."

My father simply smiled and placed a hand on my shoulder, his gesture conveying his unwavering support and pride in our decision.

However, not everyone shared our resolve. Bharat stepped forward, his voice thick with emotion. "Bhaiya, please reconsider. Ayodhya needs you. It's incomplete without its rightful king. Come back with us."

Raghunandan approached his brother and placed a comforting hand on his shoulder. "Bharat," he said warmly, "I trust you completely. You will be a wise and just ruler.

Ayodhya's future is bright with you on the throne."

"No, Bhaiya," Bharat insisted, his voice cracking. "I cannot take your place. You are the true heir."

"My decision is final, Bharat," Raghunandan stated gently. "Betraying our father's wishes and yours is unthinkable. As a Raghuvanshi prince, you must understand the importance of duty, even when it is painful. This is one such decision."

"But Bhaiya..." Bharat began, his voice trailing off.

"However," Raghunandan interjected, "if your trust and respect for me are true, then return to Ayodhya. Become the beacon of hope for its people."

"Even the brightest lamp cannot replace the sun," Bharat lamented. He then continued after a pause, "But my trust in you is unwavering. Grant me this one wish – let me take your *charan paduka*. It will guide me, a calming presence reminding me of your strength. But promise me, Bhaiya, that you will return on the very first sunrise after the fourteenth year ends. If you don't, I will relinquish everything. The throne belongs to you, and these years I will simply be your steward. You will claim your rightful place the moment you step back into Ayodhya."

Raghunandan, his voice resolute, met Bharat's gaze. "I promise, Bharat. Not a single day longer than fourteen years."

Bharat's hands trembled as he lifted Raghunandan's charan paduka. The weight of those sacred sandals wasn't just wood; it was the weight of a promise, a burden, and a longing for the brother he wouldn't see for fourteen years. The air crackled with unspoken emotions, a storm brewing just beneath the surface.

Around me, the mothers wept. Their tears were a silent symphony of grief, a farewell song for sons and a daughter who would disappear into the wilderness for what felt like an eternity. Each sob echoed in the clearing, a painful reminder of the life we were leaving behind.

Finally, the goodbyes were exchanged, somber and heavy. The royal party from Ayodhya, their figures cloaked in sorrow yet tinged with a sliver of hope, turned away. We watched them recede into the distance, the vibrant colors of their clothing slowly dissolving into the greens and browns of the forest.

Raghunandan, Lakshmana, and I – the three of us stood alone, a solitary island in the vast ocean of trees. The weight of our decision, once a theoretical concept, settled upon my shoulders like a physical burden. This was it. The beginning of our exile, a challenging yet extraordinary journey that stretched before us like an uncharted path.

A strange calm washed over me as I looked into Raghunandan's eyes. They held a quiet determination, a reflection of the unyielding strength that resided within him. In that moment, I knew, with a certainty that transcended words, that whatever trials awaited us, we would face them together. After all that he witnessed today, he stood there strong, composed, this inspired me. This exile, a punishment orchestrated by fate, might have stripped us of our kingdom, but it couldn't sever the bonds of love and loyalty that bound us as a family. The sun dipped below the horizon, painting the sky in hues of orange and purple. It was the end of an era, the closing of a chapter. But as I took Raghunandan's hand in mine, a new chapter, filled with unknown adventures, was about to begin.

The days in the jungle unfolded with a rhythm as steady as the pulse of the earth itself. Dawn arrived with the chorus of birdsong, a symphony that coaxed us from our simple leaf shelters. Lakshmana, ever vigilant, would be the first to rise, his practiced eyes scanning the surroundings for any sign of danger. But then days later when we saw him awake even at night, he told us that he received boon from Nidra devi that he would stay awake all these years for us, he wouldn't sleep for our protection, of course this mad us respect Lakshman's devotion but even more than that I respected my sister. It was her who took the sleep for Lakshman; she went for a long sleep of fourteen years; she gave up her exuberant life for us, it was her sacrifice as well that made this boon fruitful for Lakshman.

We would wake up, do the chores, meditate. Raghunandan, his gentle spirit would find solace in the quiet communion with nature. I, for one, reveled in the freedom to greet the rising sun with open arms, the cool morning air washing away any lingering anxieties.

Our days were like a paradigm woven from necessity and exploration. We learned to forage for edible plants and berries, their unfamiliar shapes and textures a constant learning experience. Lakshmana, with his keen sense of observation, became an expert at identifying safe options, while Raghunandan's quiet wisdom often led us to hidden groves overflowing with nature's bounty. Fetching water from the gushing river was a daily ritual, its coolness a welcome respite from the relentless sun. The gurgle of the water over smooth stones became a comforting background score to our lives.

The jungle, once a daunting wilderness, slowly began to unveil its secrets. We learned to read the language of the trees, their rustling leaves whispering warnings of approaching storms. The vibrant colors of the birds, the silent grace of the deer – each element of nature became a teacher, imparting valuable lessons in survival and resilience. My body, once accustomed to the comforts of the palace, grew stronger with each passing day. The sun, once a harsh enemy, became a source of warmth and life. My senses, sharpened by constant vigilance, picked up on the subtlest sounds – the snap of a twig, the rustle of leaves underfoot.

Our journey wasn't without its challenges. The nights were often filled with the haunting calls of unknown creatures, their howls echoing through the dense foliage, sending shivers down my spine. There were days when hunger gnawed at our bellies, forcing us to venture deeper into the unknown in search of sustenance. But through it all, the presence of Raghunandan and Lakshmana was a constant source of strength. A simple touch, a shared smile – these unspoken gestures spoke volumes of the love and support that bound us together.

One particularly ferocious storm left our flimsy leaf shelter in tatters. Disheartened but not defeated, we huddled together under a large banyan tree, seeking solace in each other's warmth. It was then that Raghunandan, his eyes gleaming with a newfound determination, proposed building a sturdier dwelling. With renewed purpose, we gathered fallen branches and woven leaves, working together to create a new haven. The process, though arduous, brought us closer. The shared struggle, the triumphant completion – it fostered a sense of accomplishment and a deeper appreciation for each other's skills and strengths.

Our exile, became an unexpected journey of self-discovery. We visited remote ashrams, seeking guidance from wise sages who imparted ancient knowledge on spirituality and self-reliance. Their teachings resonated deep within me, filling the void left by the opulent life we once knew. This wasn't just a physical transformation; it was a profound shift in my mental, emotional, and spiritual being. I felt a newfound connection to the universe, a sense of belonging that transcended the walls of any palace.

The days in the jungle, though challenging, were far from bleak. There were moments of pure joy – watching fireflies dance in the twilight, listening to the melodic calls of unseen birds, witnessing the breathtaking beauty of a blooming night jasmine. We shared laughter under the starlit sky, recounted cherished memories from our past life, and dreamt of a future filled with hope and reunion. The wilderness, once a place of fear, had become a sanctuary, a crucible that forged an unbreakable bond between us. It was a testament to the enduring power of love, family, and the indomitable human spirit.

The morning sun dappled the forest floor in a mosaic of light and shadow as we set out on our journey towards the ashram of Sage Atri. Anticipation hummed in the air, a welcome change from the usual routine of foraging and chores. Lakshmana led the way, his brow furrowed in concentration as he scanned the unfamiliar path. Raghunandan walked beside me, his hand resting gently on mine, a silent reassurance .

After hours of navigating through dense foliage and crossing babbling brooks, we emerged into a clearing bathed in a serene tranquility. A simple yet sturdy hut stood nestled under the shade of a sprawling banyan tree, smoke curling gently from its thatched roof. This, we knew, had to be the ashram of Sage Atri.

As we approached, a figure emerged from the hut, his weathered face etched with wisdom and kindness. "Welcome, travelers," he boomed in a voice that resonated with the calmness of the forest. "May your journey be filled with blessings."

Raghunandan bowed respectfully. "We seek the wisdom of Sage Atri," he replied. "We are Rama, Sita, and Lakshmana, and we come seeking guidance on our path."

The sage's smile widened. "Ah, Rama! Your arrival has been awaited. Come, come, enter my humble abode and rest your weary limbs."

We entered the cool interior of the hut, the air heavy with the scent of incense and woodsmoke. A gentle voice, soft as the rustling leaves, greeted us from a corner. Seated on a woven mat was an elderly woman, her eyes sparkling with an inner light.

"This is my wife, Anasuya," the sage introduced her, his voice filled with an obvious reverence. "She too bears the title of sage, for her wisdom and spiritual strength are unparalleled."

As I bowed in greeting, Mata Anasuya's kind eyes held mine for a moment. She looked strong, in full composure of herself. She had calm and yet the strength, she looked humble and yet confident. "Welcome, Sita," she said, her voice a soothing melody. "I have heard much about your strength and devotion."

A blush crept up my cheeks. "It is nothing compared to your wisdom, Mata," I stammered.

Mata Anasuya chuckled, a gentle sound that filled the room. "Wisdom comes in many forms, child. A wife's unwavering devotion to her husband is a form of tapasya as powerful as any."

The following days were filled with profound learning. Mata Anasuya, with a gentle yet firm hand, guided me through the intricacies of "*Stridharma*," the sacred duties of a woman. She spoke of loyalty, respect, and unwavering support for one's husband, weaving tales of legendary women who upheld these values.

One evening, as we sat under the starlit sky, Mata Anasuya turned to me, her eyes reflecting the twinkling stars. "Tell me, Sita," she said, "about your love story. How did you and Rama find each other?"

A smile bloomed on my face. "It was during a Svayamvara ," I began, eager to share our story. "There were many suitors, all strong and noble, but none could lift the mighty bow of Shiva. Then came Rama..."

For hours, I regaled them with tales of our courtship, the challenges overcome, and the unwavering love that bound us together. Mata Anasuya listened intently, a knowing smile playing on her lips.

It was then finally time to bid goodbye. The goodbyes were filled with a mixture of sadness and gratitude. Mata Anasuya placed a hand on my head, her touch warm and comforting. She offered me a clothing that would always remain clean and pure.

"Remember, Sita," she said, her voice filled with conviction, "your strength lies in your devotion to Rama. Together, you will face any challenge that comes your way."

She then presented me with a beautiful garland woven with fragrant flowers and a small, shimmering gemstone. "May these bring you good fortune on your journey," she blessed.

With a final bow of respect, we turned away from the ashram, the teachings of Sage Atri and Mata Anasuya echoing in our hearts. The path ahead remained uncertain, but we carried with us a newfound strength, a deeper understanding of our roles, and the unwavering love that bound us together. The wilderness may have tested our bodies at times, but the wisdom gleaned from the ashram had nurtured our souls, preparing us for whatever trials awaited us on our journey.

# XXVII

Today after a long tiring day, Raghunandan and I sat by the river. We were silent for a long time, and I love that about us. We can be silent for long hours and yet be so comfortable.

*We don't need words to conceal or express, the silence itself is raw and intimate.*

*It speaks for itself.*

After sitting in a comfortable silence for a long time, the rhythmic crunch of leaves underfoot the only sound in the otherwise peaceful forest when I moved my legs even a bit. Yet, a question lingered in my mind, a nagging thought that refused to be quelled. Raghunandan, had transformed into a protector of the rishis in our forest home. He had vanquished demons and ogres, freeing the sages from their clutches. While I admired his courage and unwavering commitment to protecting the innocent, a disquieting feeling settled in my gut.

Finally, I gathered my courage and spoke. "Raghunandan," I began, my voice barely above a whisper, "may I ask you something?"

He stopped immediately, his gaze warm and inviting. "Absolutely, Janaki," he replied. "Why hesitate? Ask anything that troubles your mind."

"I respect your vow to protect the rishis from these demons and ogres," I continued, then faltered, searching for the right words. "However..."

Sensing my unease, Raghunandan prompted me gently, "However, what troubles you, Sita? Speak freely."

Taking a deep breath, I voiced my concern. "The association with weapons is said to be akin to playing with fire," I ventured. "Out of love and respect, I suggest that while you take up the bow to defend the rishis, you should never resort to killing without absolute necessity. What connection is there, truly, between a weapon and our life in the forest? The duty of a kshatriya, a warrior, seems contradictory to the path of an ascetic."

Raghunandan listened patiently, his expression unreadable. A moment of quiet stretched between us, and just as I began to worry that I had overstepped my bounds, he smiled gently.

"You bring up a valid point, Janaki," he said finally. "And you have every right to speak your mind. It's your love and concern that compels you to remind me, and I wouldn't have it any other way. No one corrects someone they don't care for deeply."

Relief washed over me. "Exactly," I almost squeaked, emboldened by his understanding. "It's because I care so much that I spoke up."

His smile broadened into a soft chuckle. "But Sita," he began, his voice taking on a thoughtful tone, "dharma, one's righteous duty, transcends location. It travels with us wherever we go. My duty as a kshatriya remains with me, whether I am in the forests or in Ayodhya."

His words struck a chord, and I lowered my eyes, a flicker of doubt clouding my heart. But then, Raghunandan reached out, gently tilting my chin up so our eyes met.

"But my Janaki," he said, his voice filled with an unwavering conviction, "you have my word. Whenever my duty as a kshatriya demands me to take up arms, I will ensure my actions are guided by righteousness, not anger or hatred. The path of asceticism will temper my actions, even in the face of violence."

His words resonated within me, dispelling the doubts that had clouded my judgment. A sense of calm washed over me. Here, in the heart of the forest, I had discovered a new facet of love – the ability to find solace and understanding simply by sharing my concerns. It was a love that provided not just companionship but also a safe space to express vulnerability, knowing that my worries would be met with empathy and a resolute promise to do the right thing.

In that moment, I realized that true love wasn't just about grand gestures or passionate declarations. It was about finding comfort in the quiet moments, in the unspoken understanding that transcended words. It was about having someone who would be your champion, your protector, even against the imaginary monsters that lurked in the corners of your mind.

*Love is when your lover will scare away the monsters for you even when those are imaginary.*

Those monsters can be your fears, your thoughts, your nightmares.

# XXVIII

The days melted into months, and months into years. Time seemed to flow differently when surrounded by Rama and Lakshmana. It wasn't a blur, but a tapestry woven with shared experiences, whispered secrets under the starlit sky, and the comforting rhythm of each other's breaths. In those years, we'd grown as individuals, finding harmony with the wildlife around us. We understood so much more now – a silent language that transcended words. It was a language of rustling leaves, the calls of birds, the subtle movements of animals that spoke of impending rain or danger lurking nearby.

One day, like any other, Lakshmana patrolled our forest home, his senses ever alert. Rama sat in quiet meditation, his brow furrowed in concentration. Suddenly, a flurry of activity broke the stillness. A cacophony of chirps and squawks erupted from the trees, a chaotic symphony of birds scattering in all directions.

"Lakshmana," I called out, a sliver of unease creeping into my voice. "What's happening? Why are the birds in such a frenzy?"

Lakshmana, ever the watchful protector, scanned the sky. "The weather seems fine, Bhabhi," he muttered, his brow furrowed in thought. "There must be another reason."

"A foreign bird then, this happens when a foreign bird comes into their habitat" I replied.

As if on cue, a massive shadow engulfed us. A giant vulture swooped down, its wings beating a frantic rhythm. It landed awkwardly, a predator turned prey, trapped in its own fear. Before Lakshmana could react, he instinctively reached for his bow. But something stopped him. Instead, with a swift movement, he threw a net, capturing the enormous bird without harm.

The vulture remained silent, its fear seemingly paralyzing it.

"Who are you?" Lakshmana demanded, his voice firm. "What brings you here?"

But before he could get another word out, a gentle voice filled the air.

"Lakshmana," Rama said, emerging from his meditation, "lower the net."

Lakshmana obeyed, his eyes wide with surprise. As the net fell away, the vulture didn't flee. Instead, it tilted its head and studied Rama with an intensity that bordered on reverence. It then transformed into a human figure.

"It feels like I've known you forever, who are you" the vulture boomed, its voice surprisingly deep for its feathered form.

"I am Ram, son of King Dashrath" Raghunandan replied.

"I am Jatayu," he continued, a smile spreading across his beak. "Your father's friend. We've known each other for ages, fought many battles together. Where is Dasharatha?"

A heavy silence descended upon the clearing. Rama and Lakshmana exchanged a heavy glance, their eyes filled with unspoken grief. I too, understood the message conveyed by their glistening eyes. Jatayu, sensing the shift in atmosphere, lowered his gaze. A tremor of fear replaced the earlier bravado.

Before anyone could speak, Rama gestured to Lakshmana. "Bring him some food," he said, his voice thick with emotion.

"Simple fruits won't do," I interjected, ever the practical one. "Vultures prefer meat. Lakshmana, find him some fruit and vegetables with a bit more...substance."

Lakshmana nodded and disappeared into the forest, leaving the three of us. Moments later Lakshmana returned with the specially chosen fruits and vegetables. Jatayu, no longer a menacing shadow but a creature with a story etched in his eyes, devoured the food with a ravenous hunger that spoke of a long journey. Hunger sated, a sense of camaraderie settled in, and we spent the next few hours lost in conversation.

Rama, ever patient, let Jatayu take the lead. The stories he shared about our father, Dasharatha, were a balm to my soul. He spoke of his courage in battle, his unwavering loyalty, and most importantly, his booming laughter that could fill a room (or perhaps, an entire forest) with joy. It was a glimpse into a life before exile, a life filled with warmth and security.

Jatayu then turned his gaze to me, a glint of amusement dancing in his yellow eyes. "And you, Sita," he rumbled, his voice surprisingly gentle for such a large creature. "I hear tales of your beauty, empathy and wisdom that echo all the way to Dandaka. They say your eyes hold the wisdom of the forest and your smile rivals the morning sun."

"Thank you" I blushed.

He chuckled, a sound that vibrated through the clearing. " No, it's the truth. But I hear tales of your courage too, your unwavering devotion to Rama. You are a true princess, worthy of any kingdom."

His words filled me with a newfound strength. In the harsh realities of exile, it was easy to forget the life we once knew, the respect I commanded. Jatayu's words were a reminder of who I was, not just Rama's wife, but Sita, daughter of Janaka, a princess who wouldn't crumble in the face of hardship.

The conversation flowed on, a tapestry woven with stories and laughter. Jatayu shared tales of his own adventures, of mischievous escapades in his youth and fierce battles fought alongside our father. He spoke of his brother, Sampati, and the tragic wager that had left his brother wingless and him forever filled with remorse.

As the sun began its descent, casting long shadows across the forest floor, Jatayu rose with a sigh. "It's time for me to go," he announced, his voice tinged with regret. "But I promise, I will return. You have become like family to me, and I will always be a loyal friend to Rama."

"We will look forward to seeing you again, my friend," Raghunandan said, placing a hand on Jatayu's massive head. "And thank you, for the stories, for the memories."

Jatayu dipped his head in a gesture of respect, then spread his wings, casting a momentary shadow over us before soaring into the golden twilight sky. As I watched him disappear into the distance, a newfound respect bloomed in my heart for this majestic creature. The forest, once a place of exile, now held the echoes of laughter and stories, a testament to the unexpected friendships that blossomed even in the most challenging of times.

# XXIX

Years melted into one another as we journeyed through countless forests. Each one held a unique memory, a pattern beautifully woven with laughter, love, and the quiet companionship that only comes with shared experiences. Time, when surrounded by the right partner, the right family, seemed to lose its grip. It flowed like a gentle river, carrying us forward without a sense of urgency. Though a part of us yearned to return to Ayodhya and reunite with our loved ones, there was no regret for the life we built. These years of exile, far from being a suffering, had been a period of immense growth and the creation of beautiful, irreplaceable memories.

Now, we found ourselves in the enchanting Panchvati Forest. Our dwelling, though simple, felt like a haven, a place of warmth and comfort. Today, after a day filled with chores and preparations, Raghunandan and I decided to take a walk to the nearby river. As we walked hand-in-hand, a comfortable silence enveloped us. The only sounds were the rustling of leaves, the chirping of crickets, and the gentle gurgle of the flowing water. Moonlight painted the forest floor in a silvery glow, casting an ethereal light on Raghunandan's face.

After a while, I sensed a shift in the air. The usual comfortable silence we shared seemed to hold a tinge of unease. It was a subtle change, but my intuition, honed by years of living in the wilderness, picked up on it. I stopped walking and turned to Raghunandan, my gaze meeting his.

"What is it?" I asked gently, my voice barely a whisper.

Raghunandan blinked, seemingly startled from his thoughts. "What?" he replied, a hint of confusion in his voice.

"I know something is on your mind," I persisted, a feeling of concern blooming in my chest. "There's something you want to say, but you're hesitant."

He remained silent for a moment, then a wry smile touched his lips. "It's surprising how well you know me, Sita," he said, his voice filled with a quiet admiration. "Even without words, you can always sense when something troubles me."

We continued walking until we reached the riverbank. The gentle sound of water lapping against the shore seemed to create a space of tranquility. We sat down on a smooth, moss-covered rock, the cool night air whispering through the trees.

"So," I prompted gently, "tell me what's bothering you."

Raghunandan sighed, his brow furrowing slightly. "It's nothing truly important," he began, then paused. "I don't want to burden you with it, don't want to cause you even the slightest worry. But then again, I can't keep anything from you, not even the most trivial of thoughts."

My heart ached at his words. The thought of him carrying a burden alone, no matter how small, was unbearable. I reached out and placed a hand on his shoulder, my touch a silent reassurance.

"Do you trust me, Raghunandan?" I asked, my voice filled with conviction.

He met my gaze, his eyes filled with an unwavering love. "Sita," he said, his voice husky with emotion. "If you told me the moon is the sun and the sun is the moon, I would believe you."

My lips curved into a smile. "Then please," I pleaded, "tell me what's on your mind. Whatever it is."

"Sita," he began, his voice low and hesitant. "Today, by the river, I encountered a woman."

My heart skipped a beat. A woman? Here, in the wilderness? I forced myself to remain calm, waiting for him to continue. I wouldn't say I was jealous; I wouldn't say I didn't trust him, but the way he began I couldn't help but felt something was off, maybe it was intuition? Because for now I had no reason to worry, but I still did.

"She... approached me," Raghunandan continued, his brow furrowed in discomfort. "Made certain advances."

A cold wave washed over me, a storm brewing within my chest. But before I could react, Raghunandan's next words calmed the rising tempest.

"Of course," he said, his voice firm with unwavering conviction, "I told her everything. I told her I am a married man, devoted completely to my wife, Sita. My heart has no room for anyone else. My heart only belong to her and can now belong to no one else."

His words washed away the last remnants of my unease. A blush crept up my cheeks, not from jealousy, but from the sheer beauty of his devotion. I knew Raghunandan. I knew his character, his loyalty.

"So," I asked, my voice regaining its strength, "what did she say?"

"She left," Rama replied simply. He seemed troubled. But he didn't need to explain. He knew, as I knew, that he hadn't done anything wrong.

Yet, a hint of concern lingered in the air. Perhaps he sensed the change in my demeanour, the flicker of disquietude that replaced my initial shock. Wanting to lighten the mood, I decided to tease him a little.

"So," I said with a playful smile, "was she beautiful, this woman?"

Raghunandan looked at me, a surprised smile tugging at the corners of his lips. He shook his head slightly, a hint of amusement dancing in his eyes.

"Sita," he said, his voice filled with a love that never failed to make my heart flutter, "with your beauty constantly gracing my vision, how could I possibly perceive another woman's beauty? They are mere human figures to me. True admiration, true appreciation for aesthetics, exists only when I look at you. When my eyes are constantly blanketed by your beauty, how can my eyes see anyone else with that admiration. admiration for appearance comes only when I see you."

His words, even after all these years, had the power to make my cheeks burn crimson. This, to me, was the essence of love. Love that deepened with time, a faith that grew stronger with each passing day. The comfort, the familiarity, all remained, yet his expressions of love never lost their freshness, their ability to ignite a spark within me.

With that, we gently pushed the memory of the woman aside, replacing it with sweeter conversations. As we strolled back to our humble dwelling, hand in hand, the moonlight seemed to paint our path with a silver glow, a reminder of the unwavering love that bound us together, a love that would face any storm, any challenge, and emerge even stronger.

*Like a banyan, our love grows stronger with time, its roots ever-deepening, its blossoms forever new.*

# XXX

Days blurred into weeks after Raghunandan mentioned the woman by the river. A nagging suspicion clawed at the edges of my mind, a sour note in the otherwise harmonious melody of our exile. Though I tried to dismiss it, the memory flickered like a dying ember, refusing to be fully extinguished.

Today, as I prepared lunch, my back to the entrance of our simple dwelling, a sound pierced the usual forest symphony – the unmistakable jingle of anklets. I whipped around, heart hammering a frantic rhythm against my ribs. There she stood; a vision of ethereal beauty draped in a deep maroon saree that shimmered with the weight of gold jewellery.

Her smile, perfectly sculpted, lacked the warmth of genuine joy. Her eyes, long and captivating, held no depth, no reflection of the soul within. It was a beauty that felt...incomplete, almost artificial.

Before I could speak, Raghunandan appeared at my side, his brow furrowed in concern. I took a steadying breath, a small smile playing on my lips. This woman, however beautiful, admired Raghunandan. And Raghunandan, my Raghunandan, belonged only to me. That knowledge, in the face of such obvious admiration, filled me with a peculiar sense of pride.

Then, before the woman could utter a word, Raghunandan spoke. "This," he said, his voice steady, "is the woman I mentioned, Sita. And Devi, this is my beloved wife, Sita."

The woman's gaze flicked from Raghunandan to me, her expression morphing from admiration to thinly veiled hostility. Her eyes scanned me with a critical intensity, a silent judgment. Then, a harsh laugh escaped her lips.

"Well," she drawled, her voice dripping with condescension, "I thought I'd have some competition for your heart. But it seems that won't be necessary. She's just so...simple."

Raghunandan smiled gently. "You are absolutely right, Devi," he said, his voice steady and unwavering. "And that is precisely why there can never be another Sita. No one possesses the same purity, the same untarnished simplicity as my wife."

She scoffed, her perfectly sculpted face twisting in a sneer. "You say that only because you haven't experienced sparkle, Devi. Gold is what brings joy, what makes life truly rich."

I remained silent, choosing to demonstrate my trust in Raghunandan not through words but through quiet confidence. Our bond was built on something far stronger than the need to defend it with empty pronouncements.

Raghunandan's gaze remained fixed on me, a silent message passing between us. Then, he turned back to the woman, his voice firm but respectful. "I am, and forever will be, faithful to my wife. My life is complete with her by my side, and I desire nothing more, Devi. The steadiness I need in my life is what Sita gives me. Please, leave us in peace."

She opened her mouth to retort, but just then Lakshmana entered, carrying a bundle of firewood. As he placed it down and turned towards us, the woman's eyes lit up with predatory interest. She fixed Lakshmana with the same appraising gaze she'd used on Raghunandan moments ago.

"And who is this handsome man?" she cooed, her voice dripping with honeyed sweetness. "He possesses the same aura of strength as you."

"This is my younger brother, Lakshmana," Raghunandan said with a smile.

A flicker of worry crossed my mind. Lakshmana, unlike Raghunandan, was not known for his patience. I hoped the woman wouldn't test his temper with her advances.

As if sensing my concern, the woman sashayed towards Lakshmana, her movements calculated and seductive. "Don't you ever wish for a life of luxury?" she said. "A beautiful woman like myself by your side could bring you great prosperity."

Lakshmana didn't even blink. "My only purpose," he replied flatly, his voice devoid of any emotion, "is to serve my brother. That is where my true prosperity lies."

"But surely you can at least look at me before making such a decision?" she pressed, batting her eyelashes at him. "Don't you want a beautiful wife like me?"

I couldn't help but steal a glance at Raghunandan, a secret smile playing on my lips. He returned it with a knowing look, his amusement mirroring my own.

Lakshmana's response was swift and to the point. "Devi," he said, his voice still devoid of inflection, "I am a married man. I have a wife who is beautiful, loyal, and devoted. No other woman could ever compare."

The woman's face contorted with rage. Her sweet facade shattered, revealing a core of venomous anger. "You brothers are both fools!" she shrieked, her voice distorted with fury. "I offer you the gift of my presence, and you turn away like blind beggars. And all for what? This...this woman here, who adorns herself with nothing but rags! But she has you, and that's all that matters! I cannot bear it! I will end her!"

With a snarl, she lunged towards me, her eyes blazing red with hatred. The playful atmosphere of moments ago vanished, replaced by a chilling sense of danger. In a heartbeat, Lakshmana was between us, his sword flashing in the sunlight. He didn't strike to wound, but to disarm. The blade swished through the air, a sickening snip echoing through the clearing. The woman shrieked in pain, clutching at her bleeding nose.

The transformation was instantaneous. The once haughty woman was now a creature consumed by rage and humiliation. Her screams pierced the tranquil air, creating a tense and unsettling atmosphere. Despite the danger she posed, a pang of sympathy flickered within me. The woman's uncontrolled fury was a sight both frightening and pitiable. Though she was not right, but what Lakshman did, raising a weapon on a woman was unforgivable.

I turned towards Lakshman and said in an angry voice, "Lakshman, how could you use your weapon on a woman?"

He expressions were of worry and he replied, "trust me Bhabhi, I didn't do it on purpose, I was just trying to put my sword in between you and her, so she stops right where she was."

"Whatever might be your explanation, apologize right away." I demanded.

But before Lakshman could say anything, she roared, "oh stop it, stop your acts. You don't know me, I am Shurpanakha, you don't know what you did, you don't know my brother. I am sister of King Ravana of Lanka; oh, he won't spare anyone of us."

"Bhabhi you still thin what I did was wrong? Look at this woman, she had no guilt of what she did. She should be the one apologizing to you and instead look what she says." Lakshman said to me and then directed his words at Shurpanakha, "and please don't live in your delusional world. I don't fear your brother at all."

"Lakshman" I interjected in an angry tone again.

But this time Shurpanakha said nothing, screaming and crying she ran away, putting he hand on her bleeding nose. I ran behind her to follow her.

"Stop please stop, I know what happened was wrong, please stop." I called trying to stop her.

To my surprise, she did stop and turn around. She then said, "you are so proud, aren't you? You take pride in your husband, I assure you, I will snatch away this pride from you. Mark my words, I am sister of King Ravan, I can make anything possible."

After saying this she walked away, and something was int hose words, that didn't let my feet move. I know what she said was in anger, still those words made me numb, 'she will snatch away my pride?' this kept hitting I my head alike a hammer. I stood there processing what she said, and then I slowly walked back to our home.

There Raghunandan and Lakshman were waiting for with concerned faces, I couldn't tell them what she said, this would only ruin things further, and so for that even I tried to forget everything that she said.

I said nothing to anyone for a few moments and then finally I began, "Lakshman, words from an aching heart can ruin life but the mere thoughts from an aching woman can ruin lives, families, and dynasties." Then after a pause I said again,

"What you did today though unintentionally was wrong."

Lakshman lowered his head and said, "I understand Bhabhi"

Apparently all this while maybe Raghunandan too had counselled him. The weight of the day settled heavily upon us as we recounted the events to Lakshmana. While relieved by his swift action in protecting me, Raghunandan and I were both troubled by his methods. Violence, especially against a woman, was never the answer. The woman's venomous rage had tainted the serenity of our little haven, leaving a sour taste in the air. It was a stark reminder of the darkness that lurked even in this peaceful forest sanctuary.

The discussion that followed was heavy with a shared sense of disquiet. The day, once filled with the simple pleasures of preparing lunch and enjoying each other's company, had been irrevocably altered. It was a sobering realization of how a single encounter could disrupt the delicate balance of our lives, sending ripples of unease outward, tainting the once calm waters of our existence.

# XXXI

The unsettling encounter with Shurpanakha had left a long shadow, but life in our forest haven had slowly returned to its usual rhythm. Days flowed by, filled with the simple routines that brought a sense of comfort and normalcy. Today, after completing our chores, we sat beneath the dappled sunlight filtering through the leaves, engaged in quiet conversation.

Suddenly, a sharp cry pierced the peaceful silence. It was the anguished cry of an animal in distress. My heart lurched, and I rushed towards the entrance of our dwelling, eyes scanning the treeline for the source of the sound.

There, in a clearing not far off, I spotted a deer. It was limping, its gait uneven, a crimson stain blooming on its flank.

"What is it, Sita?" Raghunandan asked, his voice laced with concern, as he joined me at the entrance.

"A deer," I replied urgently. "It's wounded and needs help immediately."

I took a few steps towards the animal, but it flinched back, its large brown eyes filled with fear. Lakshmana, ever observant, spoke up.

"Don't worry, Bhabhi," he said, his voice calm and reassuring. "I'll retrieve the deer and then you can tend to its wound."

I nodded gratefully. The sight of an animal in pain always tugged at my heartstrings. Animals, unlike humans, couldn't express their suffering – their fear was a silent language of trembling bodies and panicked eyes. How could they bear such pain alone?

Lakshmana approached the deer slowly, his movements measured and gentle. But as he got closer, the deer bolted, disappearing deeper into the dense forest. Lakshmana gave chase, their figures swallowed by the thick foliage.

Time stretched on as we waited for their return. Meanwhile, Raghunandan and I prepared a healing paste from herbs and roots, readying ourselves to treat the injured animal. Every rustle of leaves, every snap of a twig made me crane my neck, hoping to see Lakshmana returning with the deer.

Finally, Lakshmana emerged from the forest, his brow furrowed in frustration. The deer, however, was nowhere to be seen.

"The deer keeps running from me, Bhabhi," he announced, a hint of dejection in his voice.

I sighed. "Perhaps the deer is scared," I mused. "It needs someone calm, someone who radiates a sense of security. I'll go. Maybe I can make it feel safe enough to come for treatment."

Raghunandan's hand reached out to clasp mine. "No, Janaki," he said gently. "You stay here. I'll go and bring the deer back. I'm sure it won't run from me. I'll make it feel safe, so it trusts me enough to come with me for treatment."

Looking into his kind eyes, I saw a quiet determination that mirrored my own concern for the injured creature.

Trusting his gentle nature and his ability to connect with all living things, I nodded in agreement.

A knot of worry tightened in my stomach as Raghunandan disappeared into the trees. He cast a final look back, his eyes holding a silent promise. "No matter what, Lakshmana," he said, his voice firm, "don't leave Sita alone."

"What's wrong, Raghunandan?" I asked, a flicker of unease crossing my mind. "I've been alone before when you both went hunting."

He hesitated; his brow furrowed in concern. "Just my worry, Sita," he finally said. "Lakshmana, no matter what happens, don't leave my Sita alone here."

Lakshmana, ever the loyal brother, met Raghunandan's gaze with a solemn nod. "I promise you, Bhaiya," he said, his voice deep and unwavering, "I will be here until you return."

Raghunandan's words echoed in my mind as he melted into the forest, leaving an unsettling silence in his wake. Time crawled by, each minute stretching into an eternity. My initial anxiety morphed into a gnawing worry. Just as the silence became unbearable, a bloodcurdling scream shattered the peace.

"Sita!"

The scream, raw and filled with terror, froze me in my tracks. It was Raghunandan's voice, laced with a primal fear I had never heard before. My heart hammered against my ribs, a frantic drumbeat against the sudden stillness of the forest.

Lakshmana, his face etched with shock, reacted instantly. His hand instinctively reached for the hilt of his sword, his eyes scanning the treeline with a fierce intensity that mirrored the terror in my own heart.

"Lakshmana," I gasped, my voice catching in my throat. "What was that? Raghunandan is in some trouble?"

The answer hung heavy in the air, unspoken but terrifyingly clear. Something was terribly wrong.

The urgency in Raghunandan's voice sent a fresh wave of panic crashing over me. Fear choked my voice, but I managed a desperate plea. "Lakshmana!" I cried, my eyes pleading with him. "It's Raghunandan! He needs you! Please!"

Lakshmana's face remained a mask of conflict. He was torn between his loyalty to his brother and his promise to me. The tension crackled in the air, thick enough to choke on.

"Bhabhi," he finally said, his voice low and strained, "I understand your fear. But Raghunandan specifically instructed me not to leave you alone. Disobeying him would be a betrayal of his trust."

Frustration bubbled up inside me, threatening to boil over. "But Lakshmana," I choked out, tears stinging my eyes, "he needs you more! He's in danger! Can't you understand that?"

Lakshmana's gaze held a depth of pain that mirrored my own. He clearly understood the gravity of the situation, the terror in Raghunandan's scream echoing in both our hearts. Yet, his loyalty to his brother, his commitment to a promise, held him rooted to the spot.

In that agonizing moment, a thought struck me. There might be another way.

I knew now if my words remain softened, Lakshman won't leave, and I can't ignore Raghunandan's help-cry.

*First step towards healing is going through pain.*

And now it was that moment. My heart hammered a frantic rhythm against my ribs, each beat echoing the terror in Raghunandan's scream. Frustration warred with fear within me. Lakshmana's loyalty, while admirable, felt like a cruel twist of fate in this moment. Realizing a desperate solution was needed, I took a deep breath, steeling myself for what I was about to say.

"Lakshmana," I said, my voice surprisingly steady, "look at me." He met my gaze, his eyes filled with a turmoil that mirrored my own.

"You swore an oath to protect Raghunandan," I continued, my voice firm despite the tremor in my heart. "Is that oath conditional? Does it depend on whether you also have to protect me?"

Lakshmana flinched; the pain of my words evident on his face. "Bhabhi," he stammered, "you know that's not true. My loyalty to both of you is absolute."

"Then prove it!" I cried, my voice rising with controlled urgency. "Raghunandan needs you now! His life might be hanging by a thread, and you stand here bound by a promise that might be irrelevant in the face of this danger! Are you going to let him down? Are you going to let him face whatever threat he's facing alone?"

My words were harsh, laced with a bitter sting. It was a tactic, a desperate attempt to break the stalemate. Though a part of me recoiled at the lie, I knew it was the only way to spur Lakshmana into immediate action.

The effect was instantaneous. Tears welled up in Lakshmana's eyes, his expression a heartbreaking mix of guilt and determination. "You... you don't understand," he choked out, his voice thick with emotion. "Disobeying Bhaiya would be... unforgivable. But to see you-"

He couldn't finish the sentence, the very thought too unbearable to voice.

"Then go!" I pleaded, my voice softening despite the urgency. "Go to Raghunandan! He needs you, and I can take care of myself for a little while longer. But if you don't go now, it might be too late, I will give up my life in your presence!"

Lakshmana's face contorted in anguish. He looked torn, his body taut with indecision. But a glint of resolve finally flickered in his eyes.

"You have driven me to choose between one horrible alternative," he said, his voice raspy with emotion, "that of disobeying my brother, and the other alternative which I consider still more horrible, to see you..." He trailed off, unable to voice the terrifying possibility.

The dam broke, and tears streamed down his face. Lakshmana's brow furrowed in a deep crease. "Alright, Bhabhi," he finally conceded, his voice heavy. "I will go. But..."

He trailed off, his eyes scanning the perimeter of our dwelling. Taking a deep breath, he stepped outside, his hand instinctively reaching for the quiver slung across his back. With a swift movement, he fitted an arrow to his bowstring and let loose. A flash of light erupted, momentarily illuminating the clearing before dissolving into a shimmering, translucent dome that enveloped our entire home. The barrier pulsed faintly, shimmering like a heat haze over the earth.

"Bhabhi," Lakshmana explained, his voice taut with concern, "I have created a protective shield around the dwelling. No one can enter, not until it dissipates." He gestured towards the dome. "You can easily pass through it if needed, but please promise me you won't leave the boundary. This is for your safety, and only on this condition will I leave."

The concern in his tear-filled eyes pierced through my anxiety. Guilt gnawed at me for the harsh words I had used, but the urgency of the situation had overridden my usual tact.

"I promise, Lakshmana," I said quickly, my voice sincere. "Just go! Find Raghunandan! Hurry!"

My mind, consumed by worry for Raghunandan, barely registered the details of Lakshmana's actions. All I cared about was getting him to his brother's side. With a final, lingering glance at me, Lakshmana turned and vanished into the green labyrinth, following the faint echo of Raghunandan's scream.

Alone within the shimmering dome, I waited, my heart a frantic drum against my ribs. The forest, once a place of peaceful refuge, now felt menacingly silent. Every rustle of leaves, every snap of a twig sent fresh tremors of fear coursing through me. The silence stretched on, punctuated only by the frantic beat of my own heart, and the weight of a terrifying unknown.

All I could do now was wait, wait for Raghunandan and Lakshman to return. I went inside and sat I meditation Panic jolted me out of meditation. The rustle of leaves and the groans of the forest were no longer a lullaby, but a menacing symphony of unease. Hours had crawled by, each one a tormenting eternity. My attempts to find solace in meditation had failed miserably. My mind, a frantic bird trapped in a cage, refused to be calmed.

Just as despair threatened to suffocate me, a booming voice shattered the oppressive silence. "Bhiksham dehi! Bhiksham dehi!"

Emerging from my meditation, I cautiously approached the source of the voice.

There, just outside the shimmering dome Lakshmana had created, stood a figure cloaked in saffron robes, the attire of a holy sage or rishi. He held a bowl outstretched, his posture radiating an air of entitlement. Relief washed over me momentarily. Surely, a rishi wouldn't harm me? I bowed respectfully.

"Pranam," I greeted him.

"I seek alms," he repeated, his voice devoid of the serene calmness usually associated with holy men. "Make the offering."

The discordant tone sent a tremor of unease through me. Ignoring the discomfort, I nodded and hurried inside to fetch some food. Returning to the edge of the dome, I held out the offering.

"Here," I said, offering the food. "Kindly bless me with your acceptance."

The rishi's eyes narrowed. "You want me to come there and get the offering? How disrespectful! Has no one ever taught you the proper way to treat a rishi? Are you not aware of the wrath we can unleash if displeased?"

His words, dripping with veiled threat, sent a fresh wave of fear coursing through me. Despite the rising terror, I forced a smile, maintaining a facade of composure. "Forgive me, Munivar," I replied politely. "But my husband and brother-in-law are not here, and I was instructed not to leave the house in their absence."

The rishi scoffed. "Very well then, stay where you are. I can listen to no more excuses! Your words reek of a blatant disregard for the intentions of a holy man. I require no alms from an egotistical woman like you!"

He turned to leave, his anger simmering just beneath the surface. A pang of guilt pricked my conscience. Perhaps he was right. Perhaps a rishi wouldn't resort to such deception.

Besides, in a time like this when Raghunandan is in some trouble, a rishi's blessings could only be beneficial.

Taking a deep breath, I momentarily disregarded Lakshmana's warning and stepped out of the protective barrier. As I approached the rishi to apologize and offer the food again, he laughed a loud and grabbed my wrist. My impulsive action was to release the hold and push him away before processing anything, but his grip tightened.

A cruel laugh erupted from the figure before me. the vessel of alms clattered to the ground as my eyes widened in horror. The holy man, with a blinding flash of light, transformed into a familiar figure, a figure I had seen before, the figure of,...king of Lanka..... Ravan!

Terror, primal and icy, froze my blood as Ravana's monstrous form materialized before me. The air crackled with a dark energy, the stench of sulfur burning my nostrils. His booming laughter echoed through the trees, a sickening sound that mocked my fear.

This couldn't be real. It had to be some terrible dream, a cruel trick of the mind. But the iron grip tightening around my wrist confirmed the horrifying truth.

"Ravan!" I shrieked, a primal yell that tore from my throat. Adrenaline surged through me, momentarily pushing back the paralyzing fear. With a desperate jerk, I flung myself back, wrenching my wrist free from his grasp.

He roared with laughter, the sound devoid of any humor, filled only with malice. "The beautiful Sita," he sneered. "Still as defiant, I see. But defiance won't save you now."

He took a lumbering step towards me, his laughter morphing into a slow, predatory chuckle. My heart hammered a frantic rhythm against my ribs, each beat a drumbeat of terror. Years of weapon training in Mithila flashed before my eyes, but the knowledge was a distant echo. Fear choked my mind, leaving me with only the primal instinct to survive.

Tears welled up in my eyes, blurring my vision. I couldn't let him touch me. The thought ignited a spark of defiance within the consuming fear. I wouldn't be a helpless victim.

Desperate, I lunged for anything that could be used as a weapon. A clay pot, a wooden cooking spoon, anything. I hurled them at him with a ferocity born of desperation. Each meager object clattered harmlessly against his thick hide, barely a nuisance.

Ravana's laughter intensified, a cruel symphony that mocked my struggle. He moved with a slow, deliberate grace, enjoying the sight of my terror. Each lumbering step felt like a cruel eternity.

"Pathetic," he spat, his voice dripping with disdain. "Such beauty wasted on such arrogance. You, Sita, are as much to blame for my sister's plight as Ram! You dared to reject me, to mock my advances! Now, you will pay the price!"

His words, laced with venomous hatred, ignited a flicker of rage within me. It was a spark against the overwhelming darkness, but it fuelled my resolve.

"You liar, deceiver!" I screamed; my voice hoarse with defiance. " Your wickedness knows no bounds, Ravana! You are a monster!"

He again walked towards me, his grotesque form blotting out the sun. I stumbled back, tripping over a gnarled root, falling to the forest floor. Pain lanced through my ankle, but I ignored it, scrambling to my feet.

Ravana once again grabbed my arm and pulled me, his laughter echoing around me like a death knell. But I wouldn't give in. I wouldn't surrender. With a final surge of desperate strength, I pushed myself forward, weaving through the trees, the undergrowth tearing at my clothes.

Behind me, Ravana's laughter boomed, a taunting reminder of his pursuit. Tears streamed down my face, a mixture of fear and a desperate hope. My lungs burned, my legs ached with every desperate step. But I couldn't stop. Not while that monstrous form loomed behind me, his laughter a sickening soundtrack to my terror. I pushed myself harder, branches whipping at my face, thorns tearing at my clothes. My heart hammered a frantic rhythm against my ribs, a relentless drumbeat of fear.

Suddenly, a powerful grip clamped onto my arm. A scream ripped from my throat as Ravana yanked me back, his ten faces contorted into a grotesque mask of glee. Panic surged through me, a primal scream clawing its way up my throat. I fought with everything I had, wrenching and twisting, trying to break free from his iron grip.

Then, a gust of wind, like a herald of doom, swept through the trees. A loud, ominous whirring accompanied it, sending a fresh wave of terror slamming into me. I looked up, my breath catching in my throat. It was the Pushpaka Vimana, descending upon us like a monstrous bird of prey.

Despair threatened to consume me. The Vimana meant I was truly trapped, any hope of escape vanishing with its arrival. With a final, desperate surge of strength, I ripped my arm free from Ravana's grasp and bolted. Tears streamed down my face, a mixture of fear and a raw, primal anger.

"You stubborn woman!" Ravana roared, his laughter morphing into a furious snarl. "Get back here!"

His anger fueled my frantic flight. But the pain in my ankle, a dull throbbing that had intensified with every step, betrayed me. Just as I thought I might reach the safety of the trees, I felt a vice-like grip tighten around my neck. A strangled cry escaped my lips, a combination of pain, fear, and impotent rage.

With a sickening ease, Ravan hoisted me into the air. My world tilted as he threw me over his shoulder and strode towards the Vimana. Before I could register the movement, I found myself deposited roughly on the cool surface of the aerial chariot. The Vimana lurched forward, rising above the trees like a monstrous dragonfly. Beneath me, the forest floor receded, shrinking into a tapestry of green and brown.

A sob wracked my body, but these were not tears of fear. They were tears of anger, a white-hot fury that burned at the injustice of it all. I, Sita, daughter of Janaka, wife of Rama, was being abducted by a monster. But I wouldn't go down without a fight.

Ravana's voice droned on, a wasp buzzing around a captive fly.

Why was ths happening to me, I thought, what had fate in plan for me. Wait, Fate! This word suddenly remined me of Mata Gargi's words, ***Faith is one thing that acts as your anchor when your life seems a storm.***

**She said to have faith in fate and only then can one take proper actions. Have faith Sita, have faith, let it be your anchor, I reminded myself.** Physical resistance had proven futile. I had to think, and quickly. There had to be a way to reach Raghunandan.

Suddenly, a spark ignited within me. Perhaps I couldn't reach Raghunandan directly, but I could make it easier for him to find me. If I couldn't send a message, I could leave a trail. A trail of glittering breadcrumbs, leading him straight to Lanka.

Without hesitation, I reached for the ornate necklace adorning my neck. It was a gift from Raghunandan, a symbol of our love. But its sentimental value paled in comparison to the purpose it could now serve. With trembling fingers, I unclasped the delicate chain, the weight of the gold feeling heavy in my palm.

A fierce determination hardened my resolve. Ignoring the sting of tears welling up in my eyes, I began to dismantle my jewellery, each piece a silent plea for Raghunandan's attention. Earrings, bangles, anklets – everything that adorned me was methodically removed.

Ravan kept laughing seeing me do this, but ignored him and is mocking laughs.

Then, with a deep breath and a defiant glint in my eyes, I flung the first piece of jewellery out of the open window of the Vimana. It tumbled through the air, a beacon against the vast blue canvas of the sky. Each subsequent piece followed, glittering sparks disappearing into the distance, a silent message carried on the wind.

As the last gleaming ornament left my grasp, a wave of exhaustion washed over me. My body ached, my heart heavy, but a flicker of hope, fragile yet persistent, bloomed within me. I had created a path, a celestial map leading straight to Ravana's clutches. Perhaps, just perhaps, Rama would see the trail, decipher the message.

The Pushpak Vimana continued its relentless journey towards Lanka, but with each passing moment, the once desolate landscape below seemed to transform. It was no longer a canvas of despair, but a potential canvas for rescue. With every beat of my heart, a silent prayer echoed in my mind: "See my trail, Rama. Follow it, and come for me."

His words, laced with a sickeningly false sweetness, were meant to taunt, to prod at the raw wound of my anger. "Taking you to Lanka," he said, his voice dripping with mock sympathy, "only if you had been a little more polite. Maybe

I wouldn't have been so... harsh."

A bitter laugh escaped my lips, a dry, humourless sound. Polite? Did he truly believe I owed him anything but my defiance? He, a monster who lusted after another, who stole me away from my husband, from my life.

Silence became my weapon. I curled deeper into the corner of the Vimana, a solitary island in a sea of his arrogance. Tears welled up again, hot and angry, blurring the world around me. The rhythmic hum of the Vimana, the wind whipping past the open windows, all faded into a dull roar.

My mind, however, was a cacophony. Images of Raghunandan, his kind eyes and gentle smile, flashed before me. How he would react to this news? Would despair consume him, as it was threatening to consume me? Panic clawed at my throat. I had to get a message to him, somehow.

Despair threatened to engulf me, but then, a flicker of defiance sparked within me. I wouldn't give in to despair. I would survive this, not for Ravan's twisted game, but for Raghunandan.

Steeling my resolve, I wiped away the tears, the anger in my eyes hardening into a steely resolve. I wouldn't let Ravan break me. He may have taken me from my home, but he wouldn't take my spirit. I would find a way to fight back, a way to send a message, a way to return to Raghunandan. In the heart of this gilded cage, a plan, fuelled by love and anger, began to take shape.

A sudden, piercing cry shattered the tense silence within the Vimana. It was a sound I knew intimately, a sound that sent a jolt of hope, fragile yet persistent, through my numbed core. Jatayu!

There, perched precariously on the edge of the Vimana, his magnificent form backlit by the afternoon sun, was the loyal vulture king. His keen eyes met mine, a silent promise of protection passing between us. In that single glance, years of shared memories, of him circling protectively above our forest dwelling, flashed before my eyes.

Jatayu's arrival was a beacon of defiance in the face of Ravan's arrogance. With a mighty screech, he launched himself at the demon king, his razor-sharp talons extended, a whirlwind of feathers and fury. Ravan, caught off guard by the sudden attack, roared in surprise.

The ensuing fight was a whirlwind of feathers and fury. Jatayu, fought with the ferocity of a cornered animal. Despite his age, his every dive and peck displayed the strength and agility honed over years of protecting the skies.

I, too, surged with a renewed sense of purpose. Ignoring the throbbing pain in my ankle, I lunged forward, desperate to join the fray. But Jatayu, sensing my intent, screeched a warning.

"Stay back, Maharani Sita! This fight is mine! I won't let any harm come to you!"

His words, laced with fierce protectiveness, brought tears to my eyes. Even at his advanced age, his loyalty to Raghunandan, his devotion to protecting me, remained steady. It was this devotion that made the scene that unfolded next all the more horrifying.

With a cruel swipe of his sword, Ravan lashed out. Sword tore through the air, a sickening sound accompanying the impact as they connected with Jatayu's wing. A bloodcurdling scream pierced the air, a cry that echoed my own growing terror.

The attack didn't stop there. In a display of unmitigated cruelty, Ravana repeated the blow, severing Jatayu's other wing with a sickening crunch. Jatayu, his magnificent form now broken and bloodied, was flung from the Vimana like a discarded toy.

As he plummeted towards the earth below, a final, heartbreaking cry escaped his beak. It wasn't a cry of pain, but a sob of apology, a plea for forgiveness for failing to protect me.

The world around me blurred as a fresh wave of tears, this time laced with a white-hot rage, flooded my eyes. Jatayu's sacrifice, his loyalty, fueled a fire of defiance within me that burned brighter than ever before.

"You monster!" I roared, my voice hoarse with fury. "You have no fear of God! Kidnapping me was a sin, one that will never be forgiven! But harming an innocent creature like Jatayu... even hell wouldn't accept you!"

Ravan, however, remained unfazed. His booming laughter echoed through the Vimana, a cruel symphony that mocked my pain. His indifference, his lack of remorse, only stoked the flames of rage burning within me. In that moment, I knew. I wouldn't break. I would fight back, not just for myself, but for Raghunandan, for Jatayu, for the very idea of justice. The journey to Lanka had taken a dark turn, but my spirit, fueled by love and righteous anger, remained unbroken.

Ravana's laughter grated on my nerves, a sickening counterpoint to the storm raging within me. "Call your Rama now," he taunted, his voice dripping with cruel amusement. "But where is he, I wonder? Lost in some far-flung corner of the world, perhaps? I bet you don't even know."

His words were laced with a venomous satisfaction, designed to twist the knife of worry already lodged in my heart. A part of me did ache with a deep, gnawing fear for Rama. But alongside the fear, a fierce pride bloomed.

"You needn't worry about Rama," I retorted, my voice surprisingly steady despite the tremor running through me. "He may be on the other side of the world, but I know this – he will come for me. He would cross oceans of fire to get back to me."

My gaze met Ravana's, and for a fleeting moment, a flicker of doubt crossed his eyes. It was a fleeting victory, quickly extinguished by his usual arrogant smirk.

"And your precious Lakshmana," he sneered. "Naïve, just like his brother. Did it ever occur to him that perhaps his precious shield should have been strong enough to keep you in, not just others out?"

The barb hit its mark, drawing a fresh wave of anger. But this time, it was a controlled anger, a burning ember fueling my resolve.

"Lakshmana, unlike you," I said, my voice ringing with newfound defiance, "is a man of wisdom and integrity. His shield was meant to protect me, not trap me. And Rama, my Raghunandan, is unshakeable like the mightiest mountain, invincible like the great Indra, and imperturbable like the vast ocean. His brother Lakshmana, a tiger among men, will not rest until the one who dared to touch his sister-in-law faces his wrath."

Each word I spoke was a weapon, a shield against Ravana's taunts. As I finished my declaration, I turned my back on him, a silent statement of my unwavering faith.

Hope, a fragile ember, flickered within me. I may be a captive on this monstrous Vimana, but my spirit remained unbroken. Rama would come. Of that, I had no doubt. The abduction was a dark chapter, but it wouldn't be the end of the story. This was just the beginning. The fight for justice, for my freedom, had only just begun. As the Pushpak Vimana roared onward, carrying me towards the unknown, I steeled myself for what lay ahead. The flames of defiance burned bright within me, a beacon of hope in the encroaching darkness. Now Ravan had to be punished not just for me but entire womankind, so no other Ravan dares to touch a woman without her consent, no other Ravan dares to deceive a woman.

# XXXII

The Pushpaka Vimana descended with a jarring thud, kicking up a cloud of dust that momentarily obscured the sight of Lanka. As the dust settled, a scene unfolded before me that sent shivers down my spine. Lanka, the fabled demon capital, teemed with activity. Grotesque figures, a motley crew of ogres and demons, lined the sides of the landing platform, their guttural roars and jeering laughter creating a cacophony of welcome – for Ravan. The sun glazed the gold structures, the entire place was made of gold it felt. What's the use of such prosperity I thought when no love, no empathy resides in the people of the place.

Among these monstrous figures stood a group of women, their regal attire a stark contrast to the barbarity surrounding them. Mandodari, Ravan's queen, stood at the forefront, I figured it from her royal cloths, her demeanour. To her side, a familiar, unwelcome sight – Ravan's sister, Shurpanakha, her single remaining eye gleaming with malicious delight. Malyavan, another familiar figure standing there with an almost proud grin. Each one of them wore heavy gold jewellery.

Ravan emerged from the Vimana first, a triumphant smirk plastered across his face. I remained rooted to the spot, a silent observer in this grotesque spectacle. My body screamed in protest against following him, but reason overruled. There would be no escape here. My only hope lay in Raghunandan, and every passing moment fueled my resolve.

Finally, with a deep breath, I stepped onto the landing platform. The crowd erupted in a fresh wave of jeers and taunts. They saw me not as a captive, but as a prize, a symbol of Ravan's power. I held my head high, refusing to acknowledge their taunts. My eyes, however, scanned the crowd, searching for a flicker of empathy, a hint of kindness.

They landed on Mandodari. Despite the gulf that separated us, despite the knowledge that she was Ravan's wife, in that moment, she was the only woman in this den of demons. A sliver of hope, fragile as a spider's web, fluttered within me. I wouldn't bow. I wouldn't submit. But perhaps, just perhaps, I could find a fragile alliance in the midst of this hostility. With a defiant glint in my eyes, I met Mandodari's gaze, a silent plea for understanding passing between us. This was a new chapter, a battle fought not just against Ravan, but against the very fabric of this monstrous kingdom. I stopped in front of Ravan's family, my head still held high.

Surpanakha walked towards me and scanned me from face to feet, she smiled and said, "well well, look who's here, how the time changes, once I was in a condition when I was pitying myself and today you are here in the same situation."

"You are wrong Surpanakha, still we carry no common ground. I am not in the same situation as you once were in, why would I pity myself? I know my Raghunandan must already be on his way to get me. I have nothing to pity." I replied, I had decided not to shed a single tear in front of these who took pleasure in my pain and sorrow.

My reply enraged her as she said, "Bhaiya Ravan, think of something, think of something to give her more pain."

Ravan sighed and said, "Enough Surpanakha, all these are child's games. I did what you asked for, now I have other important affairs to attend to. You ladies look what to do with her."

Ravan's reply was unexpected for me. A sadist like him, leaving without plotting pans to upset me, that was indeed shocking from a person like him. Ravan then left with Malyavan and another man whom he summoned as Meghnad, from what he looked like, his age, and the way he obeyed Ravan, the respect in his eyes, not of fear but of utmost respect, made it clear to me that he was Ravan's son. Then there was another man who had a flicker of what looked like sympathy for me, he looked at me with a sad face and then he too left after a pause.

"Well, then let's start by giving you the worst treatment of your life, which servant service would you prefer." Shurpanakha said with a sadistic smile.

"Surpanakha, please. Don't forget we are members of royal family, and she is too, we need to maintain the honour of royalty. She is our guest here and also a queen, she can't be treated otherwise." Mandodri said and then looked at me, "come with me, I will show you your guest room"

Though she said the words in my favour still I felt that hint of gloom and bitterness but I couldn't blame her. A wife whose husband kidnaps other women, how cans he be happy, I sympathised with her. She looked wise, she looked like a good human being, but she didn't get the blessing to be a happy wife.

Surpanakha then looked at me once again with rage and hate in her eyes, and she left storming. Mandodri then turned to guide me to the room but I said from behind, "I won't enter the palace. I won't take a single step in that direction"

To this Mandodri turned towards me and said, "I don't now how you trat your guests at your place, but here we make sure their stay is comfortable in the palace."

A taunting laugh escaped my lips, I didn't want it to but it just did. I knew it was wrong to Mandodri, she had done nothing wrong but for now for the first time in my life I thought only about what I went through. "Guest? Or a prisoner?"

"You are no prisoner, Queen Sita. I understand you have been brought here against your will, but trust me for all the time tat you are here in Lanka, no one can do you any harm in my presence." She said, her aura that of a true queen, only if Ravan had been slightly like her.

"Well, if you truly respect me as a guest of yours, then respect my decision to not enter the palace." I replied.

"Well, then where will you stay?" she asked.

I turned my head to look around for some space, and there I saw at some distance a Shimshapa tree. I said, "there I will stay there"

"There? But..." Mandodri was about to say something as I placed my hands upon her and said, "please"

This was a strange bond, I told her what I anted even when she was the wife of someone I could never forgive. She then simply nodded her head in agreement and called, "Trijata, Trijata"

In a few moments a lady appeared, she had the appearance of the people of Lanka. She came and bowed her head to Mandodri. "Trijata, you will take care after each and every need of Queen Sita. Make sure nothing bothers her. Take her to Ashok Vatika, she will be staying there."

Trijata nodded her head and Mandodri left without saying anything to me, she simply looked at me with the expression of something I could not define, was it empathy, gloom, I didn't know.

"pranam" Trijata said to me.
I simply nodded in acknowledgement. "Come let me guide you to Ashok Vatika." She spoke. I walked beside her. After moments of silence she said, "we know about you, everyone here does" I know she said his to start a conversation but I had nothing to say.
As we walked towards the Shimshapa tree in Ashoka Vatika, other female ogres and demons started crowding. Their jeers and catcalls washed over me like a putrid wave.

"Don't mind them, Princess Sita," she said, her voice surprisingly gentle. "They are ogres and demons, what else would you expect? Your beauty is a sight they haven't seen before, that's all. It makes them jealous."

Her words, spoken with a hint of sympathy, surprised a small smile onto my face. It was the first flicker of kindness I'd encountered since this nightmare began. Trijata, unlike the others, didn't radiate malice. Her dark eyes held a spark of warmth, a glimmer of understanding. Perhaps, in this den of demons, I had found a single, fragile ally.

Trijata led me through the throng, their taunts now tinged with a grudging respect for her intervention. We arrived at a grove of Ashoka trees, their crimson flowers bleeding onto the path like fallen rubies. This, Trijata informed me, was to be my new home – Ashoka Vatika.

The other female attendants, all demons with sharp features and eyes that held a predatory glint, crowded around, scrutinizing me like a rare specimen. Their whispered comments, laced with envy, stung my ears. Trijata, however, kept them at bay, her presence a shield against their hostility.

As the sun dipped below the horizon, casting long shadows across the grove, a wave of loneliness washed over me. My thoughts drifted to Raghunandan, to his kind eyes and gentle smile. A pang of longing tightened my chest. I missed him so much it felt like a physical ache.

Trijata reappeared, bearing a simple meal. "Please, Princess," she urged, her voice laced with concern. "You must eat. Starving yourself won't help anyone."

But the food held no appeal. The very thought of anything from Ravana's kitchen repulsed me. "I have no appetite," I mumbled, pushing the plate away.

Trijata insisted me again a few times, but I refused every single time. Moment later, Mandodari arrived. "I knew you would not have had eaten anything. Please eat something", she said her tone a little softer than before. She too urged me to eat, but faced with my stubborn refusal, she sighed and left.

Then just moments after she left, Meghnad, Ravan's son, appeared next. Unlike the others, he exuded an air of quiet strength. His face, unlike his father's, held no malice, no gloating. His expressions though lacked warmth, had no hint of sadistic pleasure.

"You should eat," he said, his voice deep and firm. "Starving yourself won't weaken Ravan, it will only anger him further."

"I don't care. I don't fear him" I replied.

"We all know you don't fear him" he said and then stood there for a moment. And then after a pause he said again, "it is your wish to eat or not. All I will say is if you have so much trust that your husband will come and save you then I don't see any point in starving yourself to death even before he meets you, this only shows your lac of trust in him, that he won't come" After he said this, he didn't wait for me to say anything and he left.

His words held a surprising truth. If I truly believed Raghunandan would come for me, then starving myself to death wouldn't help him find me any sooner. It would only give Ravana more ammunition to paint me as a weak and helpless captive.

a deep breath, I picked up a piece of fruit, the first bite a bittersweet reminder of a life stolen, of a love far away. The journey ahead was uncertain, but a flicker of hope, fueled by Trijata's kindness and Meghnad's unexpected words, rekindled within me. I would endure. I would survive. And one day, Raghunandan would find me.

# XXXIII

Time, that fickle jester, played its cruel games within the suffocating embrace of Ashoka Vatika. The years spent in exile with Raghunandan, with love and warmth, had somehow slipped by in a blink. Now, here in Lanka, surrounded by the mocking whispers of demons and the suffocating opulence of a stolen life, each day stretched into an eternity. The once vibrant tapestry of our forest life with Raghunandan had faded into a cherished memory, the colours dulled by the relentless monotony of captivity.

One scorching afternoon, I sought refuge beneath the shade of an Ashoka tree, its scarlet flowers mirroring the burning ache in my heart. I closed my eyes, desperately summoning a vision of Raghunandan's gentle smile, the warmth of his touch. Memories of our stolen moments, whispered secrets under a sky ablaze with stars, echoed in my mind. A single tear escaped, tracing a glistening path down my cheek.

"Still lost in your daydreams, Sita?"

The mocking voice shattered the fragile peace I'd constructed. Shurpanakha, her sole remaining eye oozing with malicious pleasure, loomed before me. Silence, I had discovered, was a powerful weapon. It often left

Shurpanakha sputtering with frustrated rage. Today was no different. A withering glare was my only response, and with a final hiss, she stormed off, leaving behind a trail of stale, sulphurous air.

Life in Ashoka Vatika was a curious dance between defiance and despair. Lesser demons and ogres, emboldened by Ravana's favour, would occasionally throw barbs in my direction, taunts about my beauty now a prisoner's adornment. But Trijata, ever vigilant, would be there in a flash, her sharp words and fiercer glare sending them scurrying away like frightened rats.

Mandodari, visited occasionally, her regal demeanour masking a flicker of sympathy in her eyes. She ensured my basic needs were met, an unspoken truce between two women bound by circumstance. One day, while meandering through the grove, I came across a tall, brooding figure beneath a tree. It was Vibhishana, Ravan's younger brother, his face etched with a weariness that mirrored my own. A tentative hello sparked a conversation, a rare exchange of empathy amidst the hostility. We spoke of the burden of duty, of the choices that shaped our destinies.

Then came Ravana. His booming voice, as he strode into the grove, shattered the fragile peace. Today, his usual arrogance was tinged with a strange vulnerability. He paced before me, his ten faces displaying a mix of emotions – irritation, frustration, even a hint of begrudging admiration.

"You cling to this dream of yours, Sita," he finally spoke, his voice surprisingly low. "This 'Raghunandan,' this prince of a forgotten kingdom. You refuse to see the power you are rejecting. Here, in Lanka, you could be a queen, by my side."

I met his gaze unflinchingly. "Power without love is an empty cage, Ravana," I replied, my voice steady despite the tremor running through me. "I may be a captive here, but my heart remains with Raghunandan. Even if he is far away, even if he never finds me, I wouldn't trade a single memory of him for all the riches of Lanka."

Ravana snorted, a humourless sound. "Such blind devotion," he said, shaking his head. "You may regret your stubbornness, Sita. But know this – I will not force myself upon you. You will be mine willingly, or not at all."

With that, he turned and stormed away, leaving me alone beneath the tree. The day wore on, and the setting sun cast long shadows across the grove. Despite the hardships, a quiet strength bloomed within me. I would not break. I would hold onto the love that sustained me, the hope that one day, Raghunandan would find his way to me. As the first stars began to shimmer in the darkening sky, I lifted my chin, a silent vow echoing within my heart: "I will wait, Raghunandan. I will wait for you."

# XXXIV

*He felt like a moon, so near and yet so far.*

For the time that we are apart, his memories weaved hope for our reunion.

The nights in Ashoka Vatika were woven with moonlight and longing. As the silvery glow seeped through the branches, casting dancing shadows on my walls, I would be swept away on a tide of memories. Memories of Raghunandan, warm and vivid, a stark contrast to the cold reality of my present.

I relived stolen glances under the dappled sunlight filtering through the trees of our forest home. I heard again the echo of his laughter, a melody that chased away the oppressive silence of my captivity. Our whispered secrets beneath a canopy of stars, promises etched on the night sky, flickered like fireflies in my mind.

*Love, is a sheltering tree, its branches strong enough to weather any storm.*

We had been that tree for each other, Raghunandan and I, our love a fortress against the hardships of exile. Now, the storm raged on, but I clung to that memory, a shield against despair.

Nights also held a strange allure. The vast expanse above, a canvas splashed with a million twinkling stars, mirrored the yearning in my heart. Each star, a tiny beacon of hope, whispered promises of reunion.

I longed to see Raghunandan, I longed to embrace him, I longed to listen to his voice. At times I thought, by any means I could get some news about Raghunandan, about how he is. But then,

*I know how he is by knowing the way I am.*

The separation, though agonizing, had only intensified the depth of my affection. It was like the sculptor's chisel, refining the raw stone of our love, revealing its strength and purity. The distance, a physical barrier, could not diminish the bond we shared.

"Distance," I mused, the word a bittersweet echo, "may separate our bodies, but our souls remain intertwined, forever bound by an invisible thread." This invisible thread, woven from the fabric of our shared experiences, laughter, and tears, stretched across the miles, a constant reminder of the love that transcended distance.

With each passing night, a new memory bloomed – the memory of this love, tested yet unwavering, a testament to the enduring power of our bond. As I drifted off to sleep, a single, comforting thought echoed in my heart: Though separated now, the stars themselves bore witness – our reunion was a certainty, written in the language of love.

Today morning felt different, the usual gloom felt to like a distant feeling. The birds chirped differently, there was something different.

The rhythmic chirping of crickets and the rustling of leaves formed the lullaby of Ashoka Vatika. Seated beneath the shade of a gnarled banyan tree, I closed my eyes, seeking solace in meditation. A sudden flurry of movement broke the serene silence. I snapped my eyes open, heart hammering against my ribs, searching for the source of the sound. But the leaves of the surrounding trees hung motionless, bathed in the golden light of the setting sun.

Dismissing it as a figment of my longing, I closed my eyes once more, focusing on the calming rhythm of my breath. A soft thud startled me back to reality. It felt as though something had landed on my lap. My fingers trembled as I reached out, a sliver of apprehension gnawing at me. Hesitantly, I opened my eyes.

There, nestled in my palm, lay a simple gold ring. A gasp escaped my lips. It wasn't just any ring. It was my ring, the one Raghunandan had slipped onto my finger the day we were promised. An emblem of our love, a promise whispered beneath the canopy of a million stars.

My heart hammered a frantic tattoo against my ribs. A wave of emotions washed over me – hope, disbelief, and a yearning so fierce it threatened to consume me. All air rushed from my lungs. "Raghunandan?" I croaked, my voice barely a whisper.

"Whoever you seek, show yourself!" I cried out, desperation lacing my voice. "Please, come and talk to me! I just need to know... is Raghunandan... is he alright? Just tell me that much!"

A rustling sound came from behind a nearby bush, and a figure emerged. It was a being unlike anything I had ever seen – a humanoid form with a long, furry tail and the face of a monkey. Panic surged through me. This had to be another one of Ravana's cruel tricks, a twisted attempt to exploit my emotions.

"Don't you dare," I hissed, voice trembling with anger and fear. "Have you come to toy with me again? This is a vile trick, a most despicable one!"

But unlike most creatures in Lanka, this one radiated a strange warmth. His eyes, intelligent and kind, held a flicker of devotion that sent a tremor of hope through me. With a deep bow, he spoke, his voice surprisingly gentle.

"Pranam, Mata Sita," he said. "I am Hanuman, a devotee of Sri Ram. I understand if you don't trust me, but look at this ring again. Do you think a mere trick could possess such an object? Only you, Mata, can recognize it for what it truly is."

His words hit me like a tidal wave. Shame and disbelief choked me. All these days, all this doubt and despair, I had questioned the very symbol of our love. Tears welled up in my eyes, spilling down my cheeks in a torrent of emotions.

Hanuman, seeing my distress, spoke softly. "Don't cry, Mata. Your wait is over now."

A whirlwind of emotions swirled within me. Relief, joy, and a flicker of anger – all intertwined. "Hanuman," I stammered, clutching the ring to my chest, "where is he? Where is Raghunandan? Why hasn't he come for me? All these days, this agonizing wait... has he forgotten me? Does he not care?"

My words tumbled out, laced with a bitterness I couldn't contain. Though a part of me knew Raghunandan must be suffering the same burning flames of separation, another part, weary and heartbroken, lashed out.

Hanuman knelt before me, his eyes filled with empathy. "Trust me, Mata," he said gently. "Sri Ram is in as much pain as you are. He hasn't rested since you were taken. He has scoured every forest, every mountain, searching for you."

A flicker of hope ignited within me. "But how?" I whispered. "How did he know where to look?"

"It was the jewels, Mata," Hanuman explained. "You, with your quick thinking, cast them down from the

Pushpaka Viman. They were found by King Sugriv, and when an alliance was formed between him and Sri Rama, the story of the jewels emerged. That's when Sri Ram knew, with a certainty that shook the very mountains, that you were here, in Lanka."

"And so, the entire Vanara sena, the monkey army, began a relentless search," he continued. "I, Hanuman, have been the most fortunate one to have found you. It was destiny, Mata."

A tear escaped my eye, tracing a glistening path down my cheek. "But how did you recognize me, Hanuman? How could you be sure it was me?"

He smiled, a gentle, reassuring smile. "The strength that shines in your eyes, Mata, even amidst the hardship, the unwavering spirit that refuses to be broken – that is what I recognized. That, and the unmatched beauty that even captivity cannot diminish."

*Hope, like a fragile flower, bloomed in the depths of my heart.*

"Come, let us not waste another precious moment. Let me reunite you with your love Mata".

A flicker of defiance tempered my newfound hope. "No, Hanuman," I said, my voice firm. "I will not sneak away from here. With all due respect, Raghunandan will claim me openly. I have committed no crime, and I will not flee like a fugitive. For my own integrity, for the respect I hold for Raghunandan, he must come here."

But vengeance also flickered in my heart. "And Ravana," I continued, my voice hardening, "must be punished for his sins. Only then can I walk out of Lanka with my head held high."

Hanuman, far from being offended, smiled in understanding. "I understand perfectly, Mata Sita," he said.

"Your strength and righteousness are legendary. Worry not, for with Sri Ram's blessings, we, the Vanara sena, will conquer these demons. We will defeat Ravan and free you with all the honor you deserve."

Then, a playful glint entered his eyes. "But before I leave," he said, his stomach rumbling comically, "might I trouble you, Mata, for a bit of sustenance? My journey has left me famished."

Relief washed over me – a sign that this wasn't a dream. A genuine smile touched my lips. "Of course, Hanuman," I replied, pointing towards the trees laden with fruit. "But please, only partake in the ripened ones that have fallen. Let the young ones remain untouched, to grow strong and fruitful."

Hanuman's eyes widened in surprise. "Even in your captivity, Mata," he murmured, bowing low, "you think of the well-being of others. Your compassion is boundless."

I watched, captivated, as Hanuman scaled the trees with the agility of a playful child. He devoured the fallen fruits with gusto, his laughter echoing through the grove like a melody long forgotten. His joy, untainted and pure, was a balm to my soul.

Finally, wiping his mouth with the back of his hand, Hanuman announced, "Now, Mata, I must take my leave. But before I go, I want to show you something – a glimpse of the force that will soon arrive to free you."

With a sudden burst of energy, Hanuman's form began to grow. He stretched taller and taller, his fur shimmering with an otherworldly light. In mere moments, he towered over the trees, a majestic giant against the setting sun.

A gasp escaped my lips. This wasn't the Hanuman I knew, the one who knelt before me and spoke in gentle tones. This was a powerful warrior, a force of nature come to life.

"Behold, Mata," Hanuman boomed, his voice echoing across the land, "the reflection of the mighty Vanara sena coming to your rescue! We are countless, strong, and unwavering in our devotion to Sri Rama. Fear not, for your liberation is at hand!"

The sight was awe-inspiring, a testament to the power that awaited Ravana's downfall. But it was his final words that truly touched me. "I trust you, Hanuman," I said, my voice steady despite the tremor in my heart. "And I trust my Raghunandan. Now, please, return to your natural form."

With a gentle smile, Hanuman shrunk back to his normal size, his playful demeanour returning. He bowed deeply; his eyes filled with respect. "As you wish, Mata. May your wait be fruitful, and may your reunion be joyous. I, Hanuman, a humble servant of Sri Rama, shall take my leave."

And with that, he turned and leaped into the gathering dusk, leaving behind a trail of hope and the promise of a future bathed in the light of liberation.

# XXXV

A newfound fire burned within me, fueled by Hanuman's words and the awe-inspiring vision of the Vanara sena. Hope, once a fragile ember, now roared like a bonfire in my heart. Raghunandan was coming. My wait, though long and agonizing, was nearing its end. Tears welled up in my eyes, this time not tears of despair, but of anticipation and a joy so profound it threatened to overwhelm me.

But just as I surrendered to the sweet embrace of hope, a chilling sound shattered the serenity of the night. A cacophony of screams, laced with raw terror, rose from the distance. The usually cool night air crackled with an uncanny heat, and a faint orange glow bled across the horizon, even through the dense canopy of trees.

My newfound peace evaporated, replaced by a cold dread that coiled in the pit of my stomach. What was happening? Was it an attack? Had something gone wrong? A thousand terrifying scenarios played out in my mind.

Panic threatened to consume me, but then I remembered Hanuman's confidence. So, taking a deep, steadying breath, I forced myself to remain calm.

There was only one thing I could do – wait. Wait for news, for a sign, anything to explain the chaos unfolding beyond the Ashoka Vatika. So, I closed my eyes, rested by head on the tree and with memories of Raghunandan I didn't realize when I drifted to sleep.

My sleep was interrupted by the voice I loathed the most, "what do you think. Tricks like these will scare me away? The king of Lanka?" Ravan said.

Confused I simply looked at him. He then said again, "That Vanara, that Hanuman, you summoned him here, didn't you?"

"What did he do?" is all I said in a low voice, not wanting to spend any energy on a man like him.

"He turned the entire Lanka with his tail" he replied.

This brought a smile on my lips; Hanuman had already begun what he had promised. Apparently, Ravan saw my smile, as he said in a more enraging voice, "I don't know what you see in that sanyasi of yours. Don't you see you can love with so much prosperity here. Forget about Ram, no matter how many weird creatures he sends, I won't set you free."

I smiled and said,

*"His love is what sets me free.*

Try your best to shackle me but I will always be freed y the love of Raghunandan. You call him a sanyasi; Well, I love that about him. Being a king, he can spend life I forest just to keep the words of his father. He honours my words; he knows how to respect women. The greatest prosperity lies not in gold but in the personae and values. But I don't expect you to know any of it."

And just like every other time, Ravan had nothing to say to it, he just hissed and walked away with thumping steps.

# XXXVI

After Hanuman left Ashoka Vatika transformed overnight. The tranquil grove, once a haven for stolen moments of peace, morphed into a war camp. The air thrummed with nervous energy. Demons practiced their battle formations, weapons clanging against each other in a jarring symphony of war. An oppressive sense of fear hung heavy in the air, a stark contrast to the carefree days before Hanuman's arrival.

This fear, however, wasn't mine. It was Ravana's. It was the fear of a tyrant facing a force he couldn't comprehend. Raghunandan's unwavering resolve had sent tremors through Lanka, and Ravana, for the first time, tasted the bitter fruit of his actions.

Days bled into weeks, each one carrying the promise of liberation. Then, a ray of hope pierced through the gloom. A message arrived, carried on the wind – the Rama Setu, a bridge built across the vast ocean, was complete. Tears welled up in my eyes. Raghunandan had literally crossed the oceans for me. The image of his determination, his love, fueled a fire within me. The pain of separation, the loneliness, all paled in comparison to the magnitude of his love.

With renewed vigour, I held my head high. The taunts and mockery of the demons meant nothing. My faith in Raghunandan was an impenetrable shield, a testament to a love that defied distance and hardship.

One day, Trijata rushed in, her eyes wide with excitement. "Queen Sita," she panted, "Ravana has finally declared war on King Rama! Meghnad, has already led an army to confront the Vanara sena."

This was the beginning of the end. The end of all monsters like Ravana, who objectify women, who presume their right over women, who think mistreating women is right. Ravana's downfall is a symbol, a powerful message to all those who see women as mere possessions. His defeat is not just the triumph of good over evil but a declaration that the era of such monstrous behaviour is over. It is a reminder that no one has the right to undermine a woman's dignity or autonomy. It is the ultimate justice, not just for me, but for every woman who has suffered under the shadow of oppression. Let this be a lesson for all: the age of mistreatment and objectification is over. A new age, one of respect and honour, begins now.

This was the dawn of a new era, an era where respect and love would reign supreme.

A gentle smile touched my lips. "Thank you, Trijata," I said, my voice calm and resolute. "But from now on, I do not wish to hear any more news from the war. I will dedicate myself to meditation, seeking the blessings of Shiva, the destroyer of evil."

Trijata's brow furrowed in confusion. "But why, Queen Sita? Why not hear about the progress of the war?"

"Because," I replied, my voice laced with conviction, "I know the outcome. I have faith in Raghunandan.

*Love, is not about seeking reasons. It's about trusting. Trusting in the person they are, in the love they hold."*

I closed my eyes, and the world around me dissolved into a canvas of swirling colours. The taunts of demons, the stifling heat of Lanka – all faded away. With each focused breath, I sank deeper into the quietude of my own being. My senses, once bombarded with the harsh realities of captivity, retreated inwards. Here, in the sanctum of my own mind, I was no longer a captive queen, but a vessel seeking solace.

The earth beneath me thrummed with a low, comforting energy. I felt it rise from the very core of the planet, a steady heartbeat that resonated within me. It was the pulse of Mother Earth, a force ancient and enduring, offering strength and grounding.

My mantra, a whispered prayer for Lord Shiva, echoed through the quiet chambers of my mind. "Om Namah Shivaya," I chanted, each syllable a brushstroke painting a picture of unwavering faith. Lord Shiva, the destroyer of evil, became my anchor, the embodiment of the fierce justice I yearned for. Just as he uprooted all that was corrupt and destructive, I envisioned him dismantling the tyrannical reign of Ravana.

With each exhalation, I released the anxieties and fears that had clung to me for so long. The longing for Raghunandan, the gnawing uncertainty about the war's progress – all of it dissipated, replaced by a quiet confidence. My heart, once heavy with doubt, found a new mooring – the unwavering belief in my love's strength.

Time, in this meditative state, became a fluid concept. Days melted into nights, the rising and setting of the sun a distant echo. Yet, there was no sense of disorientation. Here, in the stillness of my being, I was present in every moment, existing in a timeless communion with my inner strength and unwavering faith.

Visions flickered through my mind – glimpses of a majestic bridge stretching across the vast ocean, a testament to the unwavering determination of the Vanara sena. Images of Raghunandan, his face etched with resolve but his eyes filled with love, fuelled my spirit. The clash of battle, the roaring flames of righteous anger, and the triumphant chants of victory – these were the whispers of the future that reached me in my meditative state.

I didn't know how much time passed; this was a state beyond time.

# XXXVII

"They won! They won! Your trust, your faith, Queen Sita, has finally bloomed into a beautiful reality!" A voice, raw with excitement, pierced through the veil of my meditation.

My eyes fluttered open, blinking against the harsh sunlight that seemed to have gained a celebratory vibrancy. The world outside, once a canvas of oppression, now shimmered with the promise of a new dawn. The air thrummed with a joyous energy, a stark contrast to the oppressive silence that had prevailed for so long.

A smile, long forgotten, bloomed on my lips. It wasn't just a smile of relief, a celebration of victory. It was a smile brimming with the vindication of love and faith. Raghunandan, my love, had defied the odds, had crossed oceans of doubt and despair, to stand by his promise. His victory wasn't just a military triumph, it was a testament to the unwavering strength of our bond.

And in that victory, I saw a reflection of my own strength. The days spent in meditation weren't just a refuge from the harsh reality, they were a battle fought on a different plane. A battle against despair, against doubt, against the fear that threatened to consume me. And here, in this moment of liberation, I stood victorious.

But more than just a personal triumph, this was a victory for all women who had been objectified, disrespected, and treated as mere possessions. The fall of Ravana, his death, was a symbolic dismantling of the power structures that had oppressed women for generations. It was a beacon of hope, a testament to the fact that love and respect, not tyranny and oppression, were the true foundations of a just society.

Tears welled up in my eyes, tears that were not of sorrow, but of a profound joy that washed over me in waves. Tears for the hardships endured, tears for the love that had conquered all, tears for the future that stretched before me, a future bathed in the golden light of liberation and reunion.

*My heart, a bird freed from its cage, soared on the wings of hope.*

The wait, though agonizing, had been worth it. Love, nurtured by faith, had emerged triumphant. And as I rose to my feet, ready to face the world anew, I knew that this victory, this beautiful reality, was just the beginning of a new chapter – a chapter filled with love, respect, and the promise of a life lived on my own terms.

The world, a blur of joyous chaos, seemed to fade away as I focused on one thing – reaching Raghunandan. Years of longing, of silent prayers, culminated in this single, solitary desire. I took a few hurried steps, my bare feet barely registering the rough ground. I yearned to see him, to feel the warmth of his presence after what felt like an eternity.

Suddenly, a figure emerged from the throng of celebrating monkeys and warriors. Vibhishana, his face etched with concern, stepped forward. "Pranam, Rani Sita," he said, bowing low. "I come with a message from Sri Rama. He... he requests that you freshen up and meet him."

His words struck me like a bolt from the blue. A knot of confusion twisted in my gut. Freshen up? Meet him? After all this time, after the fiery ordeal I had endured, did appearances truly matter?

"Vibhishana ji," I said, my voice surprisingly steady, "I would rather see him as I am – a reflection of the grief I have carried, the tears I have shed, the turmoil that has etched itself onto my very being. Don't ask me to wash away the evidence of these long days. Don't ask me to adorn myself with jewels, creating a facade of a life untouched by suffering. Let him see me as Ravana's prison has left me – a witness to my resilience, not a fabrication of comfort."

Vibhishana stood speechless, his eyes filled with a mixture of understanding and worry. But I knew in my heart that this wasn't about vanity. It was about honesty. It was about Raghunandan seeing the true cost of his unwavering love, the woman who had waited, not in a gilded cage, but in the heart of a storm.

With determination, I bypassed Vibhishana, my eyes scanning the crowd. I yearned for a glimpse of Raghunandan, for the comfort of his presence after all this time. Let the world see me, Sita, as I was – a woman scarred but unbroken, a wife who had held onto love with faith. Let the reunion begin, not with a facade, but with the raw truth etched onto my very soul.

The crowd made space for me, and I walked and walked, and there I saw many familiar faces, but my eyes longed for only one. And there he was, Raghunandan, my Raghunandan. My eyes filled with tears; I couldn't take my eyes off him. I have waited so long for this; I was so overwhelmed that it took me some time to realise that something was just not right!

# XXXVIII

That smile, that smile of victory, that smile of reunion was missing on Raghunandan's face. The smile I had yearned for, the one that would signify the end of our struggles and the beginning of our peace, was absent. Concern gnawed at me as I walked closer to him, my heart heavy with unspoken fears

"What is it? Are you not happy to see me?" I asked, my voice trembling with uncertainty.

Raghunandan, with tears pooling in his eyes, placed his hand gently on my cheek, cupping it with a tenderness that only deepened my worry. "How can you even say that, Janaki? I have spent every single minute, every single breath thinking of you, thinking of us, thinking of reuniting with you."

"Then why is that smile not gracing your lips?" I whispered, the weight of his sadness pressing down on me, a premonition of something I could barely stand to face.

His voice faltered as he spoke, "My tongue trembles to say this, Janaki."

I couldn't bear the thought of Raghunandan hiding anything from me, no matter how bitter it was. "What is it, Raghunandan? You can tell me."

He stood silent, his eyes avoiding mine. I glanced at Lakshman, whose eyes were also filled with tears and whose face showed a mixture of sorrow and anger. Hanuman, too, had tears in his eyes, his usually resolute demeanor shattered by the moment.

"Janaki, I can't take you to Ayodhya with me, unless..." Raghunandan paused, his tears now flowing freely, soaking his cheeks.

"Unless what?" I asked, my voice breaking under the strain. His words felt like a knife twisting in my heart, but I needed to know, no matter how devastating.

"Look, Janaki, as a king, as a leader, I have to take certain decisions. And sometimes those decisions can be bitter, sometimes I might even not agree with those decisions," Raghunandan explained, his voice filled with the anguish of a man torn between duty and love. It was the tone of a healer trying to soothe a wound he knew would cause great pain.

"You can't take me to Ayodhya unless what, Raghunandan?" My voice grew louder, the urgency in my heart spilling over. I had endured so much, but this moment felt like the breaking point, a pain sharper than any I had ever known. When Raghunandan didn't respond, I repeated, this time more insistent, "Unless what, Raghunandan?"

"Unless you prove your fidelity by giving Agni Pareeksha." The words rushed out of him in one breath, each syllable striking me like a physical blow, leaving me stunned and breathless.

The world seemed to stop around me. The noise of the surrounding chaos faded into an unbearable silence, the kind that follows a devastating revelation. My heart, already fragile from our ordeal, shattered at his words.

I stood there, numb. The world fell silent, and I couldn't feel my feet or my hands. Everything went blank, and time seemed to stop. A gush of air passed by, making me shiver and bringing me back to reality. Tears streamed down my face, soaking my cheeks and making my body feel hot. I couldn't process what I had just heard, especially coming from Raghunandan's mouth.

Then something caught my eye, and I turned to see preparations already made. A pyre of fire was burning nearby. A wave of disbelief and heartbreak washed over me. "You think my character is stained?" The words escaped my lips, bitter and pained.

Raghunandan said something in response, but my ears refused to hear. It was as if the world had shut down for me, leaving only my inner turmoil. After all these years of sacrifice, this was my reward?

Raghunandan stepped closer, his eyes filled with tears. This time I could hear him. "You have been here in Lanka, separated from me all this while. That is the only reason, Sita. But I trust you. What I am asking you to do is not as your husband but as a king."

I couldn't believe what I was hearing. "Haven't you been in separation just like me? Why am I the only one who has to walk through fire? Will you walk with me as well?"

"Sita..." Raghunandan hesitated, his voice trailing off.

I pressed on, my voice gaining strength. "We are a couple. We have equal rights over each other. We share everything equally. If I need to prove my fidelity, then why doesn't it apply to you?"

Raghunandan's hesitation spoke volumes. It cut deeper than any sword. My heart ached with the injustice of it all, the betrayal from the one person I thought would always stand by me.

I looked at him, my eyes filled with the pain of all the battles I had fought, the sacrifices I had made. "If you truly trust me, Raghunandan, why do I need to prove myself? "

The silence that followed was heavy, filled with the unspoken truths and the weight of our shared history. The world around us seemed to hold its breath, waiting for what would come next.

"But Sita..." Raghunandan tried to say something, but I just focused my eyes on him and interjected,

"Make the victim the culprit,"

I began, my voice echoing through the silent assembly. "How is this right? Even for a king, how is this decision justified by any means? Why do I have to prove my fidelity? Is it because I am a woman? All these years of separation, and no one cares about the pain I endured, the suffering I faced. All that matters is whether I am pure."

My voice grew louder, the hurt and anger fueling my words. "Raghunandan, have you thought about what I went through? Every single day in Lanka, I lived with the fear and the trauma of being held captive by Ravana. My heart longed for you, for our reunion, and I clung to the hope of returning to you. But now, instead of solace, I am met with this trial by fire. I am expected to prove my purity, as if my love and loyalty are not enough."

I glanced at the assembly, their eyes wide with shock and disbelief. "Did Ravana truly die? Because I still see fingers raised at only a woman. I see the doubt in your eyes, in the eyes of the people I once thought would protect me. Is this the justice we speak of? Is this the dharma we uphold?"

Raghunandan's eyes were filled with sorrow, but my heart was too shattered to find comfort in them. "You ask me to walk through fire, to prove my fidelity, as if my love for you, my devotion, is something that can be measured by such a cruel test. But tell me, Raghunandan, if our roles were reversed, would you be asked to do the same? Would you be asked to prove your faithfulness?"

I took a deep breath, steadying myself. "This isn't just about me. This is about every woman who has ever been doubted, every woman who has been made to prove her worth in a world that is so quick to judge and so slow to understand. By asking me to undergo this trial, you are not just questioning me, you are questioning the very essence of womanhood."

My voice softened, but the intensity remained. "Raghunandan, I stood by you, I believed in you, even when the world seemed against us. I never asked for proof of your love or your loyalty. I trusted you with all my heart. And now, you stand before me, asking me to prove myself, to subject myself to this humiliation. What kind of love demands such a price?"

I turned to the assembly once more, my gaze fierce and steady. "Why must a woman always bear the burden of proof? Why must she always be the one to suffer, to sacrifice, to endure endless trials just to be seen as worthy? I am Sita, the daughter of Janak, the wife of Raghunandan, but above all, I am a woman. And I refuse to let my dignity be trampled upon. I refuse to be made the culprit for the crimes committed against me."

The silence that followed was deafening, but I could see the impact of my words etched on the faces around me. The fire continued to burn, but now it seemed to be a reflection of my strength rather than a tool of my shame.

I stood tall, my heart heavy but my spirit unbroken, ready to face whatever came next with the courage and resilience that defined me.

Raghunandan said nothing to this which shattered me even more.

So I simply turned towards the fire, my resolve hardening with each step. The voices of Lakshman and the others reached my ears, their pleas and cries mingling with the roaring flames. Even Raghunandan's voice, laced with desperation, could not deter me. But I kept walking, my eyes fixed on the flames. This fire mirrored the inferno within me, a blaze ignited by the injustice I faced, a blaze that reflected the fury in the hearts of countless women.

As I approached the pyre, the heat grew intense, but it was nothing compared to the fire that burned inside me. This was not just any fire; it was a fire that symbolized every woman's struggle, every woman's pain, every woman's resilience. The fire within me mirrored the fire that burns in the heart of every woman whose character has been questioned, whose dignity has been tarnished. It mirrored the fire in the heart of woman who was objectified, the fire in the heart of woman who was touched forcefully, the fire in the heart of woman who was touched without her consent.

The flames danced before me, their crackling sound a symphony of my anger, my strength, and my unyielding spirit.

I took a deep breath, feeling the heat on my skin, the tears still flowing down my cheeks. With each step, I embraced the fire, letting it envelop me. The flames were not my enemy; they were my ally, my voice, my declaration to the world that I was more than their doubts, more than their judgments.

In those moments, as the fire surrounded me, I felt a profound connection to every woman who had ever faced injustice. I was not just Sita; I was every woman who had ever fought for her dignity, for her truth.

And so, as the flames consumed me, I let go of the pain, the doubt, the fear. I became one with the fire, letting it cleanse me, letting it transform me. I was no longer just a queen, a wife, or a daughter. I was a force of nature; I was one with the fire around and the fire within.

# Afterword

Has Ravana truly died? Have those injustices truly perished? Are there no more women who are touched without consent, touched forcefully, who are constantly forced to prove their character and purity?

They say, "Be like her, be an ideal woman," but what about an ideal society? When there are so many Ravanas still alive, thinking that deciding a woman's fate, assuming their right over her, is absolutely right.

Have the times changed? Are there no more Mantharas, where the closest to you try to cut off your roots? Are there no more Surpanakhas, who put each other down? From movies to television, why are women often portrayed as the biggest enemies of women?

"Be like Sita," they say, while their actions mirror Ravana's. In those times, the injustices Sita faced were unacceptable, but today, those issues have only worsened. Today, too, women are touched without consent, they are judged, their character questioned. They are expected to act a certain way, to prove certain things, but only they are expected to endure these trials, to constantly spend their lives in hardships and still have to prove themselves. Prove what, and to whom?

Today, there are still Sitas with a fire burning within them—the fire of witnessing injustice, their flames constantly consuming them. Today, too, women have to give their Agni Pariksha at every moment, walking through the flames of injustice and patriarchy, bearing the burning heat of societal pressure.

This book is a reminder that the battles Sita faced are far from over. It's a call to recognize the ongoing struggles, to acknowledge the fire within every woman who fights against these injustices. Let us strive not just for an ideal woman, but for an ideal society where no woman has to endure these trials alone.

# GLOSSARY

Kaaki – a word of respect for elderly women

Ojus - "vigor" or "essence of vitality"

Rajrishi – used for King Janak, who is a king and also a rishi

Maharishi - a teacher of spiritual and mystical knowledge; religious sage: often used as an honorary title

Svayamvara - Svayamvara (self choice) is a type of marriage mentioned in Hindu mythology where a woman chose a man as her husband from a group of suitors.

Pranaam – formal respectful greeting

Devi – (here) used to refer to any lady, a word of respect

Kausalyanandan – son of Kausalya, another name of Ram

Raghunandan – another name of Ram

Chaacha shri – younger brother of father

Pita shri - father

Vidai - farewell

Lankapati – King of Lanka

Diya - Lamp

Pooja thali(s) – Prayer plate

Rani - Queen

Tulsi – Holy Basil

Yuvraj – Prince

Yuvrani – wife of prince

Charan paduka – sacred footwear

Munivar - sage

Agni Pariksha – fire test to prove one's purity